DIRTY PLAYER

STACEY LYNN

DIRTY PLAYER

By
Stacey Lynn

Editing: Amy Jackson
Proofreading: Emily A. Lawrence
Photography: Big Stock Photos
Cover Design: Shanoff Designs

Copyright 2016 by Stacey Lynn

All Rights Reserved. This book may not be reproduced, scanned, or distributed in any printed or electronic form without permissions from the author, except for using small quotes for book review quotations. All characters and storylines are the property of the author. The characters, events and places portrayed in this book are fictitious. Any similarity to real persons, living or dead, is coincidental and not intended by the author.

Trademarks: This book identifies product names and services known to be trademarks, registered trademarks, or service marks of their respective holders. The author acknowledges the trademarked status and trademark owners of all products referenced in this work of fiction. The publication and use of these trademarks in not authorized, associated with, or sponsored by the trademark owners.

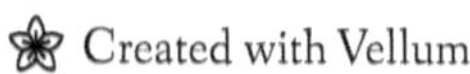 Created with Vellum

ONE

SHANNON

I slid my fingers through my hair, smoothing back the wavy tendrils that had escaped my ponytail. The sun beat down on me, the glare so bright through my sunglasses I had to squint to see him.

He stood at the fence and signed autograph after autograph. Fathers with their sons and daughters boosted onto their shoulders. Women in shirts twisted up and tied between their breasts, baring almost every asset they had—and not because of the late summer heat.

I couldn't wipe the smile off my face.

My brother. He'd done it. Drafted right after college, he'd spent the last three years playing backup quarterback, but last year, as the Vikings played the final few games of the season and their starter got hurt, Beaux had been put into the game.

He hadn't just delivered when the team needed him to—he'd kicked ass.

I had shouted so loud my voice was hoarse for a week afterward.

After the season ended, he'd been traded.

Now, he was the new starting quarterback for the Raleigh Rough Riders. The fans packing the stadium at their last day of Summer Training Camp hooted and hollered all afternoon every time he made a great play. Beaux Hale was projected to be their savior, to pull the team that ranked in the middle of the pack for the NFL into the top team.

I'd been hearing whispers of "Super Bowl-bound" all afternoon while I sat in the stands, close enough to overhear conversations but removed enough to not have to talk to anyone. The tips of my fingernails were now ragged—not that it was uncommon.

I had spent years and hours and uncountable minutes dragging him to football practices while our mom worked three jobs to put food on the table before she became too ill to work. I had been the one to drive him to practice and toss the ball around with him in our tiny backyard. I'd taken him shopping for his shoes and helmets and pads at secondhand sporting goods stores. I'd taken on summer jobs to pay his registration fees. Then I'd stayed home and gone to community college before commuting the last two years to finish my degree, so I could stay home and take care of Beaux and my mom when her illness prevented her to work. I'd foregone most of my teenage years and early twenties in order to be the caretaker for my family. Now, at twenty-eight years old, I was finally seeing my brother accomplish the dream he'd had his entire life.

I didn't regret a single second of my sacrifice.

Football had been in Beaux's blood since the moment he could walk at ten months. He picked up a football, toddled around our small living room, and never set it down. He kept it in his lap at mealtimes and cradled in his arms at bedtime. At five, he'd declared he was going to be on TV someday, playing as quarterback. It was all he'd talked about. All he'd craved.

I'd craved seeing someone in my family finally succeed at something for once. It might as well have been Beaux.

He was the best of us, anyway. He was determined on the field, full of hard work and focus, but able to flip a switch to party-master and carefree in the blink of an eye. I'd be jealous of his ability to turn off the responsibility he carried if I didn't love the twerp so damn much.

My fingers curled around the burning metal railing and I pulled them back, blowing on them to dull the pain while I walked down the stairs.

My cheeks hurt from the stretch of a smile that refused to dissipate as fan after fan thrust their breasts and pens and paper into Beaux's hand.

Only I knew that his pink-tipped ears weren't from excess sun but from embarrassment. As much as he loved the game, the attention still flustered him.

He wanted to pass a ball into outstretched, waiting hands. He wanted to break through the pocket and run for his own first down. He wanted a handoff that caused the stadium to roar so loud the field trembled beneath his cleats. The fans and the notoriety were things he claimed he never got used to.

"Oh my God," I drawled as I walked closer to him. I pressed my hand to my chest as if my heart was fluttering at a runaway speed. "Beaux Hale..."

My fake drawl, one I'd been trying to master for weeks when I finally agreed to move to be closer to Beaux, made him cringe.

"It's Beaux Hale," I repeated on a loud whisper to the woman in front of me. She was around his age, and hope flared in her eyes like dollar signs. "Can you believe it? He's so dreamy."

"He's been in my dreams every night," she replied, giving me a cheeky grin. "Now if I could just make that a reality."

Her gaze quickly scanned my body and her shiny red lips turned to a pout as she took in my breasts, well concealed behind a thin tank top, and cut-off and frayed denim shorts that showed off my shapely backside and tanned legs.

I pressed my lips together to keep from laughing that she could possibly think I'd be competition for her.

Never once had Beaux fallen for a fan. He brushed off the attention like he brushed his hair—cleanly and with purpose.

"Good luck," I replied, right as Beaux shot me a grin before turning his attention toward her.

As she began gushing over the size of his biceps and his fifty-yard pass, my eyes wandered to the row of players on Beaux's side of the fence.

They were all grinning, their smiles so firmly affixed I doubted many fans noticed most of the smiles were fake. Sweat dripped down their necks, soaking into the pads they still wore from camp.

Today was the last day. Preseason games started next Thursday. Just over one week until Beaux made his debut as a starting quarterback for the NFL.

The thrill of excitement rolled down my spine until my little brother reached out and pulled me to him.

"You fucking made it," he whispered. His large, meaty hand clasped around my neck and held me to his shoulder. At twenty-five, he was three years younger than me. Almost a foot taller at six-five and more than a hundred extra pounds, he was no longer my little brother.

He was a monster. And a machine.

And I freaking adored him.

"I did. Saw you play today—you were great."

"My short game was slow and felt too forced." He frowned when he pulled back.

Only I would catch the worry in his dark blue eyes.

"You'll warm up," I assured him, grinning. "This is your year."

The worry evaporated and softened. His fingers flexed on my neck. He said more without words than he ever could have with them, but he still tried. "I couldn't have done any of this shit without you."

He would have. The game was so ingrained into his DNA from the moment he was born that he would have found a way.

I just helped make it easier for him.

"You promised if I came out here you wouldn't make me cry."

I pushed at his shoulder only to have my hand slide off him and brush against another mountain of well-formed, toned, and tanned muscle I knew was hidden beneath shoulder pads.

"Look at you, newbie."

I looked toward the new, masculine voice. It was unavoidable. The voice instantly brought up visions of morning sex and shower sex, public sex, and sheet-clawing, multiple-orgasm, ecstatically screaming sex.

Oliver Powell.

My breath hitched as Beaux pulled me closer to the fence.

Powell was the best tight end in the league for the last six years. Five pro-bowl games. A handful of MVPs. He had awards and decorations and trophies and recognition. He had a body that drove women to distraction.

He had a voice that would make a nun drop to her knees and pray for forgiveness for her sinful thoughts.

A body that'd been plastered on every magazine cover, not always clothed.

Full lips that made you want to lean into him for a taste.

"Look at you," he drawled again, his hand coming down and clasping onto Beaux's shoulder. "One week at camp and you've already found some pussy."

...And an attitude of the biggest asshole around.

He was surly and crass. He'd been fined for refusing to give interviews, or when he did give them, he gave one-word answers. Yeah, Oliver Powell had an ass that fit his position on the field, but he was a complete prick.

I stiffened and pulled back from Beaux.

He only held me tighter, glaring at Powell. "Knock it off."

"You move in between the sheets like you move on the field, and I bet this girl's going to be screaming your name before you make it to the parking lot."

Beaux's rage started bubbling beneath the surface. He was younger, but that didn't mean he wasn't protective. His size had always made him feel like he needed to be my bodyguard.

If I didn't want to puke from the vileness of Powell's thoughts, not to mention he was talking about my brother...I would have said something.

Beaux beat me to it. "Don't be a fucking asshole right now, Powell. Save your shit talk for the locker room."

Oliver ignored the threat and kept his eyes focused on me, his gaze sweeping down my body in a leering but appreciative graze. "Wanna share? Some of these women like it. You'll see. Now that you're on the field and not warming the bench, you'll snap your fingers and get whatever you want."

Beaux leaned into him, his hand dropping from my neck. He twisted his head at the last second and whatever he whispered in Powell's ear was unheard and unseen.

As he spoke, Powell's face went blank. When Beaux stepped back, fire shot from his dark blue eyes.

I grinned and waved my fingers.

It wasn't uncommon for people to comment about my brother and me. With different fathers, we looked nothing alike. I got all my mom's features—short and curvy and all dark, from my long, chocolate brown hair and brown eyes to my olive skin. Beaux was some perfect genetic mutant with his height and build, and was the light to my dark. Shaggy blond hair he kept longer on top and trimmed short on the sides, fair skin that burned before it tanned. For anyone who didn't know us, we were nothing alike.

We were also not only best friends, but the only family we had, and that made us close. We touched a lot and hugged, and that was often misconstrued.

This wasn't the first time I had been mistaken for a woman wanting in his pants.

I tilted my head to the side and dug out a receipt from my purse.

"Can I get your autograph?" I smiled sweetly at Powell,

One side of his lips twisted up.

"Don't fucking think about it," Beaux said to Oliver as he reached for my pen, his voice still that deep and uncommon growl. "Walk away and save your shit and hazing for me for some other time."

Powell grunted, staring at my pen and paper before his eyes zoned in my breasts.

He was an asshole.

He was also beautiful.

The way he licked his lips while he stared at my body, his look said he totally knew what was going on beneath the fabric of my thin tank.

My nipples pebbled and hardened from his intensity, and when he swept his eyes back to my face, the heat in them had nothing to do with the sun at his back.

"See you later, I'm sure."

Beaux shoved his shoulder while I watched Oliver Powell walk away. The view from the back was as good, if not better, than the front. I wasn't the only woman watching him, either. Shouts and calls echoed in the air as women cried for him to come back to the fence, to sign more breasts and skin. But he sauntered away, nonchalant and unhurried, acting like he hadn't just broken his contract.

I figured he made enough millions that he preferred to pay his fines versus doing shit he didn't want to do. What's a ten-thousand-dollar fine for refusing to sign at training camp on fan appreciation day when you make fifteen million dollars a year, plus endorsements?

"Ah, fuck," Beaux moaned, pulling my attention back to him. "Don't fall for him. And please don't fuck him."

I snorted, unable to help myself. Being recently fucked over by a fiancé didn't exactly have me wanting to jump in the sack with anyone.

"What'd you say to him?"

Beaux's eyes gleamed with mischief. "Enough that he'll leave you alone."

"Did you tell him?"

"Fuck, no. If he knows you're my sister he won't leave you alone. I saw the way he looked at you."

"Really?" I couldn't help the appreciative tingle that flooded my veins. This was Oliver Powell. I mean, yeah, he was a dick...but I also bet he had a great one. He had new women around him all the time. Beautiful women. Women way out of my league.

Beaux groaned again and pushed me down the line. "Wait for me in the lot after I'm done here. Got something I want to show you. And stay the hell away from Powell. He's everything we knew he'd be like, but worse."

My face scrunched up. Not from the dismissal, but from the warning. The awareness.

Beaux had basically just told me that Powell was being a gigantic asshole to my baby brother. I should have been incensed on his behalf. The problem was I couldn't erase the way his hazel eyes had frozen on my assets...and lingered longer than necessary.

But that was trouble, and months ago I'd walked away from another kind of trouble.

This was my time, my fresh start, to do whatever I wanted and be whoever I wanted.

Being Powell's one-night stand was never going to be any of those things.

Even if I knew it'd be highly entertaining and memorable.

"YOU...I...WHAT IS THIS PLACE?"

"This is your store."

I peeled my eyes off the old, red-bricked building that sat in the arts district in downtown Raleigh. Turning to look at Beaux, my mouth still hanging open, I continued to gape. "What?"

He spun a ring of keys around his thumb before flicking them in my direction.

I caught them right before they hit the pavement. When I looked up again, I held back the urge to throw them at his face.

"Why did you—"

"Shut up. You've wanted this for years and never moved forward because you listened to that asshole say you couldn't do it. Now you have it. Be thankful, Shan."

I scowled at him. My little, dumbass, huge brother.

"Do you remember what Barclay said about rookies? What rookies need to remember?"

"I'm not a fucking rookie."

He wasn't. He had three years' experience in the league, but with this contract, these new millions terrified the hell out of me.

"You're not supposed to take care of your family," I said, reminding him what the retired NBA player had said on the news one night. Said that every professional player had the desire to set their families up so they could live large on the millions that new pro players suddenly acquired, and it was a huge mistake.

A career could vanish with one misplaced hit. Millions could disappear overnight.

I pulled my stunned gaze off Beaux and back to the building. It really was beautiful. Big without being too large. We hadn't stepped inside and I already loved the place.

It'd be the perfect home to take Stamped, my online jewelry business, to the next level.

Plus, a two-bedroom apartment above it.

All mine.

And yet I hadn't earned a penny of it.

My stomach flipped and I shook my head, handing the keys out to Beaux. "I can't let you do this."

He ignored the keys and slid his hands into the pockets of his worn jeans. Jeans he'd had since college, because while he made millions and spent it extravagantly on me, he barely used any of it for himself. Unless it was for the annual summer RV tour he took, partying it up with friends from all over the country.

"It's already done. Papers signed. I closed last week. I've also got you a booth at the summer arts festival in a few weeks, and I've ordered you new business cards with your new address."

My jaw hit the pavement. "What?"

I stared at my brother. This was too much. Too much money. Too much space. Too much responsibility. The only good thing I'd done in my life was making sure he succeeded. I'd essentially failed at everything else. Barely passed college, had shitty taste in men—a recently learned development—and couldn't hold down a real job to save my life.

My jewelry business was a fantasy, a hobby, something I did to pass the time—and while it brought in a decent amount of income and I'd dreamed of doing something bigger with it, I never thought it'd be possible. I didn't have the confidence that I could pull it off.

This...this scared the shit out of me.

"I can't do this," I whispered, my voice thick with emotion.

Beaux stared at the building. "When I was eleven, you walked me to the middle school fields one night, and when I asked you what we were doing there you said, 'I have a surprise for you.'"

My eyes began burning at the memory—his first practice. "Beaux—"

He didn't look at me, but he did reach out and take my hand in his, squeezing the keys for the building in front of us into my palm. "You dumped a duffel bag onto the ground, slapped the pads and a helmet on me, and watched me practice. You sat there for two hours doing your homework while I learned plays for the very first time. If you think for one damn second you haven't earned all of this success and money as much as me, you're a bigger idiot than I thought."

"Mom—"

"Mom wanted me to play football. She talked about it all the time. But she was all talk and working for food and then unable to do anything, while you were the one who worked to make my dreams come true, Shannon. Let me do this for you. Take the gift, do something you love with it, and finally get a slice of your own dream."

Truth fell from my lips before I could stop it. "What if I fail?"

He turned to me then, his lips tilting up at one corner of his mouth. Then, he threw my words back in my face, the same words I'd said to him when he'd learned he was starting quarterback for his high school football team as a sophomore. I'd graduated the year before and was attending community college to be close to home. With over eight hundred kids in each grade, and a football team with a huge history of winning State Championships, a sophomore starting for varsity had been unprecedented. "But Shannon...what if you don't?"

"I hate you," I whispered, sniffing over the tears burning my eyes.

My hand squeezed around the keys in my palm, gripping them tighter.

I'd give Beaux anything. I'd do anything for him.

If this made him happy, I'd do this for him, too.

"I know you hate me." He tugged me forward, uncurling my fingers from the keys so he could slide them into his own palm. "You just love me more."

I swiped my fingers beneath my eyes and blew out a shaky breath. This was it.

My future. My dream.

Coming to fruition when I knew I'd never have the guts to try it myself.

"I know," I murmured.

He slid the key into the lock and opened the door.

"I think you're pretty awesome."

"You're not so bad for a bitchy big sister. Now let's go see your new place."

TWO

SHANNON

I wrapped the towel tighter around my body and stared at the mess I'd made in Beaux's guest room.

It was a record disaster in record time, even for me. After he'd given me a tour of the building and the upstairs apartment, I'd finally submitted to his plan, his idea...his faith in me.

Yet none of it was ready and I'd left almost everything I owned back in Des Moines—where Patrick was probably currently fucking his co-worker all over my favorite couch and throw pillows.

"Ugh." I groaned and dragged a hand through my hair. The memories of him came hard and fast, unbidden, and difficult to erase once they were there.

The legs wrapped around his waist. The heels digging into his still-clothed ass as he took her—

"Shannon?" Beaux's voice rang through the doorway as he opened the door. "You okay? I knocked...shit! Cover up!"

His hand went to his eyes as I swirled around, clinging to my towel.

"What the hell?"

"Why didn't you tell me you weren't wearing clothes?"

I gaped at him, all six foot five inches clothed in jeans and a plain V-neck shirt, and looked down at my towel. It covered everything.

"You should have knocked."

"I did. You didn't answer."

"I'm covered, you idiot."

He peeked through his fingers before cringing. "Just like when I was ten."

Idiot. I was thirteen and just out of a shower. He'd gotten a full view of my naked preteen body. He claimed it scarred him for life.

Laughing, I tightened the towel around my body and rolled my eyes. "You're so stupid, Beaux. Seriously. I'm more covered now than I will be in the dress I was planning on wearing later."

He'd talked me into hanging out with his teammates. I couldn't lie and say I wasn't trying to seek attention. I'd had enough of being alone in the last few weeks, crashing on my best friend Melissa's couch while I cataloged every single one of Patrick's faults I could recall.

She'd been my best friend since college, where we'd met during our Introduction to Design class. She'd let me stay at her place after I left Patrick until I could figure out what else I wanted to do. I'd been gone from Des Moines for barely over a full day, and I already missed her like crazy.

"You're wearing...what?"

I laughed at his aghast tone.

"Just this." I held up a slinky, silver, sequined mini-dress with fringes at the bottom that only hung down mid-thigh. It'd been a Halloween costume, not something I'd wear to a bar. I had no idea how it had ended up in my suitcase.

His eyes bulged like I knew they would and a muscle popped in his neck. "You're not."

"I am." I loosened my towel a smudge, taunting him. "And if you don't leave now, you might see more than you bargained for."

He spun on his heels, the sound of the door slamming behind him barely drowning out my laughter.

"Don't wear the fucking dress!"

"Don't tell me what to do!" I shouted back, laughing harder.

My brother. The protector and athletic mutant.

The NFL quarterback superstar.

The moron.

When we were together, we still acted like teenagers.

I dropped the towel and reached for a silky black dress instead. It dipped down past the center of my cleavage. One thin strap provided support across the back and hit almost as low as the fringed dress.

It was sexy in that sinful-wanting way.

I wanted the attention. It didn't matter if it was for a night, a few hours, or a drink and just a look.

Walking in on Patrick fucking his co-worker at a party thrown for us by his firm had shaken my foundation. Damaged my ego.

But I'd promised not just myself, but also Melissa, that I'd throw my middle finger in the air as I left Des Moines and do whatever I needed to do to let go.

Even if it was only a few hours of pretending.

Fake it 'til you make it, though, right?

That was Melissa's advice. I was grabbing onto it with both hands and holding on as tightly as I could.

Once I was dressed, my hair teased and held back from my face with a few sparkly pins, my makeup heavy and smoky-eyed, and my lips a devil's red, I slipped on heels and headed downstairs, shutting my door on the mess I'd left in the room.

I'd clean it and repack over the weekend. Beaux told me I could stay at his place as long as I needed to, but the apartment came partly furnished with enough to get me started...a lumpy couch, a bed that needed to be tossed twenty years ago, and dining room table. But it didn't matter. I was twenty-eight years old and finally moving into my very own place, responsible for the success of a business I'd always dreamed would become more than just an online store.

Now that I'd had time for the idea to sink in, my mind was filling with ideas on marketing and jewelry designs, space planning and things I wanted to do to get my name out there—Arts Festival included.

"You're trying to kill me, aren't you?" Beaux asked as I reached the living room. He had a beer hanging loosely between his fingertips and he dropped it to his side as I entered the room.

"This old thing?" I spun in a circle and laughed when he cursed.

"Fucking shit. You are. You're going to kill me, probably trying to get me murdered so you can cash in on my life insurance."

"You're an ass." I swatted him with my handbag and went to the kitchen, helping myself to a beer. "When do we leave?"

"In a hurry to see someone?"

The image of a sweaty and surly Oliver Powell flashed behind the lids of my eyes.

"No."

"Liar."

I shrugged and took a swig of my drink. Cool beer. So much better than the crap Patrick insisted I drank—from the chilled sparkling wine to fruity mixed drinks.

God, what a pain in the proper ass he was.

I blinked, vanishing the reminder from my mind, and jumped when Beaux was directly in front of me.

"You hear from that asshole lately?"

"A few times," I admitted. My ability to lie to anyone, but mostly Beaux, was nonexistent. "He's been apologizing."

Which was why I needed this new start. I could barely go anywhere in Des Moines without running into memories of Patrick, the way he'd worked so hard to seduce me, to claim me in the first place.

We'd been everywhere together. Five long years flushed down the toilet. And he had apologized, but it was always in the tone of voice. The one I was only beginning to understand. The one that taunted and teased...whispered I wasn't as good as him—that I'd never done anything good on my own.

My shoulders slumped and Beaux growled—that sound he made when I knew he had his fists clenched and wanted to pummel the guy.

"It's fine, Beaux." I turned from him so he couldn't read the truth in my eyes. I wasn't fine. The breakup wasn't fine. Nothing about my humiliation and canceled wedding plans—canceled future—was fine.

"Do me a favor?" he asked, and for a moment I was grateful he was dropping the subject.

"What? Anything."

"Stay away from Powell tonight."

And then he had to ruin my fun.

Not that I had planned on it, not that I could get his attention or keep it for more than a few hours. But wasn't that what I was looking for? Oblivion?

I rolled my lips and nodded.

Beaux read my silence and threw his head back on a sigh.

"He's my teammate, Shan. And a prick. I'm serious, this guy is bad news."

"I won't do anything you wouldn't do." That was a promise. Fortunately for me, Beaux's list of *wouldn't do*s was pretty short.

He caught my meaning and scowled. "That doesn't help."

I grinned. "It helps me." Setting down my drink, I curled my fingers around his forearm. "Come on. Take me out and get me drunk so I can forget all about Patrick."

"With fucking pleasure."

WHILE THE MUSIC from the main floor beneath the VIP area was muted, the lights still flickered and the vibrations of the bass could still be felt at my feet.

Being with a dozen or more football players had its perks, definitely.

For the last hour, Beaux had taken me around to most of his teammates and some of their girlfriends, introducing me. While I had three years' experience meeting professional ball players, and more years' experience talking to ball players with egos bigger than brains and talent, it never grew old.

I had fallen in love with football right along with Beaux—from the plays and the stress to the art and finesse of the game. So many of the men I'd met, I'd watched on television or cheered for when Beaux or I were in college.

It never became less awe-inspiring. I was never less enamored shaking hands with men Beaux and I had grown up admiring or worshipping.

The club we were in whispered of wealth, from the chandeliers to the sparkling crystal glasses. Perhaps it was just the pretentiousness of the VIP area, secluded away with our own private bar and bottle service, admittance only allowed with names on a list and a bouncer at the bottom of the stairway preventing just anyone from sneaking in.

It was too similar to what I'd recently walked away from to enjoy fully. I had tried, but after the sweet, tart taste of a Red Bull and vodka and then the scowl from the barely dressed waitress when I'd ordered a beer from the tap—anything, because I didn't care as long as it was cold—I gave up on the idea of getting stupid drunk.

A slight buzz was all I needed anyway, and after a while— the murmurs of conversation going on at the high-top table around me, Beaux lost in getting to know his new teammates—I caved to my creativity that had begun its seductive whisper.

Ideas were racing through my mind. Floor plans. Set up tables. Bracelets. Necklaces and charms with matching earrings. Stamped metal designs paid pretty well, especially depending on the types of metal I used. I had started in college, making a few pieces here and there for myself and then selling them to girls in sororities. Everyone wanted something one of a kind—made for them and their personalities. While they'd been having their fun, partying away the best four years of their lives, I'd still been running Beaux around to practices, helping him with his homework, and making sure he made varsity. When he grew older and could drive himself, I still went with him on college visits to tour campuses and talk to scouts and football coaches—all while trying to take care of our ill mother.

When she passed away before she could see Beaux graduate college, the entire burden of the house and the bills and life had fallen on my shoulders. What I wouldn't have given during those years to be one of those sorority girls with wallets as deep as their dads would allow and no worries in the world other than finding a new fashionable accessory and being the first to own it.

I had envied them. I wanted to live that life now, but responsible and cautious weren't character traits easily shaken.

Plus, I hadn't had decent design ideas in months, but the historic and rugged look of the building Beaux had rented for me, lease fully paid for a year, had lit a spark.

Or perhaps that was the freedom of knowing I could finally do what I'd always wanted.

Perhaps Beaux was right. I'd earned every bit of his success right along with him. I didn't begrudge him for it. I was proud of him. There was also something to be said for having a piece of life that was all yours—although I fully intended to pay him back for every cent he'd already spent.

A large hand slammed down over the napkin I was currently doodling on.

"You are not spending the night with a pen in your hand and your face to the table."

I shrugged off Beaux's scolding tone and scrunched my face. "I finally have ideas, though."

I looked down at the designs he'd covered with his hand. Six interlocked bracelets, able to be undone, put back together, worn in six different patterns. Complicated, but replicated with different types of metals, or using one for the whole thing, I could make eight different designs and they'd all look unique.

"Well, tell your brain to shut up for the night. It's on vacation. You need it."

Before I could protest, a tray of golden-colored shots was presented and set on the table. A bowl of limes next, and a shaker of salt.

I glared at Beaux. "You're kidding me."

He threw his head back and laughed. "They're not all for you."

"Is she always this greedy?"

I turned toward the new voice and grinned. I'd been

standing next to Kolby Jones for most of the night. He seemed more enamored with the celebrities in our midst than I was.

But then again, he'd only had three months since the draft to get used to this new life. A wide receiver drafted in the first round, seventh pick, he'd gone to Raleigh lower than originally anticipated. His speed and ability to snag the ball out of anywhere in the air as long as it was within five feet of him, regardless of how many defenders he had on him, had helped lead Alabama to three national championships in a row.

He was way too young for me, but his light mocha skin and bulging muscles and kind smile made him easy on the eyes. He was also a single dad to a three-year-old girl, and more down to earth than anyone I'd ever met.

Of course, there was still time for that to change.

"I'm not greedy," I replied while I snagged a tequila shot.

"Don't let her fool you, Kolby. She's a viper."

I snorted and licked my wrist. "Right. I'm a regular siren."

Beaux caught the defeated tone in my voice and kicked me under the table.

"Your problem," he said, reaching for his own shot and sliding one to Kolby, "is that you tried for years to be good enough for some limp-dicked prick, and never once realized that you were too good for him to begin with."

"Ah, guy trouble. That's what the tequila is for."

I shot a glance toward Kolby and tapped my glass to his. "The tequila is for fun."

Screw it. I didn't need Beaux's reminder or pep talk.

Kolby sent me a smirk and our glasses clinked together before we shot the liquor.

The burn hit my tongue, my throat, clawing its way down to my stomach. I pressed my lips together and took the lime Beaux offered, thankful for the sour to help.

I still couldn't hold back the face I pulled as I took one last swallow. Nothing evaporated it until Beaux handed me another shot.

"After three it doesn't hurt so much."

"Fantastic. Once I can't feel anything then it will taste good."

"Yup." Kolby and Beaux slammed another shot with me before Kolby slid his glasses and limes into the center of the table.

I took my third without hesitating. "Where's your daughter tonight?"

Kolby took a sip of his water glass. "With my ma. They're at home, unpacking."

He shook his head, his eyes filled with that same awed look Beaux had for the entire first year of playing for the Vikings. The "how did this become my life?" look.

I still saw it spark in Beaux from time to time, but a few years in, the wealth and shock was diminishing and being replaced with a new normal.

"You moved your mom up here, too?"

A muscle popped in his cheek and I sensed I'd touched a topic he didn't want to discuss. "Ma's the only one I trust to watch Mya."

I didn't understand the love a parent had for their child—not personally—but I'd seen my mom sacrifice in order to try to give us everything. It was that memory, of my mom coming home from work only to have time to shower and go to another job, that made me slide my hand around Kolby's shoulder and squeeze. "You're a good dad, Kolby."

"Let's hope she thinks so."

"She will."

"Need more shots?" Beaux asked, his hand already in the air and waving down the waitress.

The burn of the liquor in my veins made my cheeks and chest warm. I was feeling relaxed and tipsy.

I shook my head. "No. One more beer and I should be good."

He rolled his eyes playfully. "So much for drunk and stupid."

"Oh, there's still plenty of time for stupid."

"Right," Beaux teased. "Of course."

It was my turn to roll my eyes. We both knew me. I had never been a partier and with the drinks and the warmth and the dim lights, I already wanted to get to the apartment and start cleaning the shower and floors so I could move in.

I had too much of my mom in me, and not enough of Beaux. I blamed the fact that we had different fathers.

Where he let everything roll off his back, never worrying and stressing, I had a hard time relaxing, always planning and preparing. We couldn't be any more different.

Conversation drifted then to Beaux and Kolby getting settled in Raleigh, the things they'd seen in the last few months since they'd moved out here. What they wanted to do next, their thoughts about the upcoming preseason game.

I wasn't involved in most of the conversations, so my eyes drifted along with my thoughts. Thoughts of a surly, rude tight end who had yet to appear. Disappointment uncurled in me and made me frown.

I didn't want to see him, yet I couldn't stop thinking about him either. The interaction earlier was more unpleasant than most I'd had in my life. Yet I couldn't lie—along with probably millions of other women in the country, I had pictured Oliver starring in my fantasies at some point since he began in the NFL.

Admittedly, as soon as Beaux was traded, thoughts of meeting Powell were first in my mind.

Yet as much as I teased my brother about making out with his teammates, I wouldn't do that to him. I wouldn't want to be the cause of possible tension for him in the locker room or on the field. When he was playing, my job was to support him, not make it more difficult.

With a heavy sigh, I slid out of the booth.

Beaux's gaze caught me with a questioning look.

"I'll be right back. I just need some air."

"And then a dance with me," Kolby said, flashing me a wink.

The kid was cute. I could admit that, too. He was also harmless. Safe.

"You know? I think my restroom trip can wait. Want to?"

"Hell yeah. Sexy cougar woman in my arms? I'll have to beat the men away from you." He frowned, a teasing glint in his eye as he wiggled his fingers. "On second thought, maybe we shouldn't. Can't get these hands broken in a bar fight."

I punched him in the shoulder. "Shut up." I turned to Beaux. "You mind?"

"Go kick back, Sis. You've earned it."

I rolled to my toes and kissed his cheek while I waited for Kolby to slide out of the booth. He gripped my hand and led me down the stairs, pulling me behind him so we wouldn't get separated in the crowd at the bottom. Halfway down the second flight, the hairs on the back of my neck stood up.

I paused, tugging my hand out of Kolby's, and looked around. Seeing nothing, I shook off the strange sensation and hurried to catch up to my dance partner.

The music was louder on the dance floor, pulsing through my body and filling my veins with that instant need to move.

The song was fast and perfect, and as Kolby guided us to an area of the floor beneath the VIP area where we'd sat, he set his hands on my waist, pulling me to him until my hips were against his.

We would have had to shout to be heard, so we were silent while we moved, our bodies connected. It had been so long since I'd been out. Most days I felt too old for a bar scene—not that Patrick would have ever gone anyway. And if Patrick didn't want to go somewhere, we rarely did.

I lost myself in my thoughts, my regrets, and the feel of warm and strong hands on my body as sweat began to bead at my neck.

The buzz of the alcohol beginning to dissipate as I lost myself in the music, it was just me and Kolby while he spun me in circles and we goofed around. We made funny faces and moved our bodies in time to the music.

We stayed there longer than the one song we'd agreed on, and it was at the end of the fourth when I finally needed a break. My toes hurt in my heels, and the strap of fabric across my back clung to my skin.

"I need a break!" I shouted, leaning into Kolby's arms.

He wrapped them around me. "Wondering when the old woman was going to stop. Lasted longer than I thought you would."

I shoved him playfully again and turned to walk off the dance floor, but when I went to take my first step, my feet froze in place.

Kolby bumped into me, pushing me forward, and before I could stumble, I was pulled into another set of strong arms.

"The next one's mine."

Electricity zinged up my arms and down my spine, straight to my toes where they curled inside my heels.

Powell was a force on the field. Running and catching, he could do it all with the grace of a panther. Amazing, considering his six-four frame. He looked like he'd be large and bulky, awkward, but he was fast. He was powerful.

With his body guiding me backward onto the dance floor I'd just tried to exit, he was also undeniable.

Magnetic.

Heat swirled between us as I flexed my arm and tried to pull away from him.

My mind screamed to run.

My body screamed louder to resist the urge to do so.

"What are you doing?"

His sandy blond brows pulled together, sharpening into points. For a moment I thought he couldn't hear me.

Then he leaned down, pulling me to him until my hand hit his chest. My fingers curled into his muscled firmness of their own accord.

"I'm thinking someone like you should have a real man. Not the boys you've been hanging with tonight."

He'd seen me. He'd been the one watching me. I knew it with the same certainty I knew my panties were becoming wet despite his absurd assumption.

"You don't know me. You know nothing about me."

"I know what you want."

He didn't know crap. Anything he could say or assume was wrong.

I should have pushed him away from me. I should have found the way he rolled his hips against mine repulsive.

Instead, I became malleable to every move he made, my body succumbing to his presence and the static igniting in the breaths of space between us.

His gaze dropped from my eyes to my breasts, his stare bold and unabashed before he looked back at me. "You want what they all want. The fame, the money, the right to say you've sucked our large cocks."

Yes. Repulsive. Yet a wave of excitement rolled through my body, heating it at the mere thought of his cock.

He continued before I gathered my scattered thoughts. "But what you don't know is that men new in the league are still boys, easily led by sexy pussy with tits and ass and legs for days, but they don't know what to do with it once they have it." He was talking about my brother. And my brother looking at my ass and tits. I didn't want to throw up like I normally would.

I was stuck on the fact that he thought I was sexy. How fucked up was I?

Not fucked up enough, or drunk enough, or dumb enough to not know where this was going. A quick fuck against the wall in the hallway where he'd turn me away from him, lift my skirt and plunge deep inside me, all without having to kiss or touch me.

I was lonely and still reeling from a failed engagement. I wanted a few hours of oblivion and possibly a one-night stand, but I wasn't a pushover and I wasn't an idiot. I deserved more than the sexy look he was giving me offered.

"Oliver?" I asked, my tone breathless and raw from the dancing and from the way his fingertips were running along my exposed skin.

"What, baby?"

I fought the cringe at the worthless endearment. My fingers slid from his chest to his shoulders and I pulled myself closer.

Flames shot through me as I brushed against the sizable bulge in his pants. "You don't know shit. And if you don't get your hands off me this very fucking second, my brother will kick your ass on and off the field."

He dropped his hands like I'd burned him and shot me a quizzical look.

That furrowed brow was no less sexy.

I grinned and forced myself to step back. The space was necessary. Without it I might have said fuck my morals and jumped up on him, climbed him like a monkey in a tree and let him give me the ride I knew he'd be so good at.

"Your brother? Who?" A hand scrubbed down his face.

I didn't take the time to explain. A rush of bodies pressed against us, giving me my opening.

I turned on my heels and trembling legs and got the hell off the floor, back to the VIP area and into the ladies' restroom without looking back.

My back hit the wall of the bathroom and my hands went to my face before the door closed behind me. My fingers still shook from adrenaline and lust and desire when I pressed them to my temples.

I needed to get out of there.

I needed to leave.

How could I have ever been attracted to an asshole like Patrick, just in a prettier and sexier package?

All men were the same.

They thought with their dicks and thought women should bend to their will just because they flashed a wad of cash and the promise of an orgasm.

And fuck that, my fingers hadn't let me down yet.

"Get yourself together," I murmured to myself before I used the restroom.

When I was done, I splashed cool water on my wrists and my throat. My body was still heated. The memory of Powell's body against mine. The sway of his hips. The size of his erection.

"Shit."

Squeezing my eyes closed, I tried to vanquish the memories that were so brief they should have already disappeared, but they hadn't. They were there, vivid and clear as day and equally powerful as the vision of Patrick pounding into a woman in a bathroom much like the one I was in at the moment.

The memory was a bitter slap to the face, better than any splash of cold water on my still-flushed skin.

I walked into the hallway with my head held high, my heels stable, and my resolve strengthened. Never again would I let a man use me and toss me to the side like Patrick had.

I would move on from him, but it would be with a man who knew how to treat a woman with respect, and had the ability to cherish them.

"Beaux's your brother."

The strained voice stopped me in my tracks. I didn't turn to him.

"Yes."

I waited for an apology I assumed would never come, and was surprised when it did.

"I'm sorry. I might have fucked that up down there."

Might have? He'd essentially called me a whore. I spun on my heels until I faced him directly. With Oliver several feet away, his back braced to the wall, his hands on his hips, I barely had to tilt my head up to see him clearly.

"He was right about you, though. You're a prick."

A lip curled in response. "I said I was sorry."

"Forgiven." I turned around and walked back to Beaux. He had three teammates around him, women draped on their laps, but none on his.

His eyes were on me, his face holding that look of concern I was getting so, so tired of seeing on him.

"You okay?"

"Good. Ready to head home, though."

He shot a look behind my shoulder and stood immediately. "What'd he say to you? I saw him follow you back to the bathroom."

"Nothing, Beaux. It's fine, I swear."

His gaze searched me for honesty. I was lying, and we both knew it, but I still reached around him to the table and picked up my small clutch.

"Let's just go. I'm wiped after the trip out here."

He wrapped his arm over my shoulders and pulled me to him.

As he turned me, my head twisted and my gaze locked on Powell's. He was sitting at the bar now, a glass of honey-colored alcohol in his hand. His stern expression was firmly in place and I turned back around while I still could.

With the heat in his gaze, the look of want still in his eyes, and the fact that he'd actually not only apologized but seemed genuine, I had no idea what to do about Oliver Powell.

Only that it was best if I stayed far, far away.

I TUGGED at the end of a strand of my hair and clenched the phone tighter in my other hand.

"Can you please let this go?"

Patrick's voice was like nails on a chalkboard. "Please, Shan. I'm so sorry. I miss you. I want to see you to talk about us. Don't throw us away like this."

Same old lines. Same things I'd heard for the last month.

After seeing him in the restroom, fucking Priscilla against the wall, I had taken off. I hadn't said anything, just made some choked, animalistic noise, and run from the bathroom and restaurant like hell was nipping at my heels. I was most likely halfway home before he'd realized that I was the one who'd seen him; me that I'd heard him calling her "baby."

He'd caught up with me in our apartment as I was slashing my wedding dress with the sharpest knife I could find.

The apologies had started immediately. The lies quickly followed. That it was just that one time, that he was stressed and scared about the wedding. I had stood in our bedroom that we'd shared for two years listening to his pleas and apologies for almost an hour, feeling nothing but soul-sucking grief.

I was only now just beginning to realize that the reason I'd put off our wedding for so long was because somewhere, deep down inside me, while I liked the financial stability he provided, I didn't fully trust him to take care of me. For the last year, we'd argued about getting married before I'd finally caved and set a date. He'd proposed after we had been dating for two years and I finally agreed to move in together. Then I dragged my feet in getting married, always finding an excuse or reason to continue putting it off. I should have known back then that our relationship wasn't going to work. It didn't mean it didn't still hurt to see him cheating on me.

Each word he spoke over the phone was a punch to my gut. I didn't trust that Patrick still wanted me. He didn't want to lose. He didn't want to look like a fool. He wasn't the guy women walked away from.

He was a McDonnelly. Ginger-haired and Irish to the deepest parts of his marrow, his family owned more than half of Des Moines. They still owned thousands of acres of land and businesses. No one said no to them.

I was still finding it hard to do so.

I sighed. "I'm scheduling a moving truck. I only want my stuff. Can you please let me know when's a good time for them to come and pick it up?"

"Come home and discuss this with me, Shannon. I want to see you. I want you to hear me out. I swear to you, this will never happen again. Priscilla's been moved to a different department, and I don't even see her anymore. Please."

His voice had softened, gone gravelly and determined, coaxing me against my judgment to listen, to give in like I always did. Her name on his lips was a bucket of cold water on the temptation.

I tapped a pencil to paper and gritted my teeth together. "No. And I don't have time for this. I have things to do, and if you won't be cooperative I'll figure it out on my own."

"Shannon—"

"Goodbye, Patrick."

I hung up the phone at the same time a growl sounded from behind me.

I was in what would soon be my office at Stamped. I'd scrubbed the place from top to bottom over the last week, including the cute and full-of-character upstairs apartment. Every day it settled in a little bit more that this place was mine.

All mine.

Once I got my stuff, anyway. Fortunately, I'd had the smarts to bring all my jewelry-making tools and equipment with me.

Everything was scattered about on two folding tables I'd picked up as soon as I'd cleaned the downstairs office.

With the Arts Festival opening next week, I'd been desperate to start creating. I wanted the store ready to go by then, but there were a million things I still had left to do scribbled on a ripped piece of notebook paper...somewhere in my office.

Amazing how I could make such a huge mess when I had so little.

"What did the loser want now?"

I turned to Beaux to see his arms across his chest, shoulder leaning against the door to my office. He was freshly showered, telling me he'd come straight from his late workout.

I groaned and tossed the pen to the tabletop. "Same old crap. Apologies, refusing to let me go."

I hated that there was a small part of me that was glad. Because if he didn't want to let me go, maybe everything we'd shared, everything I thought I'd once loved hadn't been a lie.

A month had given me a lot of perspective. Melissa and Beaux's persistent cataloging his faults and the things they'd always hated about him had given me greater insights into things I hadn't seen, or had refused to admit earlier.

I was angry and hurt, but beneath it there was still the love I'd thought I had for him for years, simmering. I couldn't dig deep enough to scrape it out.

"When are you moving your stuff out here?"

"Whenever Patrick tells me when I can get the movers into the apartment. He wants to see me first, though."

"Fuck that, Shannon. Melissa has a key. She can meet movers any time of the day. Stop fucking bending to his will."

"I know." I scrubbed my hands down my face and wrapped them around the back of my neck, popping my knuckles. "I know that. I was hoping—"

"You were hoping he'd be a decent human being for once."

Ugh. I hated my baby brother. Such a pain in the ass. His words were still truthful.

"Yeah." A breath fell from my puffed out cheeks. "I guess I was." I spun in my chair, my design tables between us. "How was practice? Ready for the upcoming game?"

He pushed off the doorway and walked to the tables, his fingers brushing against bracelets I'd pounded and shaped earlier.

"Won't play much the first couple games. Can't have their new stars getting injured before the season really begins."

He seemed to avoid meeting my gaze. I didn't often see him uncertain or worried, unless it came to me and my life. This was football.

His dream. His goal since he was five.

"How was practice?"

"Powell's still being an asshole. Jesus, he's not letting me get away with shit. Every play he's on my ass, screaming in my face."

The name alone sent a spark of awareness to places it shouldn't have—deep in my belly, the apex of my thighs.

I cleared my throat. "Yeah? Is he right?"

Beaux huffed and looked at a spot on the far wall. "I'm good. I know that. I'm good enough to be a starter, but every damn time I make a mistake—or when I don't, for that matter—he's right there, telling me what to do different. I'm not Madison, and I don't want to be. They got rid of him for a reason, but he and Powell were friends. I don't know if it's something he has against me, against my playing, or because I took his friend's spot." He looked at me then, a gleam in his eye. "Or if he just really wants to fuck my sister and is pissed I've cock-blocked him."

He choked over the word. I wanted to laugh at his grossed-out expression, but I couldn't. That heat in my belly unfurled into something larger.

I swallowed a lump in my throat. "Really?"

I squeezed my eyes closed immediately. How desperate would I have to be for that to happen? He was worse than Patrick. Just as big of a player but didn't feel the need to hide it.

"While this whole discussion is making me want to puke up my protein shake—"

"That's probably just the protein." I pulled a face. Those things smelled gross and tasted nastier. Add the kale, chia seeds, and spinach and it was shit in a cup.

"Shut up." He smirked and went back to looking at my jewelry. "You know he was married once, right?"

My head spun while I tried to figure out who he meant before he continued speaking.

"High school sweetheart. Gossip in the locker room is he loved the shit out of her. She used him as a meal ticket and once he made it big, she left him and took over half of everything he owned."

"Why are you telling me this?"

"Not sure." He shrugged and pulled back from a necklace charm before sliding his hand into the pocket of his jeans. "Beneath all the bullshit, all the asshole behavior, and all the crap that's said about him in the papers, I guess I don't think he's that bad of a guy."

It was as close to permission as I was going to get from Beaux. Not that it meant anything. I wasn't going to be the next woman on Oliver's arm on a photo spread of NFL player's wives and girlfriends webpage, only to be replaced the following week.

"He's been named captain of the team for a reason, you know. Is he right about you and your playing?"

For an athlete, Beaux was pretty humble. More than most. He was usually pretty open to criticism and always took feedback, evaluated it to see if it was true. Hell, he scanned his Instagram feed, reading comments from guys who couldn't pick a decent fantasy football team, to see if their Monday quarterbacking had merit.

That he'd be so angry about Powell's input told me it wasn't the criticism getting to him.

"Yeah." He looked up at me and grinned. It was lopsided and made a dimple pop in his cheek. "He might be."

"Then you need to work harder."

"And you need to get out of this office. Come to Kolby's house with me tonight. He's throwing a pool party."

"Beaux—"

"Just a small gathering. Nothing big, I swear—not with our game in a couple days."

My cheeks heated as I asked, "Will Oliver be there?"

"Fucking hell," he moaned and dragged a hand through his hair. "Probably."

"I probably shouldn't."

"You're probably right."

"I'm going."

He grinned. "I figured you would."

FOUR
OLIVER

The small crowd gathered on Kolby's outdoor patio made my skin itch.

Over a dozen kids jumped and splashed in the pool. Long Styrofoam noodles, plastic wings, and inflatables tossed all over the place made the simple act of walking a minefield.

I was trying to relax. It wasn't easy. Every year, the men on my team became younger and faster. They were tougher. They fought harder, partied louder, threw away their millions as soon as it hit their pockets.

For some, it filled them with a greater drive to succeed, to be the next big name known and shouted in small-town basements and garages all over the country for three months a year. For others, it became one big unending party...until the party came to a crashing halt.

I still hadn't figured out our new quarterback. Beaux Hale had talent. That couldn't be argued. But the man owned a fucking a RV that he drove around the country during the off season, partying wherever he parked it. He was determined on the field, a fucking clown off it. It was hard to take him seriously, and as his captain, it was fucking with our teamwork on the field.

I pushed him hard because his arrival meant we finally had a chance at the fucking coveted ring. Eight years in the league and I'd come close twice during my first two years. For the last six, it'd been a crapshoot.

Realistically I had two, maybe three decent years left in me. At thirty, I was becoming an old man. The pain in my knees, the hits to my ribs, the sore muscles...all of it took longer to recover from. I fucking ached everywhere already and the season hadn't really begun.

I wanted to walk away with that damn golden ring so badly I could taste the metal in my mouth, between my teeth.

It was all so fucking close with the team we had this year. Hale was being touted as the guy who could take us there.

I was an asshole because I doubted he had it in him, but I hoped like hell he did.

Unfortunately, I kept thinking about the way his sister's ass had felt in my hands last week on the dance floor. The fact that she'd doused my lust with her threats and then Beaux had made it clear at practice he'd follow through with them had made me a bigger asshole than normal.

Kolby, on the other hand, was the first rookie I'd ever met who seemed to have his eyes focused on the only two things that mattered: his daughter and his career. At his party, he was in the pool with her, holding on to her stomach while she flapped and kicked, making more of a splash than getting anywhere.

But he was patient, focused on only her and the other little kids around.

It forced a weight to my chest. One I hated thinking about so much that I refused to do so—but when I saw mommoments like that, I couldn't help it.

I'd lost every fucking thing I ever wanted and it was all Serena's fault. Not that I gave a shit about the money I was still forced to send her. Spousal support, my ass. She'd walked away two years into our marriage, and six years later I was still paying for her to go do whatever the fuck she wanted.

Our phone calls were once a year, her calling me, me letting it go to voicemail. The taste of regret and disgust were heavy on my tongue every time I heard her voice wondering when her annual payment was going to be deposited.

I figured the next conversation we had would go drastically different.

An elbow bumped mine and a cold beer was placed in my hand. "Take this and drink it. You look like you want to kill someone."

I glanced at Danny Rudolph. He was only a year younger than me and had been traded to Raleigh the same year I had been—the year after everything in my life went tits up. He hadn't known me before, when I had to get my shit together, but he'd been there since my downfall.

"I don't want to kill anyone," I said and realized where my glare had been.

On her.

Shannon Hale. She ignited something inside me that went beyond the thought of an hour or two between the sheets before I kicked her out of my bed, like I did with most women since Serena. It had been different from the moment I saw Shannon.

Something dark and twisted, something that told me I'd be able to do whatever I wanted to her and she'd only scream for more.

Thinking she was draping herself all over Hale to get her hand into his back pocket had pissed me off more than it should have.

The way her gaze had gone a bit hazy when she'd looked at me that first time had made me jealous of the young kid.

"You go after her and you're looking for trouble. Word is Hale's her only family. You fuck with her and he's going to go apeshit on your old ass."

I had heard that. Their mom died a few years ago. They came from nothing. Word was Shannon was more of a mom to him than his own had ever been. Not to mention they had different fathers, neither of them around. Beaux didn't hold shit back. He wasn't ashamed of where he came from.

Plus, Rudolph was right. Guy could probably take me, too, unfortunately. I might have doubted his ability, but he still had an arm of steel, built for throwing. He could be the best in the league if he didn't always fucking hesitate that half-second in the pocket.

It was going to get him sacked and concussed before the third game.

"I don't want her."

The words tasted as nasty as the swig of beer I took to wash away the lie.

I wanted her. I'd thought of a thousand ways to apologize to her for being such an asshole. They all involved her naked, her thick, dark hair spread all over my white sheets. Her jaw slack while I pleasured her, over and over again.

I caught her gaze, that same hazy, wanting look from across the pool where she stood with a half-dozen players and their wives or girlfriends.

Being the prick I was, I dropped my hand to my crotch and adjusted myself where she could see I was already growing hard.

The thought of her...the mere fucking sight of her did that to me.

I hadn't been this hard, so constantly and so easily, since

Serena had let me touch her tits for the first time when we were fifteen.

Next to me, Rudolph laughed. It was loud and gathered the attention of most of the people nearby. I glared at him, but still sensed Shannon's gaze at my back.

A little prickle of interest.

I smirked at my friend. "You're an asshole, you know that?"

"Hell yeah," he said, slapping me on the shoulder. "But there's a lot of things you are and a liar isn't one of them. Might as well get it out of your system. Let Beaux beat the shit out of you and then we can all move on. You keep looking at her like you want to fuck her naked in front of all these people and rumors will start."

Fuck. He was right. A football team was worse than a frat house when it came to gossip running rampant.

"I'll get right on that then," I muttered, setting my drink down. Last weekend's splurge at the club where I'd seen Shannon had been the last real alcohol I'd touch until hopefully February—

After a Super Bowl win.

"Can't you just go find another easy lay and fuck her out of your mind? Pretend she's someone else? This has trouble written all over it."

I'd tried that. Saturday and Wednesday.

Unfortunately I'd only pictured Shannon, and the women beneath me, their faces buried in my pillows, hadn't helped.

I wanted to see her face—those coffee-colored eyes, her pouty lips parched and dry.

"I like your first idea better." I slapped Rudolph on the shoulder. "You're right. Fuck her. Get her out of my head. Move on to the next one."

"This is going to go south real quick."

I didn't respond. I was already walking away. Toward the

woman I couldn't stop thinking about. The woman who was barely covered in a swimsuit cover—it was strapless, hitting just below her ass. A bright peach color that showed off her tan, and fuck...those legs.

Toned and long. Painted toenails to match the light blue suit I'd seen her in earlier when I'd first arrived and she was lying out on a lounge chair.

With every step bringing me closer to her, her grip tightened on her water bottle. She moved slowly away from the group of men she'd been talking to. Beaux glanced at me, but he was missing the scowl I had become familiar with this week.

The pink color blossoming on her cheeks held my attention. The slight quirk to her mouth. Lips that tilted up at one corner, practically daring me to do all the filthy things I wanted to.

I'd take her up on it, as soon as she let me. It'd been a while since I'd had to persuade a woman to let me do what I wanted, but I had a feeling she'd make it worth the effort.

"Come talk to me," I said, sliding right up next to her and not giving her any doubt what I really wanted.

Her eyes flared—hesitant and surprised at my boldness. "We are talking."

"Privately."

I held out my hand, wanting more than anything to wrap it around her elbow and pull her toward me, pull her into a dark corner where I could slide her knee to my hip and sink into her. She was short, and in sandals. I'd find a way to make it work.

But I didn't. I kept my hand still, palm outstretched.

The first move had to be hers. I'd take care of the rest.

Slowly, she nodded. Her whispered "Okay" was so quiet I barely heard her over the clamoring of the kids in the background.

She slid her hand into mine and that same shock of electric energy swam and slithered up my arm to my chest.

It was unnatural. Scared the hell out of me.

I gripped her tighter and pulled her to me. My hand went to her hair, pushing it back so I could lean down to whisper in her ear.

"You know everyone's watching this right now?"

She nodded once.

"You know what's going to happen when I get you alone?"

She cleared her throat. Her nerves were evident in the rapid blink of her eyes. "Talking."

I drew closer to her so my lips brushed over her earlobe. "We'll talk. And then you'll scream."

She didn't pull away. I was still being an ass.

I expected a punch to my back from Beaux at any moment.

But none of it came. Instead of pulling away like she should have, her chest pressed to mine.

"Then let's go talk."

FIVE

SHANNON

Almost every woman at the party stared as Oliver led me through the small crowd of players and their wives and girl-friends. They glanced at us once, quickly looked away, only to surreptitiously slide their gazes back to us as we passed them.

I swallowed hard in an effort to push down the apprehension and focused on the tingling in my stomach, the way my heart jumped and pulse pounded as he guided me inside the house. His confidence and the way he seemed to not care about what anyone thought of him—along with the sexual magnetism between us—flooded my veins in preparation for what would happen next.

What he wanted was obvious. The desire and need written all over his face from the moment we made contact was clear.

That look, along with Beaux's permission to do whatever I wanted earlier, made me want to toss my morals to the ground and stomp all over them.

I'd never had the freedom other kids had.

Now, I was to be free to do whatever I wanted. Live how I chose without the risk of screwing things up for anyone.

First, it was Beaux. If I was too hung over, too caught up in the arms of a stranger, I could miss getting him where he needed to be. I could miss a game or a practice or a meeting with a college recruiter. I could miss giving our mom her meds when she needed them, or running her to doctor's appointments.

My entire life had been spent taking care of my family, and then later, making certain I wasn't screwing up anything for Patrick or his family.

I was so, so tired of the responsibility bearing down on my shoulders, I could break at any moment.

So why not throw it all away for a quickie in a stranger's house with a sexy man whose confident and warm touch held the promise of pleasure and wild abandon?

Oliver led me through an enormous house with more floors and windows and doors than they sold in most home improvement stores until we reached a room at the end of a hall on the top floor.

I looked at everything from the incredibly fancy decor to the windows that overlooked the pool outside, to the overly dramatic chandeliers and woodwork so expensive and well-oiled it gleamed when the sun hit it.

"Kolby's house is a mansion," I murmured.

Beaux and Oliver could probably afford something like this. Oliver probably lived in something like this. With years in the league and millions to his name, he probably had houses and condos in fabulous vacation spots and private planes to take him wherever he wanted to go on whatever random whim he had. He had to travel all the time, whenever he could, to be seen in so many different places with so many different women.

"He needs a home, not a crash pad like so many of the other players," Oliver said, not looking around or swept up in anything except his intended purpose with me.

I swallowed at the thought before I realized what he said.

"And your house? Is it a home or a crash pad?"

A muscle jumped in his cheek when he finally pushed open a door and tugged me through. It was a bathroom, not a bedroom, and my resolve to live free shook beneath my feet.

He couldn't give me the courtesy of a bed?

My wants and my needs conflicted with my past and my choices and the way I'd always been.

I was a jumbled mess.

He pulled me flush against him like he'd done on the dance floor a week ago, surrounding me everywhere.

He was only wearing a thin T-shirt, a hint of chest hair peeking through the top of his collar, and bright red board shorts. Leather flip-flop sandals adorned his perfect feet and I'd smiled when I first saw them. Seeing him casual was an illusion.

As he touched me, his hand brushing through my hair again and then trailing down my arm, he was anything but casual.

Determined. Intense. Focused.

I blinked and swallowed down my nerves.

"I've thought about having you beneath me for a week now. The first time that happens won't be in Kolby's house in a strange bed where I'll never be able to picture you there again."

"Oh." The lump in my throat returned. I tilted my head back to see him looking down at me. "You wanted to talk."

"I was an asshole before."

"I have a feeling you're always an asshole."

I might have wanted him, but apparently I hadn't become a complete doormat.

My words made him laugh. It was beautiful—deep and husky and rolled over me like gentle waves.

"Touché. I'm usually an asshole, just maybe not as obvious

as I was to you. I'm sorry for making judgments and treating you like that."

"Why?"

His hands were still moving on me. Thick and large with calluses from years of hard work. Gentle yet firm—teasing. He brushed the pads of his fingers along my arms and shoulders to my upper back. He was everywhere, all over my exposed skin, making me shiver and tremble beneath him.

"Women around football players want one thing." His hips pressed against me, drawing me closer. That bulge in his shorts, the one he'd let me see him adjust earlier, pressed against my stomach. God. He was large. He was tall and big everywhere, so it wasn't a surprise.

My need grew.

"Two things, actually. It's easy to give them what they want, knowing they'll disappear afterward. When I saw you touching Beaux, and then dancing with Kolby, I didn't like it."

"That's absurd."

"I know. Can't explain it, don't really want to, but I'm thinking that we should get this attraction between us out of the way. I've got a season to focus on—nothing else can have my attention."

He was being honest.

I had to give him that.

"So a quickie in the bathroom and then I'm forgotten?"

"No." The word was clipped, showing his tension and restraint. It made my blood begin to boil beneath my skin. "After I take you here, I'll take you to my place so I can live out the fantasies I've had of you for the last week."

He'd thought of me. Fantasized about me. Somehow, that filled me with a power, a sense of control in this crazy, messed-up situation that I hadn't yet known I had.

The idea didn't seem as scary or as bad as it might have last week. After all, he had a season to focus on. I had a new job to get off the ground.

Neither of us had the time.

"Doesn't seem fair," I whispered, finally reaching out to touch him. I slid my fingers along the veins popping on his forearm. "To only get the night for you to fulfill your fantasies of me. What about mine of you?"

"You've thought about me?" His lips twitched...from humor or victory I didn't know.

Dishonesty had no place in my life, and I resisted the urge to hide behind lies now. "For years."

His hands were on my cheeks, pulling me to him. I had to roll to the tips of my toes for balance. "Tell me," he whispered, right before his lips pressed against mine. "Tell me all of them."

I couldn't. He stole my breath and my sense of decency when his warm lips brushed mine and I opened to him. His tongue slid in, not seeking or gentle. I inhaled his scent as we kissed and knew I'd always remember the fresh spice of his cologne. He smelled like summer and excitement, and I suspected some of it was just him.

He plundered me. He sent me off balance with a kiss and his firm hands pressing back to my scalp. It pulled my hair, making it sting and making me tremble beneath him.

The man was tall and strong, able to break me with a breath, a twist of his hands, and yet the bite of pain made me lean closer, crave more.

His kiss unraveled me as our tongues twisted, taking and hunting but not giving, and I succumbed to his touch, to his idea.

To the thought of him, for one night, where we could play out whatever we wanted and walk away.

It wouldn't be enough. I was smart enough already to know

it based on the heat rolling off his skin, the tightness in his muscles as he devoured me.

I was also smart enough not to say anything as he pulled away, both of us gasping for breath when he harshly growled, "Turn around. When I make you come, I want you watching."

I did exactly what he asked. I'd walked into this knowing what would happen. My body primed before he even held out his hand on the patio.

I twisted toward the bathroom mirror, legs shaking, wits scattered all over the marble floor.

"Hands on the counter."

I did what I was told, unable to think. I was pulled to the look in Oliver's eyes. Surly expression still in place like I'd made him angry. Like the thought of wanting me pissed him off.

"Oliver," I whispered. His gaze flickered to mine in the mirror. I looked wild, reckless.

He appeared firmly in control.

"Do it," I dared him when I saw his hands flex into fists at his sides.

He reached out and pulled down on my cover-up. The cheap, tube top cover I'd bought at Target just the day before fluttered to the ground and I was in front of him, barely dressed. Strapless bathing suit, twisted between my breasts, low-rider bottoms. It wasn't a bra and underwear. It actually covered more than my usual panties.

His gaze traveled down my back and my backside and then switched so he could look at me in the mirror. He stared at me like I was already naked. He made me feel like I was already naked.

"I want to see your breasts." He said it mostly to himself, but I still nodded. My silent approval. "I want to see everything."

"Okay."

His hands slid up my back, taking their time, trailing large circles over my skin. His thumb flicked over the clasp at the back of my suit. My hips rocked forward in response and the surliness in his expression faded to something else...something scarier. Something that looked like rapture mixed with desire.

His thumb rested on my strap again, tightening at the clasp. I inhaled a steadying breath while he deftly worked to undo it.

"Tell me. Are you wet for me already? After a kiss and some touches?"

Pink burned my cheeks and chest. "Yes."

I was past the point of being embarrassed, too turned on, too needy to care.

"When?"

"When what?"

He finished working on my suit and let it drop to the floor. I stared at my breasts in the mirror, knowing that was where he was looking.

His hands slid from my back to the sides, fingertips brushing the sides of my breasts, and I gasped.

"When did you get wet?"

He stepped closer to me, until I could feel him at my back. He was so tall. This position would never work. I opened my mouth to answer when his hand covered my breast and he brushed the side of his thumb over my nipple.

A delicious scrape. It sent fire to my sex.

"When did you get wet?" he asked again, moving to my other breast, my other nipple. "Tell me. I want to know. When I kissed you? Before?"

"When I saw you talking to Rudolph."

His smile lit up the small bathroom like I'd pleased him.

"I didn't even have to touch you?"

It was teasing, a hint of maliciousness, like he knew how easily he could have not only me, but any woman.

"Yes."

"Good." His hips pressed against me again and he bent his knees.

His cock nudged against my ass and my head fell forward, unable to bear the weight of the sensation.

Shit. He was huge. Thick. I licked my lips.

"I've been hard since I saw you at training camp. A fucking week, Shannon, and I haven't been able to get you out of my fucking head."

"Oh my God." His truth burned my skin, lava rolling down my spine.

I needed that. This tryst in the bathroom meant nothing, not long term. I still needed to know he'd thought of me more than just when he'd seen me.

"Oliver."

"You need something?" His hand ran across my stomach, his other still at my breast, lazy flicks over my hardened nipple. "Need something more than this?"

In reality, I could have orgasmed from the breast play and his words alone. It didn't take much. Never did—at least, not until the last couple of years.

My hips rocked forward, seeking his hand at the top edge of my swimsuit. "Yes."

"My fingers? Do you want them inside you?"

God, the asshole was going to make me work for this. My lip curled in frustration when he trailed along the edge of my swimsuit, teasing me.

His eyes gleamed with satisfaction.

"Make me come, Oliver."

"My fingers or my tongue. Your choice."

Oh God. Just the idea of him dropping to his knees either

behind me or in front of me sent a full body shiver rolling through me.

His fingers brushed against my swollen and hot center and he groaned. "Fuck this," he muttered and yanked down my bottoms.

"I want you too much. So fucking hot and wet for me, I can feel it through your suit. I'm going to torture and tease the hell out of you later, though."

It was a warning.

It made me smile.

The smile immediately vanished when he pressed his fingers against my clit and slid them through my wetness.

"Fucking soaked," he growled, his eyes on mine in the mirror. I saw him watching me before my eyes dropped to his hands.

One gripping my breast, the other fingering me, sliding through my flesh, teasing my clit before he pressed one finger inside me.

"Oh God," I moaned, my mouth going slack. "So good. More."

"So fucking greedy."

Yes. It'd been months since I'd had sex with Patrick—a clue I should have recognized, since previously we'd frequently had sex.

I brushed the thought out of my mind.

"More," I mewled again and let out a satisfied sigh when he pressed another finger inside of me. His hand at my breasts squeezed tight, finger and thumb playing with my nipple.

I rocked against him as he began fucking me, holding me in place with his touch on my breast. Every move forward rocked me into his hand, his thumb brushing my clit. Every pull back shot fire from my nipple.

I was throbbing, sweat beading on my hairline when he

pushed against me. His fingers slid out of me, causing me to cry out. He dropped his shorts before settling himself against me.

"Not fucking you here," he said, when he saw my eyes go wide. "But fuck if I can't wait to feel you against my skin."

I nodded once. I didn't want to be fucked here. His fingers returned to my cunt, sliding and pushing, and then I was overwhelmed with sensation. His cock sliding through my crease, gathering wetness, his fingers rolling and pressing, his fingers squeezing my nipple.

My whimpers became moans. All of it was overwhelming. He was everywhere, leaning over me, his chest brushing against my back, the press of his hips against my ass telling me he was just as close as I was.

"Oliver," I gasped, my body beginning to shake.

"Come for me, Shannon. And fucking look at me."

My eyes flew to his in the mirror and then rolled back before I could focus on him, the gritted words he spoke, and the harsh lines around his jaw.

I shattered when I saw him—when I noticed the pain it was taking him to stay in control.

The way his body, his muscles, his fingers and hands, and his thick cock pressed against me.

Chanted pleasure fell from my lips as my spasms began rolling through me. I quaked and shook and fell apart before his hand left my breast and went to his cock.

I lost the ability to stay on my hands and dropped to my elbows so I could watch him, looking over my shoulder.

He tugged and pulled on his erection, bigger and thicker than I had imagined, and I suddenly did want what he was going to do.

"Wait." I gasped, his fingers already beginning to slow inside of me.

I pushed him back with my hips, spun, and dropped to my knees.

I couldn't help it. I wanted him in me, wanted the feel of him losing control inside of me ingrained in my mind, keeping me warm when he was just a memory.

My fingers wrapped around his cock and he swore. "Fucking shit, Shannon."

I didn't tease him. His balls were pulled tight, his thickness hardened steel covered in silk.

I wrapped my lips around him and sucked him deep. Quickly, without pausing, I began taking care of him.

His hands dug into my hair again, holding me in place but letting me do the work.

He was heaven. Delicious and large in my mouth, I used my hand to help. His balls swung, hitting me in the chin with every thrust forward. I popped off his dick and stuck my tongue out, sucking them into my mouth.

"Holy fucking shit, get your mouth back on me."

I complied after tugging on his balls one more time, feeling them rise and tighten, the flesh warm and rigid.

My mouth went back to his tip and I swirled my tongue around him, playing with him and sucking him deep. His thrusts increased in speed until his fingers dove into my hair, tugging painfully.

"Coming in your mouth," he warned, his teeth pressed sharply together.

I nodded as best as I could, not that he'd seemed to ask my permission.

And then he pushed forward, gagging me at the back of my throat before he cursed and pulled back.

"Fuck. Sorry. So good. Holy shit," he chanted as the first spurts hit my tongue, holding me steady, his hips shaking from the stress of not plummeting into me again.

I sucked him off, swallowing until he was done and his hands went slack on my head. I gave him a final lick, bathing his cock with my tongue and the taste of us mixed together.

I was still coming down from my own high—my own orgasm and the power of giving him one he seemed to enjoy so much—when reality slammed down on me in the mere breath of a question.

"Fucking hell, how in the hell are you single with a mouth like that?"

I flinched and reached for my bathing suit, scrambling for it while on my knees.

"My fiancé thought it was more fun to fuck someone else, I guess."

SIX

OLIVER

"What?" I reached for her as she stood, pulling her back to me.

She jerked out of my touch, and I took the moment to pull up my own shorts. Fuck, that was hot. The last thing I'd expected was for Shannon to drop to her knees and suck me off like she'd been starved for it.

I was still reeling from it. Still shaking and trying to catch my breath when the words slipped from my mouth.

"I didn't mean it badly." I scrubbed my hands down my face. I had to get control. "And any man who lets you go after that is a moron."

The irony wasn't lost on me.

She shot me a look over her shoulder that told me she thought the same.

"I'm sorry. Give me a minute. I think you might have sucked my brains out through my dick."

She laughed, and I knew it was despite herself because she was still getting dressed like she couldn't wait to get the hell out of there.

Hell. I'd had blowjobs before. Lots of them. I wasn't

kidding when I told Shannon that women everywhere wanted to wrap their lips around an NFL player's cock for the sole point of being able to brag about doing so.

I can't exactly say I'd been particular before, but nothing compared to her excitement, her lust for it. The way she'd acted like she *had* to have it inside of her.

My dick hardened all over again just thinking about the way she looked on her knees. Eyes wide and watery. Lips stretched and bright pink.

Damn it. I adjusted myself and put my thoughts in order.

"Can I start over and say that was fucking amazing? And ignore the part where it hurt your feelings?"

"That'd be fine." She smoothed down her hair, running her fingers through it. It was useless. She looked well fucked and wild.

What she didn't do was look at me in the mirror.

I wanted us back on track. Back to the talk of fantasies and filthy words she didn't cringe from when I spoke.

"I should go," she said, turning to avoid me.

I stepped in front of her, resisting the urge to shake her. If she thought I was letting her walk away from me now, she was out of her ever-loving mind.

Besides, I was strangely curious about this fiancé. Not that I'd ask.

"Come home with me. I want you in my bed."

She made a sound of disbelief, arms crossed over her now-covered stomach like I hadn't had my hands all over her body moments ago.

No woman had ever acted like she wanted to hide from me. It was quite the opposite, generally.

I liked this new game.

I couldn't resist. Reaching out, I slid a finger along her cheek and smiled when she shivered from the slight touch.

She felt this...whatever it was that existed between us. I just had to find a way to burn it out quickly.

"I think this was a mistake."

"No way in fuck it was. It was going to happen, and it'll happen again."

"Threatening me?" She arched a brow, a challenge in her eyes as her shoulders rolled back.

I shook my head. "No, I'm talking about living out those fantasies of ours. I still want to hear the ones you had about me, and maybe if I'm feeling generous, I'll give it to you."

She swallowed slowly. A battle raged in her eyes. I was promising her nothing but hot fucking.

I couldn't promise her more than that—I wasn't built for it. Not anymore.

"One night."

I fought the urge to grin. "It's going to take longer than that."

The words were out before I could reel them back in, yet I didn't resent them either.

"What are you thinking?"

"Through preseason."

My half-hard dick was apparently calling the shots. No one ever spent more than one night in my bed, much less a month.

Her eyebrows jumped on her forehead, arching into perfect points. "Excuse me?"

I was as baffled as she was.

I pulled her toward me then, her chest against mine, and peered down at her. She was so small in my arms, so soft against me.

"You feel this," I said. "You know I'm right. One night is only going to make things worse. We need to burn out this attraction between us."

She flinched for a moment, and I thought I'd lost her. I'd deserve it.

She'd essentially told me her guy had cheated on her, and I wasn't offering anything more stable. Plus, she had to have known my reputation.

But after Serena left, I didn't give a shit who I fucked.

"I won't fuck another woman when I'm with you. You have my word on that."

Because cheaters were worse than players. They were liars. I was as honest as they came, except for maybe with myself.

"A month." She tested the words on her lips, thinking it over out loud. "I have a new job to start. I can't be distracted."

I'd assumed she was living off Beaux's income. Fortunately, I was smart enough to hide my surprise. I wouldn't ask her what she did. It didn't matter.

"Tell me. If you go home tonight, and are in bed alone, will you be thinking of me? Running your fingers through your wet slit and wishing it were my cock?"

She shivered again, her silent answer.

"Take me up on this, Shannon. I think you need it as much as I do."

"What makes you think that?"

"Because you just had someone use you and treat you like shit. I might use your body, but you'll always have my respect."

Her lip curled in that unhappy manner and I wondered if I had crossed a line.

Surprise ignited my senses when she smiled. "Okay. Deal. One month."

I turned to unlock the door. "Let's go tell Beaux we're leaving then."

"Oh no, no, no, no." She pressed her hand against the door, her eyes frantic. "There's no way I'm going back out there. Not after this...thing." She waved her hand between us, and I smiled.

"This...thing?"

"Yes." She gasped and tugged at her hair.

I was quickly learning that playing with her hair was her nervous habit.

"They'll all know. All of them. The team...the women. Oh my God!" Her eyes flashed wide and feral. "They'll think I'm what you think I am!" Panic struck her then and her palm went to her chest. "That's what they'll think of me. That I'm just some gold-digging slut, someone who spreads her legs—"

"Enough." I pulled her toward me without thought and slammed my lips over hers. It was bad enough when I heard myself say the words, a thousand times sharper when she repeated them. She leaned into the kiss, surrendering and submitting like I wanted her to. Perfect.

I pulled away. "No one will say shit, and if they do, I'll fucking handle it."

"You don't know what the women are like. How catty and vicious. Jesus, I've seen it before, heard it before, but now what they're saying is true."

"And none of their fucking business. Whatever girlfriend down there says shit, it says more about them than you or us. We know what we're doing and that's all that matters."

"Do we?"

No. I had no fucking clue what we'd just agreed to.

"Yes. We're giving each other what we need, no secrets, no hidden motives. Who cares about them?"

I sure as hell didn't.

Before she could panic again, I threw the bathroom door open and pulled her out of it. "Go downstairs and out the front door. I'll go talk to Beaux."

"No. Just...let's go. I'll text him so he doesn't worry. Tell him I'll be home later."

"Tomorrow morning."

This was getting out of hand faster than I could stop it. My mouth kept speaking what my dick wanted.

"I have to be at work early," she mumbled.

I couldn't remember a time when I had a woman on my arm thinking more about her job than the orgasms I'd promised to deliver.

Strangely, it wasn't a hit to my ego.

"Early tomorrow," I agreed, unable to hide the satisfaction in my smile. "Promise."

"Okay." She nodded and flitted her eyes to me, questioning. "Okay then. We're good to go, then."

She was trying to convince herself. If I were a gentleman, had any morals or values left inside of me, I'd ask her if she was certain she wanted this. I wasn't going to force myself on someone.

Coercing gently, though...that was another matter. Not giving her time to change her mind, I pulled her down the stairs, weaving through the maze of hallways in Kolby's mansion and out to my car.

It took work to get my Audi A8 out from the line of cars closely parked together, and not for the first time, I rued the day I'd sold my pickup in favor of a sports car.

Look the part, play the part, be the part. It was something my old man had drilled into me since I first caught a whiff that I could be good enough for the NFL.

Old and beaten pickup trucks screamed small-town hick, not athletic superstar.

Still didn't mean I didn't miss it, though—especially when the urge to go off-roading and mudding took hold during the off-season months. A man, a truck, a few beers...God, sometimes I missed it when life was simpler.

~

"THIS IS YOUR HOUSE?"

She covered her mouth with her fingers to stifle her giggle.

I glared at her. "Yes."

I loved my house. Liked that it was out in the middle of nowhere so on the rare occasion I brought a woman home with me and then took her back to wherever the next day—if I didn't just call for a cab—there was no way in hell she could find her way back. Plus, it was the only place I could find a few years ago when I wanted to get out of the city and back to where I was most at home.

"You have a barn." Her eyes widened further as she took in the horse paddock and the white barn to the left of the house. "Horses?" She spoke slowly, as if I was hard of hearing or didn't understand English.

"Why do you sound like you're about ready to go into shock?"

I knew why. No one expected this of me. The few teammates who had seen my house still gave me shit for it. No one ever saw it during the daytime. Bringing women to my house was a rarity, and on the nights I had company they were gone long before the sun rose.

Usually, I took them to the hotel room I kept during the season.

My home was my secret. My place. All me.

Why I chose to bring her there during the day when she could actually see it was something I hadn't considered until I saw her expression.

"It's so small." Her eyes were back on the house. It was. A small, yellow ranch that I kept meaning to paint in the off-season but continued putting off. I could have hired someone, but I wanted to do it myself. "And yellow."

She lost the control on her laughter then and let it loose.

My knuckles tightened on the steering wheel as I pulled the car into the garage before I relaxed.

I had essentially bared who I truly was to her, by accident, and she was laughing in my face.

For some reason, I didn't want to pull out and take her back home. "Keep laughing at me and you'll be sucking my dick for dinner."

That stopped the laughter. Her head whipped around to face me and her lips parted. Pink bloomed on her cheeks and it was my turn to laugh.

"Holy shit, it makes you so fucking sexy that you like the thought of that."

I couldn't help myself. She kept getting better and better. Every disgusting word I spoke seemed to light something inside of her.

"Shut up," she murmured before blushing harder and putting her hand on the door handle to escape. Not like she could go anywhere. I had thirty acres of empty land all around me. She could run and hide in a few of the buildings sprinkled throughout the property, but I'd enjoy searching for her.

"I like it." I reached for her arm before she could get out of the car. "It makes me hard all over again thinking about the way you liked my dick in your mouth. No fucking joke, Shannon, hottest thing I've ever seen."

She relaxed under my touch, and I released her, climbing out of my car and meeting her at the passenger side as she got out.

"So. Tour of the place or do you want to go straight toward my bedroom?"

"Tour."

I knew she'd say that. I didn't know the last time I'd offered. But for her, I knew just where to begin.

"You ever been on a farm?" I asked, sliding my hand to hers until they were entwined together. I didn't have to think about it.

Touching her was natural; so was her being here.

She shook her head, her gaze on the barn I was walking her toward. As we stepped on the gravel I stopped her and cursed.

"Shit. You don't have decent shoes on."

"What?" Her brow furrowed and she looked down at her feet.

I pointed toward the ground. "Stay here."

Turning, I rushed into the mudroom of my house, not looking back to see if she stayed.

When I reached the room, I kicked off my sandals and pulled on my work boots. Then I searched through the closet and dug out the ones my mom wore when she visited. She hadn't been here in over a year and the leather was dusty and hardened, but I figured they'd work. My mom wasn't that much taller than Shannon. If they were too big, they'd still be better in the dirty horse barn than the sandals she was wearing.

I walked out of the house and back through the garage to see the spot I'd told her to park it empty.

Instead, I found her at the white fence. One arm draped over the top railing, her other hand blocking the sun while she looked out at the fields.

I paused in my tracks, taking in the view of her delicious, barely covered ass before I walked toward her.

She was beautiful. Curvy but thin, so soft in my arms. My dick was already half-hard again by the time I reached her.

"It's so beautiful and quiet here." Her voice was soft, almost as if she was talking to herself.

"You're from Iowa—land of farms and corn and soybean fields."

From her profile, I saw her lips tilt into a smile. "Yeah, but I lived downtown Des Moines. It's not a big city, but it was never as quiet as this."

It shouldn't have made me smile that she liked where I lived.

I held out the boots to her. "Put these on."

She looked at my outstretched hand and frowned. I knew what she was thinking. She'd be a shitty poker player. Every expression she had was plain and unhidden on her face.

"They're my mom's. No one's worn them in a year, but they'll keep you cleaner than the sandals."

Her eyes flickered to me before she finally took them from my hand.

Once she'd kicked off her sandals and slid on the boots, she stood up and grinned.

And damn it if that grin didn't burn straight to my chest. She kept nothing hidden, not her fear or her happiness.

It was that moment I knew that whatever we'd decided was a mistake. A stupid agreement for meaningless sex—even if it was dirty, raw, and fucking amazing sex—was going to ruin every wall I'd built since Serena walked away from me.

I was smarter than this. Knew what I needed to do to keep my head in the game and my eye on the ball. I should have picked her up, thrown her in my car, and taken her to Beaux's immediately.

I didn't do anything I should have when she looked at me, giggling before she looked down at both of our boot-covered feet. "We look ridiculous. Swimsuits and boots."

Still thinking with my cock, I reached out and took her hand in mine and pulled her toward the barn.

"I've got three horses," I said as we walked. "You ever ride?"

"Once. When I was ten."

I looked down at her and waited for a better explanation.

"I had a friend who wanted to ride horses. She took a

bunch of us for her birthday party to a place where we could ride horses on a trail. It was only an hour and I was so young."

"But you liked it." I could tell by the way her eyes went hazy as she pulled the memory to the front of her mind.

"Yeah."

That one word made me happier than it should have.

I opened the door to the barn, dropping her hand from mine to unlock the double doors and push them open. As we stepped inside, the unmistakable smell of horseshit and hay and dirt made her crinkle her nose.

But she said nothing. She walked forward, down the row to the last few stalls where the noises from the horses grew louder.

"That's Winne," I said as she stepped up to the first mare. If I was honest, she was my favorite horse. I'd bought her when she was two and she had been mishandled and skittish. It took forever to tame her and get her to trust anyone, but the results had been worth the work.

Now she was kind and gentle, all brown and black. Shannon stepped closer to the door and Winne's large eyes turned excited as she blinked at the newcomer.

She neigh, pulling her lips back, and Shannon yanked her hand back in surprise.

"It's okay," I murmured, speaking quietly to calm Winne. I reached down and took Shannon's hand in mine and I held both of our palms out toward the horse. "She'll sense if you're nervous. Let her sniff you and she'll let you pet her soon."

"Okay." Her voice trembled much like her fingers and I tightened my grip on her hand.

It only took a few seconds for Winne to register my scent and Shannon's before she dipped her head, took a step closer, and turned her neck.

"There you go," I whispered to the horse as much as to Shannon. "That's a good girl."

I laid my hand on Winne's neck and held it there while Shannon gently began brushing her hand up and down the horse.

We were silent, the only sound coming from the other horses stepping on their hay, eager for their turn and snacks.

"Keep petting her. I'll get her treats."

I needed space. My heart was pumping faster than it should have been. Seeing Shannon in the barn, touching my horses—lovingly—an ache grew deep inside my gut.

Only an hour into a month-long agreement and I was already debating if I should end this as fast as I could. I should have known this would be her reaction. So far, she'd busted through every preconceived notion I had of her. What the fuck did I think was going to happen when I brought her in here?

I grabbed a couple handfuls of apples from the horses' snack bin and walked back to Winne, holding an apple out to Shannon.

We'd feed them. Then we'd fuck.

And after eating dinner, fuck again.

"She's so beautiful," Shannon said when Winne reared back and gobbled the apple out of her hand. Shannon squealed as the horse's lips grazed her palm.

"Don't close your fingers—keep them straight out or she'll eat those too."

Shannon flashed me wide, disbelieving eyes, and I shrugged, juggling the remaining apples in my hands.

"Did you name her?"

"I did."

Her lips pressed together. "It's a pretty sweet name for a horse."

"She was a rescue." Why was I bothering to explain? After tonight there was no way in hell I was ever bringing her back to this place. She was already looking too comfortable and we hadn't yet gone inside.

From now on, I was fucking her at the hotel.

"She hadn't been taken care of and was hard to train. But since then, she's been the gentlest horse I've ever had. She needed a name to match."

I looked away when Shannon's eyes went soft. She was thinking things about me that she shouldn't.

I broke the moment and walked to Ralph's stall. He was old, probably wouldn't live much longer, but I'd had him since I was in high school. He was the first horse that was all mine and the reason I'd bought the damn land to begin with. After living without horses and space for so long, I couldn't stop missing him.

There was something that was so freeing about getting on a horse at the end of a shitacular day, when every muscle ached to the bone and I'd royally fucked up at a game. Ralph had always understood what I needed.

Now, he was too old to ride too often, but I still made sure he got the exercise he needed. He'd lost the energy and pep he used to have and when I walked up to him, knowing Shannon was following me, he brushed his head against mine.

"Settle down, boy," I said and handed him an apple. He took it slowly, knowing I'd give him an extra one. He always got two—because he was old and my first and I babied the shit out of him.

God, I had never realized how big of a pussy I became around my horses until I was taking care of them under Shannon's soft and watchful gaze.

I rubbed him down, whispering words to him that I wouldn't let her hear before I turned back and saw her walking to the stallion's stall.

"Don't get too close. He's still nervous around new people."

Hulk was a monster. Eighteen hands tall, all shiny black stallion. Beautiful and graceful and powerful as hell. He gave me the thrill these days that Ralph no longer could.

But he was also an asshole. To prove it, as Shannon stopped three feet back from his stall, he reared onto his hind legs and kicked at the door.

She jumped back, and I wrapped my hand around her back so she didn't fall.

"Told you. He can be an asshole."

"Is that why you like him?" She looked up at me, smiling. "Remind you of someone?"

"Yes." I didn't grin, but it was true.

Hulk was the untamable. He'd never fully submit, and because of that I had to be careful with him. Only Lee—the caretaker who helped me with the horses during the season when I was busier and traveling—and I rode him.

My own father wasn't allowed to ride him anymore.

I clicked my tongue with my teeth and walked toward Hulk. "Come here, boy."

He shuffled back to the far end of the stall, not taking his eyes off Shannon.

"It's okay."

He shook his head back and forth, disagreeing with me, and I couldn't help but smile.

"He's a stubborn prick, too."

"Again," Shannon mumbled. "Sounds familiar."

When I flashed her a mock glare, she arched her brows, raised her shoulders. "I didn't imply it was you, but if that's how you took it..."

Her voice trailed off as I held out the apple to Hulk. "I've only had this guy a year. He's still a bit wild."

"And the one you were hugging?" She pointed her thumb back to Ralph without taking her eyes off me.

With that look, the question, and the fact that I was fucking introducing a woman to my horses, she ripped me wide open.

Bare and naked and vulnerable in the worst way. Something twisted in my gut.

"Ralph's old. Mine from home and the reason I bought this place."

"You love him."

My lip curled at a corner. She was pushing, pressing too hard, without realizing it.

For a moment, my chest heaved from her knowing gaze. Like she'd finally figured out who I really was, deep down, where I hadn't let anyone in since Serena.

Anger bubbled inside me at my own stupidity.

Raw, dirty fucking. Fulfilling fantasies. Burning out this insanely ridiculous attraction that had invaded me since the moment I saw her.

She was just pussy...hot and sexy pussy, but pussy I'd grow tired of nonetheless.

"I didn't bring you here to meet my horses," I finally said.

I took a step toward her, licked my lips, and peered at her with wicked intent.

I had actually wanted her to meet them. What a fucking mistake that was. I should have just pulled her into my house and taken her to my bed, gotten rid of her like everyone else.

The barn was a fucking mistake I'd rectify.

"You didn't?" Her breath hitched and her pulse fluttered at the base of her collarbone as I walked closer.

"No." I put my hand around her waist and pulled her to me. My cock was already straining inside my board shorts, my balls thick and heavy, filled with need for her tight and wet cunt. "I brought you in here to fuck you."

I gasped as his other hand hit my waist and he lifted me. On instinct, I gripped his shoulders and tightened my thighs around his hips. "What?"

"You heard me."

He walked toward the front of the barn, and for a moment I thought he was leaving before he pushed a stall door open and continued walking until my back pressed against rough wood.

I quickly took in the small but clean space. "Oliver."

My tone was questioning, something he silenced when he looked down at me before glancing at a spot above my head.

His intense expression shifted to something darker. Sexier and wicked.

My thighs trembled with expectation.

"Lift your hands."

"What?" I tilted my head back to see a heavy, thick hook hanging from the wall.

"I want you to hold on to that hook so I can drop to my knees and lick your pussy I can fucking feel through our clothes until you shatter. Here. Inside this barn." One of his brows arched. "That enough of an explanation for you?"

It was more than enough. My swimsuit bottoms grew wet as he talked. But I saw something else in his eyes as I pulled my fingers off his shoulders and did what I was told.

It wasn't satisfaction with my obedience. It was the way he had so quickly closed himself off when I'd asked about the horses. He wasn't the man I'd thought he was.

He wasn't the man I'd read about in magazines, all arrogant and cocky and sexy as hell.

Sure, he was, but he was also more than that. For a moment, when he'd whispered to the horses and fed them and talked softly...hell, this whole house he lived in...this was who he really was.

Yet he hid it.

It was none of my business. I knew the agreement we'd made and I was okay with it, but I also knew that as hard as it'd now be for me to not fall for him, it would be equally hard for him to be vulnerable in front of me again.

He'd made that clear with the quick change in direction.

My fingers wrapped around the warm metal until I clung to it. With a hand on my stomach, Oliver pushed me against the wall, holding me steady until he dropped to his knees in front of me.

"Shit. I can smell you already," he murmured, adjusting my legs so they dropped over his shoulders. With the height of the hook he'd hung me from, I was at the perfect level for him to do what he wanted.

He didn't remove my clothes or my swimsuit bottoms.

Sliding his fingers over my clothed, hot, and swollen flesh, he pushed the gusset to the side and leaned in.

"Damn it." I gasped as he licked me. "Shit."

"Oh." He pulled back and grinned up at me—that wicked, dirty smile. "If you scream you'll scare the horses. So be quiet."

I could barely suck in a breath before he dipped his head. His fingers dug into my hip, holding me steady while his other hand held me open and ready for him.

My entire body shook as soon as he touched me again. Giving me no time to prepare for it, he penetrated me...my pussy, my body. He was everywhere, deep inside me as his tongue worked in evil, soft circles, driving me crazy and burning with need to release as soon as he touched me.

But I'd been like that as soon as we'd arrived. Hell, as soon as we'd finished at Kolby's I was already wanting him again. This attraction between us was something I'd never experienced. It was unexplainable, unavoidable.

"Oliver," I mewled as he added fingers to his teasing and touching. It was too much—too much heat and too much friction as the rough wood at my back abraded my skin.

I squeezed my eyes closed and everything besides the feel of him and the way my body began to tighten and pulse disappeared.

My thighs began to spasm on his shoulders as he held me pressed open. My fingers ached from clinging to the hook.

"Quiet," he muttered against me. "You're so fucking delicious. I could eat you all day, but you're going to come soon, aren't you?"

His fingers twisted inside me, pulled and pushed, pressed against the perfect spot, and I whimpered.

"Yes," I moaned and bit my lip to stop from screaming like he'd warned me. "Yes, I am. Please..."

"So fucking delicious." He groaned before his mouth opened. And then the teasing was done.

He didn't just lick and taste me, he *ate* me.

He devoured me, sucking on my clit and nibbling with his

teeth. Pulling and feasting on me like he could never get enough.

The onslaught of sensations was too much—his fingers, his mouth, his tongue, and his teeth. The spasms hit my body out of nowhere and powerfully. My body shook from the pleasure, from the surprise of it. My orgasm coiled at my center and shot all the way to my toes and fingertips.

I shouted his name as I convulsed around him. My thighs tried to close around him, but he didn't stop feasting until he'd pulled every wild shudder and quiver straight through me.

The horses neighed. The sound of one hitting its stall door surprised me and I yelped, pulling back and hitting my head against the wall.

"Please, stop." I gasped as his tongue began to draw slow, swirling circles on my clit. "Too much."

"You can go again. I can feel it."

I dropped my head then and glared down at him. We were both still clothed, the top of my peach cover-up bunched in his hand at my hip.

I could barely see him. It didn't matter.

When he dipped his head again, eating me like he had all fucking day to keep me propped against a barn wall, he was absolutely right.

It took moments before another climax hit me, this time deeper but slower, less dramatic but no less powerful.

I chanted in a whisper, nonsensical sounds and gasps of his name and curse words repeated. *Please, no, stop, too much, oh shit, fuck, yes, coming...* They all fell from my lips without thought.

Only ecstasy coursed through my body until he finally pulled back, adjusted my bottoms, and stood, pulling me into his arms.

"My dick is so fucking hard for you right now," he said as I draped my arms around his shoulders.

I was listless in his arms, barely able to help hold myself around him as he took us out of the barn, pausing only to make sure he locked it behind us. My eyelids drooped, heavy from the pleasure he'd given me, and I was barely awake when he walked inside, kicked off his boots, and pulled mine off in his mudroom before he walked through the small house into a massive bedroom.

He dropped me onto the bed, then whipped off my cover-up before I could blink and look around.

Then his shirt was gone, his shorts dropped to the floor.

His hands went to my swimsuit and I squirmed enough to remove my top for him.

"You okay for a little bit more?" he asked, already reaching into his nightstand, pulling out a condom, and covering his hard dick. "I can let you recover, but this is going to be fucking quick, I know it."

I laughed softly at his honesty, unable to help myself. Brushing hair out of my eyes, I grinned up at him, unashamed I was spread out naked before him.

Standing in front of me was a man who could be carved out of marble and no one would know the difference. Every muscle in his chest and abs, his sides and his hips down to his thighs... everything I saw made drool pool in my mouth. Heat began to curl inside of me all over again.

I spread my legs and reached for him as he bent over me, the bed shifting from the weight as he crawled onto it.

"I'm good," I said, my voice breathless and my throat dry. "Go as quick as you need."

He smirked, pressed one hand next to my shoulder, and I wrapped my legs around him.

His other hand wrapped around his erection, he slid it through my slit and groaned. "You're wet again. Fucking shit."

Embarrassment flooded my cheeks and I glanced down, watching him slide his thickness through my folds.

"Don't blush," he whispered as he pressed the head of himself at my entrance. "It's sexy as hell." He dropped his head and groaned, and we both watched as he pressed into me. "So fucking tight."

"Go slow," I whispered. My body was unaccustomed not only to sex but to someone of his size. I ached from the rawness of what he'd already done to me so many times today and from my muscles stretching to accommodate him.

He pushed in slowly, pulling back out even more so. His arm next to me quivered from the strain of control.

"You okay?" he asked, lifting his head to look me in the eyes. We were inches away from each other, close enough that I could lean up and kiss him. I didn't.

We'd been intimate enough, and the look in his eyes—the intensity along with the confusion—made me pull back.

He wanted to fuck me. He didn't want to like me. I'd wanted the same until I saw his eyes go soft when he whispered into one of Ralph's ears. It had been endearing and sweet, something I knew he hadn't intended for me to see.

"I'm good." I nodded and inhaled a deep breath. "Move how you need to."

My permission shot through him like the snap of a rubber band. He didn't ask for my certainty again. He just shoved his hips, pressing into me with a quick, hard movement until he was fully inside.

I pressed my head back into the pillow beneath me, my fingers clawing at the muscles in his back.

He went wild as he began thrusting and pulling back. The quick thrust of his hips against me would leave bruises. His muscles, the weight of him, it all sent me spinning and flying as I hung on for the wild ride.

"Feel so good. So tight. So fucking wet."

His eyes were closed, his lips twisted with rapture and concentration as he dropped to his elbows. His coarse chest hair brushed against my nipples, hardening them into painful points with every scrape of his body against mine.

I tightened my grip just above his hips, my body heating and igniting with every wicked thrust.

"Oliver." I chanted his name, unable to control myself. I met his movements, pulled him to me.

His lips parted and his head dipped. He pressed his mouth to mine, his tongue instantly invading, and I was surrounded by him.

By his kisses, his weight, his scent, his muscles, and the powerful pistoning of his hips hitting the end of me every time he moved.

Our tongues swirled together, matching the movement of his cock. He fucked my mouth like he fucked my pussy. He grew more frantic and we swallowed each other's groans as my pussy clenched around him, tightening and flexing with another orgasm. It came unbidden but was as reckless as he was. My abs tightened, heat shot from my spine to my sex, and I gripped him, nails digging into his skin so hard I knew they'd leave marks, but it only seemed to make him crazed.

He lifted his mouth from mine abruptly and then he buried his head into my neck as he seated himself harshly inside of me, balls-deep.

He groaned against my skin, his hand moving to dig into my hair, and he held my body tightly to him, molded to him as his own orgasm rolled through him.

I held on to him, loosening my grip to place my palms to his flesh. He was hot and sweating, muscles everywhere, and my palms easily slid up and down the length of his back.

"I'm crushing you."

I liked it, more than I could or would admit. "Mm-hmm."

Once his breath caught, he pulled back and I released my hold on him reluctantly. Surprise enveloped me as his gaze searched mine. I'd expected him to pull out immediately and clean up, not look at me with wide-eyed wonder. Instead, his gaze carried the same confusion I knew mine did. The worry that we'd somehow crossed a line.

That all of this…the day, our lust for each other, how good it felt when we were together…it was all too much and too unexpected.

His eyes left mine and trailed over my face, and then around me. "Fantasy one fulfilled," he whispered quietly, a soft, pleased smile on his lips. "You look more gorgeous with your wild and crazy hair all over my pillow than I thought you would."

I chuckled softly.

He pulled me back from the heaviness of my thoughts and reminded me of what we were without being an ass about it.

"You weren't so bad yourself."

I patted his ass and gasped as it made him move inside of me.

"Fucking hell. I need some recovery time," he said, his lips twisting into a smirk.

"Good." I shifted beneath him, unable to move, but he seemed to understand my intent. "Then maybe you could feed me and give me something decent to wear before we go again."

His eyes searched mine, and I wondered if for once I was able to hide my lies behind my expressive eyes. He seemed to buy it enough, either because I had suddenly grown the ability to lie or because he wanted to believe the easiness in my words as much as I did.

"Shirts in the top drawer, shorts beneath them. Help yourself to anything you want."

He hesitated before leaning forward and pressing his lips to mine. "I'll go get cleaned up and leave a cloth for you in the bathroom."

I LOOKED at Oliver over my shoulder where I was digging through his fridge for something else to drink. We'd already eaten grilled steak and vegetables, but I was thirsty.

He had a dozen prepackaged containers labeled for shakes lined up and stacked to one side of the small, regular white fridge.

Everything I'd seen of Oliver since I slid into his lusciously leathered and beautiful car had thrown me for a loop.

"Do you need a protein shake or water?"

He lifted his brow before shaking off whatever thought he had. "Both. I can get the shake, though."

"No problem." I turned back to the fridge and pulled out the small container along with two bottles of water.

The blender was already out on the countertop, so I helped myself to it, dumping in the contents of the veggies before reaching for the jar of protein powder on the counter.

"You make these a lot?" Oliver asked as he reached around me and twisted off the top of the water bottle. "Beaux make you take care of him?"

I stiffened at the mention of my brother—how anything I'd done to help him succeed was because he'd made me. "No. I make them because I care about him."

He was silent for a moment while I dumped in the powder,

and then the only sound in the room was the whirling of the blender. I blended it longer than necessary, stabbing buttons to turn it off, unable to hide my irritation.

"Tell me about him. What's Beaux really like?"

I frowned at the question. "He's Beaux. I'm not sure I understand."

Taking the mixer out of my hands, Oliver twisted and reached for a glass, dumping the thick green sludge inside.

He slammed it back, chugging it in one swallow, and cringed before he cleaned his mouth with the back of his hand.

"I have a hard time reading him. And in order to trust him, I need to know him."

"Perhaps it's his trust you have to earn." I arched a challenging brow. Yeah, Oliver was the veteran on the offensive line, and he was team captain. But Beaux was still the QB. He had to trust who he was throwing the ball to, not the other way around.

"Can we talk about him without you getting defensive?"

I ground my teeth together. Was that what I'd been doing? For so long, it had just been Beaux and me against the world. It was a hard wall to drop.

"Sorry. What is it?" I reached for my own water and took a seat at the small but cozy kitchen table.

This time, Oliver seemed to measure his thoughts before speaking. "Is he really as laid-back as he seems?"

I tilted my head. "Yeah. I guess. He doesn't let anything get to him. Is that why you've been such a dick to him? You don't think he takes this shit seriously?"

"There are men who join the game for the game and not the work."

I snorted. If he only knew. "How cute. I'll tell Beaux that. He'll think it's fucking hilarious. You think he made it as far as he has based solely on natural talent and not his work ethic? How fucking hypocritical of you."

Oliver's water bottle crushed inside his death grip. "He lacks intensity. It worries me."

"He has confidence in his ability and the members of his team in spades. That keeps him loose."

It hit me then, why it bothered him so much. My irritation that had prickled at the first question began to flicker and disappear. "That's why it bothers you, isn't it? He's enjoying himself out there. Playing his hardest, loving the ride and the life and the game and hell, everything else he has to do in order to get on top and stay there, and it pisses you off he does that while still having fun."

His lip curled. I'd made my point.

"Tell him he's hesitating a half-second too long in the pocket. He needs to speed up his throws or he's going to get sacked every game."

"Maybe you should get open quicker."

Another lip curl. Another wave of irritation rolled off him like a tidal wave. Something else I couldn't miss sparked and burned brighter.

"Fucking hell," Oliver growled. "How is it that you're pissing me off, and all I can think about is bending you over this table and fucking the attitude out of you?"

A delicious, warm shiver rolled down my spine.

"You want that?" He stepped forward, setting the damaged bottle on the counter. "Do you know how fucking hot it is that I can read every thought that flashes through your eyes? You hide nothing from me."

That could be a disaster at some point.

I swallowed a huge gulp of water to settle my nerves and stood from my chair. "Exactly how would you like it to happen?"

I turned my back to him then and pulled his gray shirt, which I'd thrown on earlier, over my head.

I'd barely gotten it tossed onto the floor when one of his hands was at my hip, the other between my shoulder blades, pushing me down.

And then my shorts were pulled down, my legs kicked apart.

His lips hit my shoulder and I heard the tear of foil right before his cock drove into me, not giving me time to adjust—but I was already wet and ready for him.

When we were done, he learned that even a deliciously hard fucking that was quick and powerful wasn't enough to erase the attitude from me.

I moved more hay into Winne's stall, my back hurting worse than it should have been. It'd been bugging me for months now. Not painful, but a dull ache that never seemed to go away despite pain meds and deep tissue massages and chiro appointments.

Yesterday and last night's activities had made the pain flare up, but I wouldn't change a damn thing.

I was still hoping to finish cleaning out the stalls before Shannon woke up. The sun was just starting to rise, and while I knew she said she had to get home early, I figured I still had time.

I had plans for her before I had to take her back to her brother's.

We'd reached an impasse yesterday when I'd talked about Beaux. Her defense of him along with the fact that she'd read me so well made me not want to jump into that topic of him ever again.

He wasn't going to kick my ass for fucking his sister. And I might try to be less of a dick to him.

I pushed people.

I always had. I wanted to be the best and needed to know everyone else on my team wanted the same thing. Seeing someone so kicked back and chill over practices and incomplete throws and bad plays ate at something deep inside me.

Shannon had also been right—not that I'd admit it. I'd lost the enjoyment of the game a long time ago.

I loved football. It was rooted down deep in me, inside my marrow. Over the last few years, it'd been too hard to stay on top. Too much work to stay the number one tight end in the league. Too much work to stay pain free. I was kidding myself if I wasn't getting tired of it. Plus, at thirty, retirement was knocking on my door, whispered through the halls and in the voices of sportscasters—not to mention in my own head, late at night when the sounds of birds and crickets were all I heard.

It was barreling down on me. I had another two or three years at most, and that damn gold ring was calling to me—laughing at me in the distance, mocking my inability to take my team there earlier.

And yeah, maybe that was why I drove Beaux harder, pushed him more than I ever would have Mason.

I wasn't pissed that Mason had gone free agent and Beaux had been traded. I was pissed that Mason and I hadn't been the ones to bring the Super Bowl win to Raleigh.

I wanted it. I wanted the parade and the madness and the recognition that my team was the best.

We had it in us.

Next to me, Hulk battered against the door of his stall, anxious for his early morning ride I didn't have time for.

"Settle, boy." I moved the remaining hay around Winne's stall before propping the pitchfork on the far wall. I went to the stall she was waiting in and moved her back into hers before locking the door and going to see Hulk.

His black eyes narrowed when I came closer, that distrust so similar to Shannon's when I spoke dirty to her.

She didn't trust me, and she shouldn't. So far I'd worked to earn Hulk's, but if things went according to my plan with Shannon, there was no point in earning hers.

She'd be gone before there was time anyway.

Hulk whined and bucked against the door again, thrusting his head out of the stall and toward a noise I couldn't yet hear, but I still turned to look at the barn doors just in time to see Shannon rush through them.

Her curly hair was wild and untamed, flying out behind her when she slid in the dirt and braced herself against the doorway.

"I've been looking everywhere for you." She was breathless, a hand pressed to her chest. She'd also already thrown back on yesterday's barely existent outfit of her swimsuit and cover-up.

I scowled at the look. She'd ruined my idea of waking her up with my mouth all over her.

"I'm here." I walked toward her and checked my watch. "What are you doing up? It's still before six."

"I told you I had to get home early today."

She had, but early by most people's standards wasn't before seven. Another way I'd underestimated her, apparently.

"Do you have to go now?" I asked, cutting the distance between us by half. "Because I'm done here, and I was thinking of joining you in bed, my mouth on you, your hands digging into my hair, your legs spread open for me."

Her breathing faltered when I reached her. I placed my gloved hands on her hips, smiling as she shivered at my touch.

She was so transparent. So pliant. Her pink tongue darted out and swiped her lips.

Instead of taking me up on my offer, she stepped back and pushed her hands through her unruly hair.

"I can't. I really have to get back to town and get to work. There's so much to do." Her voice thickened as she looked up at me, long black lashes flickering wildly as pink burst onto her cheeks. "And, well, I'm really sore."

The thrill of victory burst in my chest, and I couldn't stop my grin. "I made you sore?"

She nodded.

"I made you hurt in a way that will make you remember yesterday and last night."

She cleared her throat. "And early into the morning, yes."

"Do your hips ache? Does your pussy hurt?"

She looked away from me then, the pink spreading to her throat and chest. "Don't be so vulgar."

"You have to know that's the hottest thing I've ever heard."

Not that I'd done it. We'd been wild. Hell, my dick was sore, too. Not so sore I couldn't—and wouldn't—go again, but she'd drained me dry.

"You say things to me that I think should gross me out."

"But they don't." I pulled her to me, my hand at her hip. "And that's why this will work. You like my filthy words. You like that they turn you on. This next month...you get to enjoy whatever the fuck you want to do, knowing you have someone willing to do whatever you want."

"And you? What do you get?"

"Someone who gets off on doing whatever I want."

Her pulse jumped into her throat and she swallowed. For a moment I thought she was going to take me up on the idea I'd had about waking her up. I could use a shower, and a long, relaxing one would do my tight muscles some good before I had to get to the stadium.

"I should go," she whispered, pulling away.

The rumble of Lee's engine echoed in the distance, growing closer.

She turned her eyes to me. "Who's that?"

"Lee." I pulled off my work gloves and tossed them on a nearby shelf. "He helps with my horses during the season."

"And off season?"

"I do it."

She didn't hide her surprise. "You? All of this land? The work in the barn and the horses?"

I couldn't hide my scowl. Or the fact my next words fell with disdain. "Not all of us can tour the country in party buses."

It was what Beaux had done last summer, and the summer before. The day the season ended, he'd hopped into a tricked-out RV, gathered friends from wherever, and took off. Last year there'd been an Instagram feed devoted solely to *"Where's Hale?"*

Shannon stiffened at the comment. I didn't take it back. Seemed as if I wasn't the only one underestimating a person, and I didn't care enough to apologize.

"Hey, Ollie," Lee shouted as he climbed out of the truck. He took in Shannon's messed and unruly appearance without hiding the surprise on his face. "Hello," he said, walking directly toward her. "I'm Lee. Powell's caretaker. And you are?"

"Leaving," Shannon whispered. Her angry burning eyes flashed to me. "I'm leaving soon."

Lee tipped his hat in her direction and wished her a good day, giving me a scathing look as he passed.

"If you give me a few minutes to change and grab my workout bag, I'll get you home."

She cleared her throat. "I'll wait for you by the car."

She walked away to the fence as Lee guided Ralph out to the paddock. There, he saddled him. Ralph would roam the circle for a while before Lee would come back out and give him his morning ride.

I tried not to look back this time, but when I reached the door to my house, I couldn't help but watch Ralph canter over to Shannon and nudge her hand with his nose.

I went inside and kicked off my work clothes, threw on a clean outfit, and washed the smell of horseshit off my hands before I walked back out to the car.

Shannon was still at the fence, arms folded on the top rung when I approached. Her smile was soft as she watched Lee ride Ralph in circles but never leave the pen.

"He's older than the others," she said.

"Almost sixteen. An old man in horse years."

She said nothing then before she turned to me. "You're nothing like I thought you'd be."

"I'm exactly what you thought I'd be," I said, warning her.

I was the playboy she had read about. I used women. I bent them to my will before I tossed them aside. I couldn't stand immaturity on the field and had no problems letting a ref know when he'd made a shitty call. I was the asshole she was expecting.

"Don't let the horses fool you," I said, dropping my voice. "I'm worse than anything you read about."

She smiled, reached up, and stroked my unshaven cheek. "Okay, Oliver. Ready to take me to Beaux's?"

No. That soft touch stirred something inside of me. It stretched and glided inside my gut. It woke up parts of me I'd long since put to sleep. "Sure."

I walked next to her as we moved back to my car, my hands at my sides and not holding on to her.

She unsettled me. Saw things she shouldn't. Knew things she couldn't.

Distance helped me regain my bearings when we climbed

into the car and I pulled out, taking back country roads where I could push the mettle of the Audi without fear of traffic or cops.

THE DRIVE back into the city was mostly quiet. The radio volume was turned down so we could talk over it, but we didn't say much.

Next to me, Shannon curled a strand of hair around her finger before letting it pop back. She did it repeatedly, her other finger tapping along to the music on the side of her door.

She was fidgety and nervous, and there wasn't much to say to make her feel better. I wondered if she was regretting the night, changing her mind about our agreement.

That she might actually do it made me keep quiet for most of the drive. I didn't want to hear her say that yes, she regretted it. No, she didn't want to see me again.

I hadn't had repeats in my bed in years, but this girl...she was proving herself different from all the others.

So far, she'd challenged me. She'd shocked the hell out of me, and she'd made me shoot my brain out through my dick.

She impressed me at every turn, which was what finally made me speak as she quietly gave me directions to Beaux's as we got closer.

"Where do you work?" I asked, breaking another long stretch of silence. I shouldn't have cared. Yet I already knew her answer wasn't going to be cheerleader or assistant or wannabe model/actress, like most of the women I met.

Shannon had a depth to her, a seriousness that hid her playful side. Somehow, I wanted to dig through all of it and explore every side of her—the sweet and shy and easily embarrassed to the dirtiest places she imagined.

"Stamped. It's an internet-based business."

"What?"

Her lips twisted and her finger went back to her hair. *Twist, pull, spring.*

"I have my own business. It's nothing too exciting. I make metal jewelry, stamping it into the shape I want it. So it's called Stamped."

My interest was piqued along with my irritation. She had to leave my house before fucking to go make jewelry?

"You only sell it online?"

She hesitated a moment before answering. When she did, she turned to me and I saw a spark of fear, maybe excitement, before her hesitancy took over. "I've done that for years, but Beaux leased a building for me in the arts district. Said he wanted to help my dream come true like I'd always done for him. I've spent the week cleaning the building along with the apartment I'll move into as soon as I can get my stuff from home."

She frowned and looked out the window.

"There's a street fair coming up next week I've been getting ready for. I have no idea how busy it is, how many customers I could get, but I've barely slept while trying to get everything prepared." She pointed to a corner. "Turn here. His place is the second on the left."

I skipped the turn, and she shot me a look. "I'm just driving around the block so you don't have to cross the street when I let you out." I knew these streets. The row of brownstones didn't have parking except in alleys behind them, and parallel parking was a bitch.

"Oh." That sweet blush hit her cheeks. "Thank you."

My fingers twisted around the steering wheel. "You coming to the game this week?"

She turned to me then and grinned. "I wouldn't miss it for anything."

It was the first time I'd seen her seem truly free since I'd met her. Her pride in her brother seeped out of every one of her pores, almost making her shine.

It made me feel like an asshole for being rude to her about him.

I quickly pulled around the corner and placed my hand over hers before she could get out. That heat that was always between us grew and inflamed in the cool car.

I wrapped my hand around the back of her neck and pulled her to me, holding her steady as my lips pressed against hers. She opened for me immediately, her tongue seeking mine, and it wasn't just me kissing her...but her kissing me back. She wasn't just taking it, allowing it...she wanted it.

I swallowed her soft whimper and pulled back before I had the overwhelming desire to fuck her in my car.

Honesty spilled from me before I could stop it. I blamed the sexy-as-hell kiss and her soft, pouty lips. "I had a good time with you."

She licked her lips before answering. "Me too. But I should go."

She turned to open the door, and something about the moment —her hesitance in wanting me while she made it obvious—had me reaching out to her, the only way I knew I could get her attention.

"I'll try to be less of an asshole to Beaux."

She grinned at me, looking over her shoulder as she opened her door. "I'll tell him to throw faster."

"When can I see you again?" And why did I feel so fucking desperate for it?

"I don't know." She winked and slid out of the car, bending over to face me once she was on the curb. "Call me."

"I don't have your number." I smirked, holding out my hand to ask for her phone.

She smiled at my hand and then sent me a devious look—one I wanted to spank off her before I fingered her to the brink of orgasm. "I think you can figure out a way to get it."

She shut the door then, but I heard her laughing as she walked away. When she reached the door to Beaux's place, she waved at me, the smile still ingrained on her cheeks.

She was going to make me ask him for it if I wanted it.

She was going to make me work for her.

As I pulled out into the street after she disappeared inside, I realized that I was okay with it.

I hadn't had to fight for anyone I wanted in years, and she'd be worth it.

At least for a month.

"DON'T FUCK HER OVER," Beaux whispered as he handed me Shannon's number.

Sweat still dripped down my back. I still had my pads on. For once it wasn't Beaux moving slow in practice; it had been all me.

I couldn't find a fuck to give. I'd been waiting for this moment the entire practice. Waiting for him to threaten me or punch me in the face.

I'd deserve it, and I'd take it, once.

"She understands where we're at," I told him. I hoped like hell she did.

He made a gagging sound and held up his hand. "Please. Fucking spare me. She told me the same thing earlier, and I almost puked all over her. I don't want to know what's going on between the two of you. I just don't want her heart broken again like her fiancé just did to her."

"Understood." I did, too. I sort of wanted to beat the asshole up, too. I reached for his shoulder as he turned away from me, stopping him until he spun back around.

"Yeah?"

I swallowed the criticism I wanted to give him. He'd played a great day. I'd been off my game. He was still moving too slow. "Good practice today."

His eyes narrowed and he put his hands on his hips. "Even if I'm too slow in the pocket?"

I popped my jaw. Was he teasing me? I assumed Shannon had told him what I'd said, but had she made me seem like the asshole I probably was? I didn't want to ask. I didn't want to know if she'd shown up at his place this morning ranting about me.

"You'll get there," I replied. "Takes a few weeks and it's a new team. You'll adjust."

His eyes narrowed further. "If you hadn't just been with my sister last night I'd ask if you somehow slipped your dick into magical pussy to make you nice today." He held up a hand again. "I don't want to know. Honest. So don't tell me."

He grinned then and shook his head, almost as disbelieving as me that we might actually be getting along.

"I'll up my game," he responded. "Anything else?"

He seemed honest—sincere and open to anything I could say. We'd reached some detente. He wasn't going to be a jerk about me screwing his sister.

I could trust that Shannon was honest about how much he wanted his team to be successful.

"Yeah." I grinned and stepped back, out of his punching range. Then I held up the paper with Shannon's number. "Voodoo pussy. Not magical. Thanks for helping me get more."

He lunged for me, but I jumped back, straight into Rudolph. We both tumbled to the floor, a round of shouts and *What the fucks* echoing in my ear from the surprise of our movements.

I rolled to my back and off Rudolph only to get his elbow in my ribs. Hale's body landed on me with a thud.

The madness of the locker room took over and soon I was on the bottom of a fucking dog pile of men who had never outgrown their teenage years. We acted like assholes, pushed and punched and shoved until I realized that my abs weren't hurting so hard from the playful hits and kicks I'd taken from my teammates, but from the fucking laughter that wouldn't stop.

NINE
SHANNON

The crowd around me rose to their feet as we shouted for the amazing forty-yard pass Beaux had just made. It landed soft and perfect in Oliver's outstretched hands, where he ran another seven yards for a touchdown to move the Rough Riders ahead.

Twenty-one to seventeen. The team was doing it. It was late in the third quarter, but I couldn't relax. Beaux had played the first quarter and then the first string had taken the bench until late in the third quarter. I had seen what Oliver meant: Beaux hesitated in the pocket more than normal, like he hadn't quite found his rhythm.

I'd chewed off my nails—which had grown since summer training camp—during the first quarter, but when he took the field again he looked more relaxed. More confident. More like the Beaux Hale people were used to seeing, and the crowd ate it up.

I stayed on my feet, cheering, and gave him a thumbs-up as he hurried off the field. I'd done it since he was in the youth leagues in Iowa and never stopped. It didn't matter that most of the time he couldn't see me.

He'd bought these seats. He knew exactly where I was. I was still surprised when he trotted off the field, slapping Oliver on the back for the leaping catch he'd had to make, and his eyes came directly to me.

He hit his hand to his chest and flashed a peace sign in my direction. My grin exploded as the fans around me whispered, "He's looking right at us."

Fifteen rows up from the fifty-yard line behind the Rough Rider's bench, I had the perfect pair of season tickets.

I tilted my chin toward Beaux, in acknowledgment, and then looked at Oliver. He was still standing next to Beaux, the animosity between them either having disappeared or been expertly hidden, when I saw him looking directly at me.

His hands went to his chin straps and he ripped them off before yanking off his helmet.

His eyes met mine and my breath faltered. Amidst the crowd of cheering fans, I still knew he was looking directly at me. I hadn't seen him since he'd dropped me off at Beaux's earlier in the week, although we'd spoken.

Most recently it was this morning, when he'd called me only to whisper in his gravelly voice, "Tonight, after the game, I'm going to do wicked things to you."

I'd barely been given time to agree before he hung up, leaving me on edge and unfocused for the rest of the day.

All those feelings magnified while he held his helmet in one hand. I saw him listening to the offensive line coach, nodding. He never took his eyes off me.

The crowd cheered again, returning to their feet when the special teams kicked the extra point.

Coach Marks turned from Oliver to talk to someone else,

but the whole time Oliver's gaze stayed fixed on mine—unyielding. Relentless.

Powerful.

It was as if he could see me quiver, my thighs heating and that burning desire I had for him spreading through my veins.

A smirk twisted his lips. That arrogant, cocky smirk I wanted to kiss away to see the quiet and confident man I'd seen on his farm.

A fucking farm. He lived on one. Or on enough land to have a farm. But the mysterious tight end lived in the middle of nowhere and took care of horses, whispering to them in soft, quiet murmurs while wearing board shorts and T-shirts and didn't seem to care what I thought of him.

For some reason, he'd invited me into his personal space. He'd let me see who he really was, giving me very little information.

I had gleaned enough.

He wasn't the guy the world knew him as.

It made it harder to keep my heart from getting involved, yet I was still determined to do so.

I had less than four weeks with him. I wanted every second to count.

All of that conflicted with the way my heart quickened as Oliver smiled at me, pressed his fingers to his lips, and dropped his hand to his side before flashing me his signature wink.

I liked him. I didn't know him well, but it was more than physical attraction that swirled and built into a combustible moment whenever we were around each other.

It'd been days.

It felt like months since I'd been with him, since I'd touched him, since he'd been deep inside me.

"Did you see that?" the woman behind me whispered to her friend. They'd gossiped about the players the entire game, their dates or husbands or partners on the other side of them, ignoring them.

"I saw it. He looked at us. Powell looked at us and blew us a kiss."

The other woman huffed.

I resisted the urge to turn around and check them out.

They hadn't been focused on the game for a single second, but had been whispering about the men in their tight pants and what they'd do to the players if given the chance. I assumed the men they were with would be getting the ride of their lives later, the women living out wicked, dirty fantasies in their beds, or the men would be left high and dry while the women searched out the players.

I had great seats—seats where I didn't mind watching the game alone. Most of the people around me were people I'd be seeing all season. No one said anything about the empty seat next to me, but those questions would come. Eventually they always did. Why Beaux bothered to buy me two seats when he knew I'd rarely bring anyone other than Melissa to the games was beyond me, but I never argued.

For the rest of the game, I cheered when we had great plays, jumped to my feet and stayed there when there were forty-five seconds left and the kicker lined up a field goal to seal the win.

When it was done and they'd won, I pushed through the crowd, headed toward the back hallways where only family had access, and waited for Beaux, and Oliver, to make their appearance from the locker room.

The hallway was packed with media and sportscasters. Cameramen lined up outside the locker room. From inside, the chants and cheers of the victorious team reverberated through the hallway like a dull roar.

"You're new. You family or girlfriend?"

I turned toward the female voice and smiled, holding out my hand. "Shannon Hale, Beaux's older sister."

Her face lit up with recognition. "Oh! We didn't get a chance to meet the other day. I'm Jillian Rudolph, Danny's wife."

"Nice to meet you." I'd met Rudolph at the party. He'd pointed his wife out to me from the distance, and up close she looked just as pretty as she had in a white, one-piece swimsuit with cutouts just above her hips. Rudolph was a defensive end player, large and strong and had a great game earning one sack. "He played great tonight."

"He'll play better later," she said, wiggling her eyebrows. "I bet Oliver will, too."

I jerked back, and she laughed at my surprise.

"They're good friends. Trust me, there isn't a thing Oliver does that Danny doesn't know about. And I've been hearing about you all week long."

"Um." Nerves suffused my veins and speech was difficult. This was for fun, sure, but he'd talked about me? "We, um...just met and we're friends."

She rolled her eyes playfully. "It's okay. Us girls need to stick together. Did you watch the game from a box?"

"No. Fifty-yard line. Beaux's always gotten me tickets there."

"Oh. Those are wonderful! Danny always gets the seats for me in the box with other player's wives." She leaned in and lowered her voice. "But between you and me, it's hard to watch the game from there."

"You can always join me," I said, my mouth moving before I could stop myself. "Beaux gets me two, but I watch the game alone."

"That'd be great! And you and Oliver should come for dinner some night. Or just us. Girls' nights are more fun anyway, you know?" She nudged my side and it took me a moment to regain my bearings.

I was used to women using me to get close to Beaux. I wasn't used to women seemingly being so open and honest. But as my gaze roamed over Jillian, her kindness and friendly smile made it easy to trust her. Blond hair pulled back into a ponytail with Rudolph's jersey, skinny jeans and faded, well-worn gray Chucks on her feet, she lacked the pretentiousness so many athletes' wives seeped from their pores.

"I'd like that," I found myself saying. "The game, at least. Oliver and I...we're just..." Heat bloomed on my chest as I tried to find the words. "Having fun. Friends."

"Right." She winked. "Of course you are."

The doors burst open then. Lights flashed and media personnel shouted their questions to players as they began exiting the locker room. All wet-headed and dressed in suits, you could tell they'd celebrated and showered quickly before leaving.

Beaux came out early and was instantly surrounded by the reporters. I stayed back, next to Jillian. Beaux twisted around his Rough Riders baseball hat so the team's logo was in front and began answering questions.

His eyes met mine and he smiled. I held his gaze, silently encouraging him and letting my pride for him shine through until a different current hit me.

Oliver exited the locker room, hat pulled lower over his eyes, covering his dirty blond hair. His head dipped and he thanked the reporters clamoring for his attention, but he seemed to pay them no mind while he pushed past the small, congregated crowd before making his way to me.

"Yeah. If you two are just having fun, I'll eat my husband's hat." Jillian nudged me again, playfully.

I didn't turn to look at her, but my lips lifted into a smile.

Whether it was because I liked her and found her funny or because Oliver didn't stop moving until he was directly in front of me, I didn't know.

"Ready to get out of here?" he asked, his voice rough and thick.

I was sure I answered.

Certain I tried to.

It felt like a handful of cotton balls were lodged in my throat as my mouth opened and closed.

His hand gripped mine and he tugged me toward him and whispered, "I told Beaux where we'd be. He said he'll see you in the morning."

I caught Beaux's gaze, his eyes tightening as he saw me leaving, and then I was pulled through the maze of hallways, unable to gather my thoughts while Oliver guided me toward his car.

"YOU GUYS HAD A GREAT GAME," I said once we were settled into his car.

We'd made a brief stop at Beaux's car, where I'd left an overnight bag earlier, and then a strange silence had permeated the fancy vehicle while Oliver guided us out of the underground parking garage for players and season ticket holders and onto the packed streets of downtown Raleigh.

His hands flexed on the wheel.

"You don't think so?" I asked when he didn't answer.

"I never think we play as great as we should."

It didn't surprise me. Oliver was intense and focused off the field just as much as he was on it.

"It was still a great touchdown you made in the third."

His lips went from a pressed line to a hint of a smile.

Shaking his head, he looked at me. His expression softened a bit. "You love the game."

"Well, yeah, it was either find a way to love it growing up or hate all the hours I spent at the fields and driving Beaux around. I could have either become bitter and jealous of his success or been a part of it. I chose the latter."

"Yeah, but you still didn't have to like the game. You could have supported him without it."

I grinned then. "It's more fun this way."

He fell silent after that, seemingly lost in his thoughts.

After several blocks where he seemed to be twisting his car around the streets of downtown instead of heading out to his place, when he spoke again, he surprised me.

"I have to admit—that catch was awesome."

"Soft fingers," I whispered. "It was incredible to watch. Everyone around me went insane when you hurdled the defender."

He pulled up to a building and shoved the gearshift into park. We idled at the curb, and I looked at where he'd stopped us. A hotel.

Disappointment uncurled in my stomach.

I closed my eyes and let a soft breath fall from my lips.

"Trust me," he said, reaching out to open his door. "When I get you to my room, my fingers will be anything but soft."

The desire that was there before sparked, but fizzled quickly as I realized what we were doing.

What I was doing with him.

A hotel. A one-night stand.

Was I really prepared for all of this? For the whispers and the gossips and being treated like his latest fling?

I had never been one to live so recklessly.

Yet hadn't I earned it? Didn't I deserve a month of hot sex

and fun and no strings and everything else single people experienced all through their twenties?

It was that realization that made me force down my disappointment and the increasing unease as my door was opened.

"Good evening, Mr. Powell. Good game earlier."

"Thank you, Frank," Oliver said, lifting his hand toward me as he stood next to the bellhop who had opened my door.

Frank was old, his hands speckled with liver spots, leathered skin telling me that when he was younger he spent too much time in the sun and used too little sunscreen. His eyes met mine with a kind smile. "Good evening, miss."

"Shannon," Oliver said, pulling me out of the car. He'd already grabbed my overnight bag and it was thrown over his shoulder. "She'll be here frequently."

A glimmer of excitement hit Oliver's eyes as he made his intent clear.

"Very well, sir," Frank said and closed the door behind me. He took the keys from Oliver and gripped them in his palm. "Straight to the garage tonight?"

"You have a break coming up?"

"Always plan on it when I know you're coming."

"Then take it for a spin, but be kind to her."

"Will do, sir."

Oliver rolled his eyes. "Call me Oliver, for the love of God, Frank."

Frank winked at me before shaking his head. "Can't cross all the lines with my job. You know that."

Oliver smiled at him—the first genuine smile I'd seen on him all night. I had watched the entire conversation slack-jawed. When he slid that grin in my direction, my mouth snapped closed.

"Just don't crash her."

"Never do," Frank said as he opened the driver's door and

slid inside. He peeled out onto the street so fast I wondered if he'd looked for traffic first.

As the lights disappeared around the first corner and the sound of screeching tires evaporated, the smell of burned rubber remained.

"Come on." Oliver tugged on my hand, and I stumbled on my feet, trying to catch up to him.

I'd assumed he'd brought me to the hotel for a random hookup, treating me like any random woman he'd picked up off the streets. His conversation and obvious affection for Frank told me something different was happening.

We didn't stop as we walked through the lobby. Oliver moved quickly and with purpose, and when we reached the bank of six elevators, he pulled me toward the farthest one and slid a key through a reader before pressing the button.

The door opened immediately and we stepped inside, my mind still whirling with the quickness of how everything had happened. Had he checked into the room earlier?

"Frank's been the doorman at this place for almost twenty years. Lost his wife to cancer shortly after I met him. From what I've been able to figure out about him, he doesn't have much in his life, so when I stay here he drives my car for a few minutes before parking it in the valet."

It was a really long explanation that didn't answer any of my questions. Like, what made Oliver begin speaking to him in the first place? How did he take the time to learn all of that, and what had happened that made them seem so close?

It all contradicted his assurances of being an asshole.

I stared at Oliver through the mirrored reflection of the elevator door, too nervous to face him, too scared of what he'd see on my face. Yet as everything began clicking into place, I couldn't stop the smile.

"Asshole," I teased. "Right. You're such a prick."

His eyes widened and he stepped in front of me, pushing me to the back of the elevator without touching me.

His strength and his size made him immoveable in front of me and I couldn't see around him to see the look of surprise I knew was on my face.

"Have I told you tonight how sexy you look in my team's jersey?"

I was in jeans and sandals and an oversized jersey with Beaux's number on it. My hair was pulled back so the wild curls stayed out of my face during the game.

There was nothing sexy about how I was dressed, yet when Oliver began trailing a finger along the length of my jaw, I felt like I was in a ball gown.

"You might have forgotten that part."

He leaned forward. His hand on my jaw tightened and held me in place. "Forgive me."

His lips pressed to mine, stealing my breath, and I clung to him immediately. It'd been days. My body ached for him immediately.

He held me against the wall with the frame of his body, and the kiss changed from soft and seeking until he devoured me. His tongue slid along the seam of my mouth and pushed through before I could receive him, but I met him then, kissing him back and raising my hands to his shoulders so I could get closer. Deeper.

A thud sounded on the floor and then his hand was at my waist, pulling me toward him, ripping my shirt from my waistband until his hand was pressing against the small of my back.

The chime of the door and the sudden stop of the elevator made him jump and we separated, both of us breathless, his dark hazel eyes more tawny than green. Mine were just as wild as he looked down at me, his gaze tracing every feature in my face.

"When we get inside my place, we're going straight to my room where I'm going to spread you out all over my bed, taste every inch of your skin, and eat you until you're screaming my name and begging for more."

My mouth went dry and wetness seeped into my panties. Everything he said did that to me. He had a way of looking at me like I was the only woman he'd ever seen. Like stripping me naked and making me bare for him was his highest priority.

"You say such filthy things," I whispered as he bent to grab the bag he'd dropped earlier.

"You fucking like it."

I did. I didn't argue with him about it. I wanted sex with him and his filthy words more than I cared to admit. Even when my sex life with Patrick had been at the pinnacle, we were always more of a one-and-done couple when it came to sex and orgasms.

Multiples in one night had been rare.

With Oliver, I knew the opposite with him would hold true. He wasn't the kind of man to stop until he'd gotten everything he wanted. Lucky me that he seemed to want me.

At the very least, he wanted my body. My heart could take it. I had gone into this eyes wide open, understanding everything that was happening between us.

So I would take my screaming orgasms whether they happened in a hotel or a house, and hopefully I'd be able to deliver some of my own to him.

Her hand in mine, my hand on her skin, the buzzing of the door behind us, I was only thinking one thing.

Bringing her to the hotel room I kept during the season was as big of a mistake as taking her to my home. When this was over, I wasn't going to be able to go anywhere to escape the memory of her flushed cheeks, wild hair, and her body splayed out wherever and however I wanted.

"You want that?" I asked, when she didn't answer me the first time. I pulled her out of the elevator, walking backward so we stayed pressed together. Fuck. I couldn't get enough of her. Seeing her at the game, cheering on her feet, her smile wide and unrestrained when I scored a touchdown had twisted something inside me.

The only thing I didn't like was that she'd done all of that with Beaux's number plastered to her generous breasts instead of mine.

"You want me eating you, sucking and licking your pussy until you come, over and over again? Until you're so sore you think you can't take any more?"

She nodded frantically, unable to hide her lust for me, and fuck if it wasn't perfection. She had no motives. No hidden agenda. She wanted my dick and my body, and I didn't give one shit if I was using her.

She was using me, too.

"Yes. Yes, I want that."

I dropped my hand from her back only long enough to dig my keycard out of my pocket and slide it through the door. There were only two rooms on this floor and I knew the other owner.

A country singer whose visits to The Mayfield Tower were as sporadic as mine. We'd actually gotten drunk together one night in the bar downstairs and then, like jackasses, autographed our names onto each other's skin with permanent marker.

My team had just lost the AFC Championship game earlier that night and Bethany had been plastered all over the gossip rags for screwing another country singer—a married one. She swore she had thought they were already divorced. The fact that they were legally separated never made it into the papers or the gossip columns, so Bethany and I had bonded over failed nights and shitty decisions.

She became a friend after that and I knew she was on tour, currently playing in arenas all over the western part of the country.

For once, I was thankful she wasn't around to see my one-night stand leaving in the morning and that she couldn't possibly hear us through the walls.

"So you have both," Shannon said as we stepped inside and the door shut behind us.

"What?" I shot her a quizzical look.

She waved her hand out to the large living room. The suite wasn't overly large or ostentatious. Two bedrooms with king-sized beds. A passable living space and a small kitchen. I didn't need large and massive. I needed a place to fuck and crash on the nights I didn't want to drive back to my home late at night, or when we had to get up early to leave for a game and I didn't want to get stuck in morning traffic.

It worked, and besides clothes, there wasn't a personal effect around. At first I had thought this would make it a better place to bring Shannon. Her curiosity knew no bounds. I was quickly learning that she didn't need photographs and decorations to figure out who I was, or who I used to be. She saw enough as it was.

"I asked you at Kolby's if you had a home or a crash pad. You have both."

"Right. I keep this place during the season. It's easier to get to the fields."

"And to fuck faceless women."

Yeah, she saw too damn much. Unfortunately, I was also quickly learning that she'd never be faceless. Her face and the memory of her would linger in this damn place and in my home long after the scent of her was gone.

"You need something to drink?" I dropped her bag and headed to the kitchen area that would be stocked with drinks and food for me. I didn't cook when I stayed there, but I made sure I had other food to eat and protein drinks.

After a game like tonight's, I usually downed a few of them.

My head wasn't thinking about nutrition at the moment, but on changing the fucking subject.

"I'm not offended," she said, following me. "I was just curious."

"Don't be," I clipped, harsher than I intended. I saw the look of pain flash in her eyes. But it'd do her good. If she wanted to walk away, it'd probably be better for both of us.

I sure as hell wasn't going to be the one to do it.

"You're awfully temperamental for someone who's made it clear what they're looking for."

Stunned from her flippant remark, I stood frozen while she walked around me and helped herself to a bottle of water from the small fridge. I took in the curve of her ass, the way the stupid-ass rhinestones on the pockets were like a homing beacon for my eyes.

"Get over here, Shannon."

My voice deepened. My hands balled into fists. She had too many clothes on and too much sass in her. I planned on fucking it all out of her.

She shut the fridge and turned to me, twisting the top off the water bottle and taking a long sip. Nervousness flashed in her chocolaty eyes before she could hide it. "Are you going to be nice to me?"

"No." I shook my head, letting my intention be clear in the slow movement and the drawl of my voice. "I plan on being very, very filthy with you. I'm also certain I just told you to do something."

The bottle shook in her tight grip as she set it off to the side.

She made her way to me, three long, slow strides. Fuck if she didn't know what she was doing. Listening, but disobeying at the same time.

I knew her game. She'd give me what I wanted, but it'd be in her own time, her own way.

I pressed my hand against my hardening cock as she closed the space between us, her eyes gleaming with pure intent and unabashed lust.

Fuck if she wasn't beautiful. I'd thought it the first time I saw her in the stands at the training camp. She didn't know that. I wasn't planning on telling her how much the fact that she'd been there—cheering for everyone but separated from the large crowd of fans—had turned me on from halfway across the field.

She gave everything her all while holding herself back, a dichotomy I wanted to understand more than I should.

"Now that I'm here?" she asked, her hands held loosely at her sides as she tilted her head. "What are you going to do with me?"

"Take off the jersey." Someday I'd fuck her while she wore nothing but mine. My number would be on the fabric abrading her nipples while I slammed into her. The last thing I wanted when I dirtied her up was her brother anywhere in the room.

Her hands went to the hem and she crossed her arms before pulling it over her head in slow...fucking...motion.

I pushed down the urge to smack her ass. People, women especially, didn't play games with me. They bent to my will as soon as I crooked my fingers. Someone else drawing out antici-pation wasn't something I was accustomed to.

I didn't hate it as much as I thought I would.

I licked my lips as her hair bounced and flopped from the movement of the shirt being ripped over her head. I trailed my eyes over her beautiful skin. The curve of her sides, the soft indentations around her abs that told me she worked out but didn't kill herself doing it.

"Take your hair down."

"Are you going to touch me or make me do all the work?" She teased while her hands went to her hair. She tugged and pulled and untwisted a band in her hair until she dropped it to the floor along with her jersey.

Her hair tumbled and fell all over the place and her hands went to smooth out the wild waves.

"Don't. You're fucking sexy as hell when your hair is untamed."

"It's a mess." The blush burned her cheeks and it was the

first time since she'd begun her seductive dance that there was hesitancy in them.

I reached out and trailed my hand through her hair, tangling my fingers in it before I yanked her against my body and looked down at her.

"If I didn't think you were so damn sexy, you wouldn't be here. I know what I want and it's you, as messed up and dirtied as I can possibly make you."

Her pulse kicked up, a jump of blood beating faster in a vein behind her ear. My thumb brushed it before I stepped back and removed my own shirt.

"Your bra," I said, when she stood frozen, staring at my chest. I flexed my muscles and made her eyes jump to mine. "Take it off."

"Your pants," she bravely ordered as her hands went to the back of her bra. I heard the click of the satiny fabric unsnap before she winked at me. "Take them off."

My hands went to my hips. "I don't think you understand who's in charge here."

But damn if being on the receiving end wasn't sexy as hell.

"I'm not someone who sits on the sidelines and blindly follows orders."

We'd see about that. Someday I'd have her blindfolded and following orders and she'd love it.

My hand went to the zipper of my dress pants and I dropped them so they pooled at my feet before I kicked off my shoes and socks.

My boxers were next. They fell to the floor and I wrapped my hand around my cock, keeping my eyes on her until she followed my movement.

"Get naked and get over here," I said, walking to the counter. I didn't take my eyes off her while her fingers fumbled at the button of her jeans and then her zipper.

"Beautiful," I murmured, the praise falling unbidden from my lips. With curves and tits and legs for days, I didn't know where to start with her.

I dropped my hand from my dick and gripped her hips, lifting her and placing her at the edge of the counter. She was so short that fucking her from behind hadn't been easy. At this height, I could slide my dick straight into her.

"Spread your legs and place your palms on the counter behind you."

"Oliver," she whispered, her voice husky. "I'm already wet for you."

"I know." I smirked. "And I want to see it, watch you play with yourself before I fuck you and eat you and do all the things to you I've already promised."

Another dozen ideas flashed through my mind as she slid her legs further apart. Her wetness, her desire for me, slickened the insides of her thighs and made her pussy pink and glistening.

Fuck, she was beautiful. I wanted my come all over her. Her tits, her ass, her stomach. I wanted to mark her. Claim her.

She's temporary.

My lip curled at the loud reminder shouting at me, but my dick was in charge all over again.

"Wider," I demanded and began tugging on my dick so she could see what she was doing to me. "Slide your fingers through your pussy."

Her muscles tightened at my command. Little breathless pants fell from her lips. Her chest heaved, making her breasts shake with the movement. Every time they did, I wanted to wrap my lips around the hardened, darkened nipples until my mouth was full of her.

"Help me," she whispered, adjusting herself on the counter but still listening. "I want you to help me."

"Help you come?"

I received an immediate nod.

"No fucking way. This first time you're doing it yourself, showing me what you like and what you want. Show me what you did to yourself this week when you were alone in bed, naked and thinking of me."

My eyes met hers when she inhaled a gasp.

Dirty, dirty girl. God, I loved that. The look she gave me made my cock harden even more.

"You did, didn't you? You slid your fingers deep inside your pussy, only to be frustrated it wasn't my cock inside you."

"Shit." She gasped as her fingers began sliding around her clit. Her fingernails were painted a light pink, lighter than her flesh. The sounds of her wet sex filled the room, magnified by her quick breaths.

"Yes," she whispered, her hips bucking into her hand. "I thought of you."

It was all I wanted to hear, needed to hear it more than I understood.

I stepped forward and continued running my hand down my long and heavy and hot shaft. My head brushed against her clit as she teased herself. I couldn't wait to be inside her, but I wanted to drive her crazy first.

My balls were already pulled tight, my spine heated as her fingers continued pressing against her flesh, her clit, slow circles then fast as she widened her legs and her inner thigh muscles began to tremble.

"Do it," I whispered, not taking my eyes off her quivering pussy. "Fuck yourself and let me see you come."

"Oh God," she whimpered.

I pressed against her thigh with one hand to hold her steady. She rubbed more, teased more, slid her fingers inside and around her lips until her fingers shone from her own wetness.

"Oliver." Her hips pressed and rolled. "So close."

I teased her with the head of my cock, getting it wet from her own ministrations.

And then she shattered beneath me. Every part of her tightened and bucked with abandon. She fell back, and I leaned forward until I could taste her pussy. Then I ate her.

Her hand went to my hair as I strung out her orgasm, pulled it from deep inside her as my teeth and tongue took over.

She slid against my mouth, wet and slick, and it only made me keep going while she chanted for me to stop.

"No more. Please. Too much. Oh God."

Everything repeated, dulled by the roar in my own ears at the way this woman went fucking wild.

"Oh God, going to come. Again. Oliver." Her fingernails dug into my scalp and I flinched from the pain, used it to press deeper. My hands went to her thighs as I stretched her open as wide as she could get.

I buried my tongue in her, lapped her juice, and licked everything I could devour. My tongue fucked her, mirroring the movements my cock would be doing to her soon.

"Oliver!"

She screamed my name like I'd wanted her to. I didn't stop. I fucking couldn't. I was going crazy with the taste of her and the way she seemed to not stop coming all over me. I stood up some, grabbing her ass in my hands, and continued licking until her shakes began to subside.

She threw an arm over her eyes and shivered. "Holy shit," she murmured over and over again as I gently set her legs down.

I chuckled. Fuck. She was wilder and crazier than I'd thought she'd be, and every time she was more fantastic than the last. My hand ran up her stomach, through the center of her chest until it settled at the side of her throat. Her pulse and heartbeat pounded against her heated skin.

"You okay?"

She shook her head back and forth. "Dying."

"Come on." I pulled her so she was sitting and then I picked her up, laughing against her when she could barely wrap her legs around my waist. "You'll have to recover quick," I said as I carried her down the short hall to the less-than-impressive bedroom. "I haven't even fucked you yet."

I stretched when I woke, feeling the dull ache in my thighs as I stretched out my legs. It took a moment to remember where I was. The plush cover pulled up to my chin and the softest pillow beneath my cheek helped me remember as soon as I opened my eyes.

As my legs moved, my foot brushed against Oliver's legs behind me and I rolled over.

He was still asleep, lying on his back with one hand thrown over his eyes to block out the sunlight from the blinds he hadn't shut the night before.

Not that there'd been time. He'd done everything to me he promised he would, ravaged me until I was listless. He wrung so many orgasms from me that I lost count. My abs hurt when I pushed myself up to an elbow to get a better look at him.

The last time I'd spent the night with him, he'd woken and left the house before I was awake, so I hadn't gotten to see him like this.

He slept with his lips slightly parted; the dark blond stubble on his cheeks was short but thick and coarse. When he'd scratched his face against my thighs the night before, multiple times, seemingly unable to get enough of me in his mouth, that hair had done wicked things to my senses.

Oliver Powell didn't go down on me like it was a job or a duty, but like it was his destiny to be between my thighs.

I took in the long lines of his body hidden beneath the thin white sheet and smiled as my gaze trailed his length. One leg was straight, the other bent to the side and exposed. One arm was set across his abdomen, almost cupping his morning erection tenting the sheets, covering what was quickly becoming my most favorite part of him.

Not that his body wasn't firm and defined and tanned and absolutely perfect, but the things he could do with his cock would give me memories to masturbate to for the rest of my life.

"If you're going to keep staring at my dick, you might as well get a closer look." He dropped his hand from his eyes and turned to me with that surly, bossy smirk of his. His eyes were open into slits, almost challenging me.

Morning sex had never been a thing for me. There was the smell of sleep clinging to skin and morning breath in mouths. As delicious as the thought was, to wake up and suck him hard and deep into my mouth, my lips twisted.

"The thought disgusts you? After last night I didn't think there was anything you wouldn't do."

His statement was a challenge, a dare, but not quite the command that turned me on so much.

I gave him honesty, because this would never work between us if we began hiding things. "Morning sex doesn't do it for me. Sort of grosses me out."

"Oh God," he groaned and rolled to his side to face me. He grinned as his hands went to my hair—always tangling in my curls like he couldn't be close and not touch me. A shiver of awareness rolled down my spine. "Don't tell me you're one of those women who cares about morning breath and shit."

The face I must have made was my answer.

He rolled his eyes and then pushed himself to sitting, groaning as he moved.

I was sore from sex, but the bruises forming on his sides told me the groan was one of pain.

"You okay?" I asked and sat up, following him.

He dropped his head to his hands and let out another pained grunt.

I reached for him before I could stop myself, dragging one fingernail down the ridged bumps of his spine, careful to avoid the bruising. "You didn't get much time to rest your body last night."

He glared at me over his shoulder, eyes darkening with memories of what we'd done, what he'd done to me. "It was worth it. Today's practice is no pads and only a few hours. I'll be fine by Monday."

"Do you need any meds? I can get you some."

He scowled. "I'm not Beaux. Don't act like you have to take care of me, Shannon."

I held up my hands and pulled back. "Grouchy before your morning shake?"

I tried to make light of the moment, but his comment stung. The look of remorse he gave me before he slid out of bed helped.

"No. Fuck, I'm sorry. I'm sore as fuck, though." He wiped a hand across his mouth and his shoulders fell when he faced me, both of us on opposite sides of the bed, the space between us larger than the monstrous bed. "I'm not used to someone wanting to take care of me or being worried about me."

I looked at the floor for my clothes and my bag. I understood. I still had the urge to flee.

"Go shower and get cleaned up," he suggested, his voice warmer. "I'll go get your bag. Dropped it by the front door last night and you drove me so fucking crazy I forgot about it."

I arched a brow. "I drove you crazy?"

"Yes. The mere sight of you drives me fucking insane. Not used to that either. Go shower."

The admission seemed to surprise him more than it did me. He was out the door of the room like a bat out of hell when I realized I was still standing in the bedroom staring at his beautiful retreating form. Both of us were in deeper than we imagined.

I shook it off.

I could dwell on his rudeness or accept him as he was. Beaux wasn't the nicest guy in the morning, especially after game days, either—win or lose. Their bodies took a pounding and sometimes Beaux told me that fucked with their heads, made them feel weaker than they thought they should be.

I tried to shake it off, tried not to take the comment personally as I turned on the water in the shower. I used the restroom while I waited for the water to heat before I climbed in, still naked from how I'd fallen asleep.

Water sluiced down my body and I slid my hands along my arms and stomach, waiting for Oliver to return with my bag that contained my shampoo and hair-taming crème. I'd need more than hotel shampoo and conditioner to deal with the frizz.

The door to the bathroom opened, letting in a burst of cool air before the sliding door to the shower opened behind me.

He was naked when he slid his body against mine, his hand reaching to my front and showing me he'd thought to grab the shampoo.

"Thank you." I took it out of his hands and squeezed a large amount into my palms before I turned and stepped slightly out of the spray so he could get wet. "Joining me in the shower?"

"Figured the quicker I got us cleaned up, the quicker you could put your mouth where you wanted it earlier."

He rocked his hips forward, drawing my attention downward.

"You're an ass," I whispered, scrubbing my hair but still unable to take my eyes off his hand wrapped around his long and thick erection.

He was beautiful. Strong and sinewy and every muscle in his abdomen bunched and flexed as he slowly stroked himself.

He was a jerk, or he could be, but he was also quick to apologize as if he couldn't believe the things he spoke sometimes. Like he didn't want to be who he'd become, but didn't know how to stop it.

"Tell me you don't want my dick in your throat, that you don't want to leave today with the taste of my cum in your mouth."

I rinsed my hair before he stepped into the spray, washing himself.

Soap rolled down his body while he scrubbed himself with his hands, cupping his balls and cleaning off his dick.

I stood frozen, and my hands fell to my sides as I licked the drops of water off my lips.

"You want it, don't you? You want me more than you think you should, but you can't help yourself."

He read me like an open book. I still challenged him by arching a brow.

"And you?" I asked, unable to stop myself from moving toward him and reaching for him. He was right. I did want the taste of him deep in my throat. "Does it piss you off that you want me so much?"

I dropped to my knees and licked along his shaft. His hand fell from his dick to my head, pushing water off my forehead.

"Fuck. Yes, it pisses me off."

I looked up at him from on my knees. Satisfaction trilled through my veins at his admission.

"Suck me harder. Deeper."

His commands shot through me, making me flush. Never had I been so excited to get on my knees for a man, or had I thought being told what to do would be such a fucking turn-on. Out of bed, it rankled me.

Inside of it, or in the shower—or anytime I had my hands on Oliver or his were on my body—it made me needy, desperate for him.

I wrapped my hand around his shaft, pulling and tugging as my mouth went to work on him. His hands cupped my cheeks, holding me in place while he fucked my mouth. Every thrust of his hips forward drove me crazy, making me gag, and tears fell from my eyes.

"Relax your throat," he whispered, gentling his hold on me. "Open it and take me deeper. You can do it.'"

He pushed forward slowly, the tip of him scraping against the back of my throat.

I began to take more of him while he slowly moved forward and retreated. He gave me time to breathe and adjust. Every glide of his dick against my throat made me grow wetter until I dropped one hand to my center and rubbed my clit.

"That's it," he murmured encouragingly. "Get yourself off because I'm not coming in your throat. I'm coming all over your fucking gorgeous tits."

My body trembled at his words, but I complied.

I wanted whatever he wanted.

"Faster," he said. "Spread your legs. Your mouth feels so full, so fucking good on my dick."

I built up the heat in my body as his thrusts came quicker.

"Fuck," he groaned, his movements becoming more erratic.

I whimpered around his cock, my orgasm coiling inside me.

It was barreling down on me, making my pulse speed. My movements around his dick turned frenetic from the impending rush that would flood my veins.

"Fucking hurry, Shannon." He grunted, moved faster, and I put my hand back on his shaft to stop him from pushing too hard.

He slapped my hand away and glared down at me. "You'll fucking take what I give you and you'll love it, every single fucking time."

The warning, the threat...the promise, was all I needed. I squeezed my eyes closed as he hit my throat at the same time I exploded beneath him. My knees hurt from the travertine-tiled floor, but it was all secondary to the pleasure that rolled through me, bright lights sparking behind my closed lids when he quickly pulled out of me.

I opened my eyes just in time to see his hard cock in front of me, and his cum splashed against my chest like he'd promised.

He braced himself with one hand on the wall next to us, his other wrapped around the length of him. He tugged harshly as he grunted his climax, shooting in long, thick spurts all over my wet and soapy breasts.

I waited until he was done and then my hands went to my chest. I washed it away while at the same time rubbing it into my skin, smiling when I realized what I was doing.

"Fucking hell," he said, his voice harsh and dry. "I don't think I've ever had someone suck my dick like you do."

It was meant as a compliment as he reached down and helped me to my feet before quickly brushing his lips against mine.

I tried to take it that way. I still turned and put my back to the shower, not wanting him to know how it hurt me. The reminder of the women he used for sex, that I was here, at his crash pad and not his home, where we'd just fucked like rabbits for hours and slept very little.

His hands slid to the front of my stomach and he pulled me against him. His lips glided down the side of my throat as I cleaned myself, keeping my eyes closed.

"I feel like you took that the wrong way, or it came out the wrong way. I just meant that I liked it. Fucking loved it. Will be something I always remember."

At least that was a bonus. When I was gone, when we were done, he'd remember my lips around his dick.

"I should get going," I said, stepping out of the water and practically jumping out of his grasp.

"You're hurt, and I'm not sure what I did to do that."

I didn't know either. Maybe because this simply wasn't me. I was moving on from Patrick. I wasn't willing to get lost in someone like that again, someone whose very presence made everyone want to put their own desires to the side and give them whatever they needed or wanted.

I could see it happening, from the way I responded to his commands to the way I'd thought about him all week.

Perhaps I wasn't cut out for this after all. It wasn't my heart I was worried about, it was my own passions, my own desires and dreams. I was suddenly terrified that spending time around Oliver would make me get all wrapped up in him and his desires and that mine would get pushed to the aside.

Again.

This was supposed to be my hour, my time to finally throw myself into everything I'd always wanted. Getting lost in Oliver Powell and his magic cock with his wicked words had the power to throw it all off-kilter if I let it.

"I'll let you shower," I mumbled and stepped from the steamy, enclosed space before he could stop me.

"You leave before I get out and I'll tan your ass," he said

over the din of the water falling. "Not fucking kidding, Shannon."

I wasn't planning on it. I was afraid, but I wasn't a coward. I didn't enjoy running from something difficult, even though I'd done that too. Sure, I missed Beaux and wanted to be close to family, but at the epicenter of my decision to leave Des Moines was the fact it was too hard to face the memories of Patrick and our life together.

I didn't want to do it again, though, but it also didn't mean I had to hop back into bed with the man either. I didn't have to throw everything I wanted away just because he commanded it.

I was dressed and in the kitchen, drinking coffee and mixing him a protein shake when he walked in dressed in workout clothes, running shoes already strapped to his feet.

"Not trying to take care of you," I said before he could snarl at me for the shake. "Old habits die hard."

"Thank you. That was nice." He took a sip and pulled the cup away from his mouth. "Would you like to explain what happened earlier?"

I shook my head. Nope. I didn't. I still wasn't certain myself. "I have to get to work. I'm swamped and everything's happening so fast."

I meant the business and the street fair and my own personal fear of failure, but I allowed Oliver to take it as between us.

"I see." He drained the last of his shake and reached for his keys. "Am I taking you back to Beaux's?"

"*Stamped* is closer. You can take me there."

"IF YOU THINK you're the only person shaken from this

attraction between us, you'd be wrong." He spoke so quietly when he pulled in front of Stamped that I almost didn't hear him.

The ride had been quiet and tense, neither of us speaking minus the directions I had to give him.

I'd had one hand on the door handle to make my quick escape, but when he dropped that bomb, I turned to him.

"Maybe you're right to run," he said and scrubbed a hand down his face. "Maybe it makes me a bigger prick than you think I am to make it so you can't."

"You consume everything, everyone around you. I don't want to disappear in your shadow." I looked at Stamped, the first thing to have potential to be all mine, the first thing in my life. "I'm just out of a five-year relationship. Rebounding maybe?" I shook my head. That wasn't what this was turning into, at least for me, and I didn't want to cheapen it. "I don't know what I want right now."

I didn't miss the teasing tone in his voice. "I think you like when I consume you."

I flashed him a look over my shoulder, part annoyed, part scared, equal parts amused. "You know what I mean."

He pulled his eyes off me to the front door of Stamped. The windows were covered, but the metal sign out front had been hung before the game yesterday. It was polished and perfect, giving a sense of what was inside. And behind those covered windows, I was really freaking proud of what I'd done in a week.

"Maybe you're right," he finally muttered. "But I'd still like you to give me a tour of your place. Show me what you do."

"Why?"

He gave me a shrug, looking as uncertain.

"Fine." I dug my keys out from my purse and opened the door. "But no making fun of my stuff."

The beauty of an online store was that I got to have my anonymity. No one bought anything from me because I was the sister of an NFL player. The downside was that I never saw anyone's reactions when they bought my jewelry and fell in love with it. Were they as thrilled as they pretended in their thank you notes I received or were they just being polite?

Seeing Oliver walk through my small store as I opened the door and led him through made my pulse race in a way it hadn't yet around him.

I'd always had Beaux's support. It was what we did for each other. I'd made decent money in college selling to other college students. I made decent money now with my online-only store, in addition to making simple items in bulk and selling them to online boutique clothing stores like Modern Vintage.

Yet seeing Oliver Powell walk through my building, glancing through the display cases and running his fingertips along the edge of the glass like he was afraid to leave a smudge, created a lump in my stomach..

"You make all of this?" he asked, staring at some simple, thick bracelet cuffs. "How?"

I cleared my throat and walked to him, setting my purse near the register counter on my way. "In the back. I have a workroom where I design and make everything."

"Show me."

I looked at the clock on the far wall. That space was personal. And a disastrous mess. Letting Oliver into that sacred space of mine would show him more of me than I wanted to reveal.

I didn't answer. I stared at the door that led to the workroom and private restroom. That lump in my stomach grew larger.

"Shannon?" Oliver asked. "Can I see it?"

It was a tipping point to something I didn't fully understand. I would essentially be baring myself to him, not my body, but my soul and all my innermost desires…if he could see it through the chaotic mess I lived in.

He walked toward me, his presence growing larger and heavier until he was next to me. From the corner of my eyes I could only see his profile, the way lines popped and appeared at the outer corners of his eyes when he ran a hand through his hair and exhaled harshly.

"I'm guessing this is how I felt when you saw me with Ralph and Winne."

I laughed before I could stop myself. "Stripped raw? Vulnerable?"

I couldn't look at him. My palms were sweating and my pulse was racing.

"I didn't know why I wanted you there, then you were and I didn't know what the fuck to do about it."

Another harsh laugh fell from my lips. I swiped my mess of a hair off my neck, which burned under his seeking gaze.

I nodded once, understanding what he was saying in a way I didn't think anyone else could.

He held himself away from people—whether from his past or maybe because of his notoriety, I didn't know.

I just knew I did the same. I was Beaux Hale's sister, and with that I was used to putting up walls, not allowing many people to get close to me for fear of being used. Patrick had broken through and then blown it to smithereens. Only Melissa had ever been someone I fully trusted.

Granted, I could walk through malls without recognition or being hounded for autographs, but there were plenty of times my name had been paired with Beaux when pictures of us out for dinner or at the ESPY awards surfaced.

"Okay." The word was a whisper, pulled from my throat before I could choke it down.

He followed me through the rest of the store while I stalled and moved as slowly as I could. I realized halfway there that Oliver wasn't following me. He was lingering, looking at every single piece of jewelry I'd made with softness in his eyes. He had an appreciation for what I poured my heart into.

Damn him and his hidden kindness.

I was trying to walk away from him, and he was pulling me closer to him without a word or a touch, just his respect.

My keys jangled in my hand, getting his attention from a selection of leather-wrapped cuffs with silver accents around the edges.

"I have a friend who would love these," he said, pointing at a pair of braided leather cuffs, gold metal stamped along the border. They were edgy and country and I loved them. I'd made them the other day after walking past a bar where country music had filtered through the doors.

The music, the sudden realization I was in the South now and everyone loved their country down here, had inspired a whole new selection of designs. Those were the only two I'd completed.

"I just made those the other day," I admitted, feeling something churn in my stomach at the mention of a friend. A female one.

He was allowed to have them, after all.

I turned away and unlocked the back office/workroom before he could see that it'd bothered me. I had no right.

"Holy fucking shit," he whispered when he walked up behind me. He still wasn't touching me. I suddenly wanted him to be. "Did someone break in?"

TWELVE
OLIVER

I didn't know where to look first as I took in the crowded and destroyed space. Wherever I looked, it was a disaster. Buckets of metal, different sizes and different colors with smaller buckets and drawers pulled open, their contents scattered all over the place.

Tools and paper littered the tabletops. I spied a small area with a laptop, and remnants of takeout and bills and more paper and more tools covered what I assumed was a wood desk. It was hard to tell.

The room looked like it'd been invaded and trashed by someone desperate.

Her laughter pulled my eyes off the space and to her, where a furious red heat bloomed on her cheeks. "No. I'm just...really messy." She waved her hand out, but she didn't need to—it was obvious and I had never been so surprised by anything about this girl until this moment.

And why this was what shocked me, rocking and knocking something hardened loose inside my chest, I had no idea. "But you're always so put together."

I was baffled and I couldn't hide it.

"Beaux's made fun of me for it, for like ever, I think." She shrugged and walked toward what I assumed was her desk. She picked up a pile of papers and set them down again. "I've never been good at cleaning, or picking up, and my mind works better in the chaos. Does it scare you?"

Strangely, my dick twitched and hardened beneath my shorts. I saw her guarded and careful, quiet and held back, almost too proper and perfect in the few times I'd seen her. This...this rattled me...made me see her in a different way. A woman who was frantic and hurried and creative, someone who lived inside her head more than out of it.

"No. It doesn't scare me."

She caught the gravelly tone in my voice and quickly glanced away. "So this is it. This is where the magic happens."

She picked up a set of pliers and tossed them into the bucket. From the top of it, I saw handles to other tools. Behind it, some sort of table saw and a handheld circular saw.

I thought of her wielding it, slashing through metal, and my dick hardened further.

This wasn't sexy. It was a disaster and messy, but I wanted to be making a different kind of magic.

Her jewelry was incredible. Beyond what I could have possibly imagined. I had pictured tiny jewels and flamboyant rings. Typical charms on silver and gold chains.

Nothing I thought of came close to the creative magnitude that had stolen my breath as soon as I saw it.

She was letting me see it, despite thinking we were moving too fast, despite wanting to run from me. A part of her, I knew, felt the same way about me that I did about her. There was a pull between us, magnetic and strong and fierce. Neither of us necessarily wanted it, but it also couldn't be denied.

Running was futile.

Burning it out, impossible.

I memorized plays and studied my opponent for a living. I studied game films and had played football long enough to adjust my game plan in a split second on the field when I saw a defender barreling down on me.

For the last seven years, since I'd played the field since Serena walked away, her pockets lined with millions, no one had ever made me want to change my game plan.

This woman...this sexy as fuck, intelligent, beautiful, kind, guarded, and fucking messy as hell woman rocked everything beneath my feet.

I struggled with what was happening inside me before I realized she was watching me, waiting for my judgment.

"You're talented," I admitted. A strange buzzing whirred maniacally in my ears. "Incredibly talented. Everything I can see is absolutely stunning, and I'm not just saying that to get in your panties."

I flashed her an awkward look, one I hoped like hell she let slide.

My chest burned. My shirt or my skin was too tight. I needed to get out of there and I suddenly understood her reaction that morning in the shower.

I was too much for her.

She was too much for me. She made me feel too much, think too much, question fucking everything.

"Thank you," she muttered, the bright red on her cheeks fading to a dull pink.

I had the urge to reach out and smooth it away with my thumb. Tell her how much she impressed me. Spill my guts at her feet and hope like hell she didn't stomp all over them.

I shoved my hands to my hips to stop myself. She had shown me her inner sanctum, and doing so had blown everything to smithereens.

"I should let you get to work," I mumbled, looking around everywhere except at her.

"Okay."

She didn't stop me. Didn't move or seem to notice the insanity burning deep inside me. And it was all her fucking fault.

"I need to go work out."

"I'll let you get to it then." She set a stack of bills she'd been flipping through down on the desk and walked toward me. "I'll walk you out."

"Okay." I stepped back and out of the room, hoping like hell the open warehouse feeling of the front area would fill my lungs with a cooling breath. Everything buzzed brighter and hotter as she walked me to the front door.

I could barely look at her when she pulled it open, stepping aside so I could walk through. What in the hell would she see on my damn face? The look of a man who had just realized that for the first time in over a decade he actually thought he was falling for some woman?

It was bullshit. I'd known her over a week, seen her a total of four times—five if you counted this morning. I didn't believe in that "first sight" fantasy bullshit unless it was lust.

This was more, though—headier—and it made my head spin.

"I'll see you later?" I asked, barely able to choke out the words. I was lost, free-falling.

"Bye, Oliver."

I heard the hurt in her words, the total misunderstanding from everything that was slamming inside my brain, and I couldn't articulate it.

I didn't correct her, either. There was no fucking way this was goodbye.

I wouldn't say goodbye to her. Not ever.

Where in the hell did that come from?

I jerked my head when I got to my car. She was still standing in the doorway, arms crossed protectively over her stomach like she was trying to shield herself from me again.

I didn't think.

I hurried back to her, not caring that she jumped in surprise when I rushed her. I pressed my hands to her cheeks. My rough and callused palms scraped her soft and tender and fucking delicious skin.

I kissed her. I kissed her hard and long and shoved my tongue deep inside her mouth as she gasped in shock. Without words, using the only thing I could think of—my hands and my tongue and my sudden erection clamoring to get out of my shorts—I fucking showed her everything I was thinking and feeling.

The sudden onslaught of emotions, the thick desire to slam her into the door and fuck the daylights and brains out of both of us, had me pulling back, both of us gasping for breath, her eyes just as wide and feral as mine.

"What in the hell was that?" she asked, wiping across the bottom of her lip.

I followed her finger, pressing less furious kisses long her bottom lip.

"I don't know," I said, gasping for breath. "I don't fucking know. I don't know what's going on, but that wasn't goodbye. Don't say that to me."

I was desperate. Sinking and soaring. Falling and flying. Twisting and unraveling.

Nothing made sense except the taste of her on my lips and the feel of her trembling body against mine.

"I'll see you later, Shannon."

I let her go before I did everything I wanted to do to her.

But I'd see her later. I'd be drilling my cock deep inside

of every inch of her, claiming her and making her mine before either of us realized it could be the worst thing we ever did.

～

"ICE YOUR ANKLE, twenty minutes on, ten minutes off."

"I know how to handle it." I barked at the athletic trainer wrapping my ankle. I had no one to be pissed at but myself. And thankfully, it wasn't sprained, just twisted and swollen. I'd be fine by next week, but the fact that I hadn't been able to clear my head, focus on the game and the practice like I usually did still pissed me off.

Fuck, I'd gotten hurt in a practice where we didn't even wear our pads.

Coach Pomville pushed through the door, slamming it so hard it banged against the windowed wall. "What in the fuck was that?" He shouted at me like I'd lost the Super Bowl.

I had no one to blame but myself, but I didn't cower to the coach. Not anymore. I had too many years under my belt. Too many bad games and bad practices.

"I'll get it together," I assured him. "Just a misstep, is all."

"'Just a misstep, is all.'" He mocked my words and shooed the trainer away after he set an ice pack on the table. I was still in my shorts, although I'd ripped my shirt off before I was back to the locker room.

I looked Coach directly in the eyes as he stalked toward me.

"You know what we have riding on you this season? A fucking contract extension. You can't pull shit like this. You can't be distracted for a single fucking second. You understand that?"

I understood. More than he did. My five-year contract was up at the end of this season and I was getting old.

One bad game would be the difference between millions of dollars and retirement.

"I said I'll get it together."

"See that you do."

He left as quickly as he had entered, already barking down another player's throat, with the door slamming shut behind him.

Coach Pomville was an awesome coach. He knew when to motivate, knew when to kick ass and smack helmets. I admired him, had mad respect for him both on and off the field.

I'd been off today. I was still sore from last night's game because the hits weren't as easily shaken off anymore when men almost ten years younger and stronger than angry bulls charged at me.

I needed to be more focused.

I would be, too, after I settled shit with Shannon. While I should have been focused on plays and receiving and running and taking off from the line of scrimmage, I had been thinking about black curly hair all over my pillows and heaven-scented pussy.

Before I could talk myself out of it, I picked up my phone and called her.

"Hello?" She sounded distracted when she answered, more than a little irritated.

"You still at Stamped?" I asked, barking out the question like Pomville had just snapped at me.

"Oliver?" The phone went quiet. "Oh, sorry," she said. "I didn't look at the ID before I answered."

"You always this rude to unknown callers?" A grin tugged at my lips, the urge to tease her unbearable.

"No." She sighed, and I imagined a finger going to those curls, wrapping it around her finger before she tugged and let it pop back into place like a spring. "Just a crappy afternoon. What are you doing?"

"Headed to your place. I want to see you. We need to talk."

"Talk?"

"Yes."

"About?"

"I'll tell you when I get there." And then I'd show her. "Where are you?"

"Um. I'm at Beaux's. I can meet you…"

"No." I wanted her in whatever bed she slept in for once. I wanted her to wake up knowing she'd never get the memory of me washed out of her sheets. Like I gave a shit if Beaux heard me. "I'll be there in thirty."

"Um, maybe we can—"

"Thirty minutes, Shannon. Be ready for me."

I hung up before she could reply, but not before I caught the quick intake of her breath.

So fucking responsive. So beautiful.

Soon she was going to be all mine, because I had two choices: get rid of her before the season started so I could focus on only the game, or go all in so we could stop this ridiculous bullshit uncertainty between us.

And only one choice was acceptable.

I hopped off the bench, tossing the ice pack to the table.

"Hey," the trainer, Alan, called after me.

"Ice it, twenty on, ten off. I got it." I raised my hand as I headed out the door, listening to him grumble about how we didn't know shit.

I walked carefully, my ankle tender and twisted but not sore enough that I couldn't put weight on it.

The fact that I was injured, mildly, only gave me ideas on how Shannon could take care of me later. With her hands, her mouth, her thighs clenched around my hips as she rode me, taking us both over the edge.

"Hey." Beaux slapped my shoulder, and his voice along with his touch was just the bucket of ice I needed to drown my erection. A hard-on in athletic shorts was too obvious. "We're partying tonight, heading out. You coming, old man?"

I couldn't help myself. "I'll be coming. But not with you."

The kid's skin went green and he covered his eyes. "Jesus. Fuck. Don't say that shit to me. I'm fucking serious. I don't need that image—" He scrubbed his face and shook his head. "Seriously, you're an asshole, Powell, you know that?"

I slapped him on the shoulder. "Have fun tonight. We won't wait up for you."

"Aw...hell. You're doing it at my place now? Stay off the furniture."

I hadn't planned on being on it. At least not for long. I still wiggled my eyebrows as I pushed past him on my way to my locker.

"Dick!" he shouted and turned toward his own locker on the far side of the room.

Because we were men, and we thought with that part, and in the locker room everything went, I reached down and grabbed my semi-hard dick and shouted Beaux's name.

"She likes it, though, you know? I think it's good for her."

"Damn, Powell," one of our defensive linemen groaned. "That's just nasty."

"You're nasty," I shouted back. "Hale can take it."

"Oh the innuendo in that one. The things I could say," Rudolph muttered, earning another round of groans throughout the room.

"Don't fuck with the quarterback," someone else shouted.

I thought it was the safety, Smith, but I turned back to the locker when I saw Hale's cheeks had turned bright pink with embarrassment like Shannon's did. I might have gone too far, but the safety kept talking.

"Quarterback's pissed off at you and you won't get the record for tight end receiving touchdowns this year."

"I wouldn't fuck with his record," Hale said.

I turned to him, the fact that I'd forgotten all that lay in the palm of my hands...all that rested in his had been momentarily forgotten while my judgment became clouded with pussy.

"Swear to fucking Christ, Powell, I wouldn't pull that shit on you, no matter how much you piss me off. Don't fucking hurt her. You do and I'll kick your ass, but that shit won't filter onto the field."

I examined him then. It was the most serious I'd ever seen him, most determined about anything. Beaux was always so fucking laid back it was hard to trust him, but I couldn't find a single part of him that didn't seem one hundred and ten percent honest about his statement.

Something grew between him and me in that moment. Respect.

I needed it from him like I needed to give it to him, and that would earn his trust, both on and off the field.

"I hear you, kid," I said.

I dropped my shorts and wrapped a towel around my waist. I only had a few minutes for a quick scrub-down before I could be at Shannon's when I told her I would be.

I didn't need to spend any more of it bonding with the men.

SHE ANSWERED the door to the condo as soon as I knocked, her hair disheveled and flying out behind her, and a little breathless. None of it matched the fury flashing in her eyes that she tried to hide as soon as I stepped in.

"Beaux called, said he and the team were going out tonight. Did you plan that?"

I grinned. "Fortuitous, I think, but no, I didn't. Is that why you look ready to strangle someone?"

She groaned and moved toward the kitchen. "No. I've been on the phone with my friend Melissa all damn day because Patrick's being a douche-nugget about my furniture." She yanked the cork out of a wine bottle and filled a glass with deep red liquid. "Sorry, you want some?'"

"I'll help myself to water. Who's Patrick?"

"My ex."

My head was buried in the fridge when she muttered the word. When I looked back, she was swallowing the wine like she was in a college chugging contest.

"Hey." I walked to her and took the glass from her mouth, smiling as she leaned forward to get one more drop and then licked her lips to get any remaining ones that fell. "What's going on?"

She shook her head and looked over my shoulder. "That's not why you came here. Not to talk about that." Her brow wrinkled and she looked at me. "Why did you come here? This morning...I thought—"

"We'll get to that." I opened my water and chugged half of it. I was stuck on her ex being an asshole—an asshole that fucked around with another woman and was stupid enough to get caught. Red blurred at the edges of my vision. "Tell me what happened today. Is that why you were irritated when I called?"

"Irritated, pissed, distracted and too busy to handle all this shit on my lap? Yes."

"Whoa." I handed her wine back. She was babbling and manic. Maybe the alcohol would settle her down. "Calm down. You eaten dinner yet?"

"No. I ordered pizzas a while ago."

Pizza and massive carbs would mean a four-hour workout tomorrow instead of three. I didn't say shit. She looked like she could reach for a butcher's knife and fling it at the next thing that set her off. It wasn't going to be me moaning about pizza.

"How about we sit and talk," I suggested and then opened the door to the freezer. I was helping myself like I lived there and she didn't say a word. I dug through bags of frozen vegetables until I found an ice pack.

"You're hurt?" Her eyes jumped and her gaze quickly roamed my body before meeting mine.

"Twisted my ankle. No big deal, I swear."

Her shoulders slumped a bit and for the first time since I'd arrived, I think she breathed.

I walked to the living room couch and sat down, propping my foot onto a pillow on the coffee table to keep it elevated. Once I was settled, I put my arm on the back of the couch and gestured for her to join me.

I tried not to let it bother me that she sat just out of my reach instead of curled into my side like I wanted.

We'd get there after she bitched about Patrick and after we talked about where I was taking us. She didn't trust me yet and she shouldn't. I'd been way too fucking mercurial.

"Talk to me." I waited for what felt like forever before she began.

I'd been on a rollercoaster all day long. After Oliver's abrupt departure this morning—not knowing at all where we stood, but feeling like something had shifted between us, something moving past this four-week arrangement we'd agreed on—I'd received a call from Patrick.

The day went downhill from there.

I set my glass of wine down on the table and tucked my feet under me on the couch and faced Oliver.

He'd gestured for me to sit next to him, but I was still too raw, too dizzy to trust his touch.

Now, just out of his reach, I wished there was a way I could move closer without being obvious. I wanted to be closer to him, pressed against defined chest and enclosed in his sinewy arms.

Under the right circumstances, it would be a safe haven.

I didn't know if we were there yet, so I held back, trying to be smart.

"Patrick and I lived together," I started after I tried to piece together the day enough to tell it so it made sense. "But he moved into my apartment. I added his name to the lease after the first year, and I've since had my name removed from it, but all the furniture in it is mine. He's refusing to give me a time that movers can be there to pack it up and move it out here until I agree to see him so he can apologize."

"He wants you back."

Oliver's voice went steely and I sighed. "Yeah."

"And you want?"

"Gosh." I shook my head and messed with my hair. "Not that. I think he's embarrassed and pissed that someone of my caliber of lifestyle walked away from him."

Oliver's brows jumped up his forehead.

"I know," I said as I laughed softly. "His family is really wealthy. Think they might have owned all of the Iowan land at one point, and they've sold it off."

It was an exaggeration, but their wealth overwhelmed me on the best of days. They either currently owned something, or had once owned the land most of the Des Moines area had been built on, not to mention the buildings they owned, too.

"Anyway, I'm just a girl from a rundown home, with a single mom who had two kids with two different dads and could barely afford to raise us."

"That's not you," Oliver snapped. He was so serious.

I couldn't pull my eyes off his tawny eyes.

"That's not who you are."

"It is, though." I shrugged. I wasn't ashamed of my past.

Compared to Patrick and his family, who hosted fundraisers for politicians and didn't eat anywhere except a restaurant with valet parking—a rarity in Des Moines—we were common. Lower class.

I waved away his statement. "It's not a big deal. Beaux and I came from nothing. I'm proud of my mom. She worked her whole life, paying for it in the end, and I didn't mind taking care of her or helping Beaux succeed. I don't even think Patrick wants me. He just doesn't want to lose."

"So how are you getting your stuff?"

"I've considered staying with Beaux until I can afford new stuff for my apartment above Stamped."

"There's an apartment there?" Oliver's eyes lit with interest. "You mean, when I was there earlier, we were ten yards from a bed and didn't end up in it?"

The teasing glint in his eyes relaxed me and I laughed, tilting my head against the back of the couch.

"Surprising, huh? But no, the bed is nasty and I could live there, but I want my own stuff. Patrick can afford to replace everything with the snap of his fingers. He's only holding onto it to maintain some twisted sense of control."

"So what are you going to do?"

"My best friend Melissa has a key. She's going to meet the movers there next week, or as soon as I can get everything scheduled."

She was ecstatic about the idea.

When we had talked earlier, she'd told me about a photo she'd seen online of Oliver and me leaving the game together. We'd laughed and over-analyzed everything that had changed for me in the short time I'd been here. When I told her I was happy, she'd reluctantly agreed not to cause potential problems with Patrick—even if she was gloomy about me making her promise not to slice and dice all of Patrick's expensive suits like she'd mentioned.

While I had struggled with my frustration with Patrick all day today, I also realized something important.

I was over him long before our relationship was over. We'd been roommates mostly for six months before we broke up, before I caught him cheating. We'd drifted apart before he began cheating, bored and too placated with our lives after only a few years together. If a relationship could be that dull after such a short time, we had no business spending a lifetime together.

I wanted passion and excitement. I wanted friendship and respect. I wanted laughter and late night movies in bed and marathon, athletic sex sessions. I didn't want those moments to dull before the *I Dos* were spoken, and with Patrick they had years prior.

It might have been my stubbornness that made me hold on for so long, something Melissa reminded me of when we spoke. I'd been unhappy for a long time and before I was unhappy, I'd been uncertain of the future.

I loved that she waited until she knew I could handle hearing the truth before stating it.

"Hey." Oliver tapped my hand that was near him and when I pulled my gaze to his, he was smiling. "Where'd you go?"

I laughed and shook my head. "Sorry. I was thinking of Melissa. I miss her, I guess. We talk almost every day, but it's not the same."

His lips twisted, quirked up on one side. "What'd she say about me?"

The question threw me before I realized he was teasing. I teased back. "Said if you have a cock as big as I'm proclaiming you do, I'd be the biggest fool in the world not to ride it as long as it's offered to me."

The words flew unbidden from my lips. I blamed the wine I'd chugged. One glass before he'd even arrived. As the blush hit my cheeks, Oliver leaned forward to get close enough to wrap his hand around my wrist.

He tugged me to him, pulling me until I straddled him, careful of the leg he had propped on the coffee table.

"What exactly did you tell her about my big cock?" His

thumb stroked the inside of my wrist and sent shocks up my arm to my chest.

I rolled my hips, unable to stop myself. Beneath me, his bulge hardened. "I told her everything. Everything you do to me. Everything you make me do. Everything you make me feel."

His hands dropped to my hips as he groaned. He stilled me, held me against his hard length between us, and met my eyes. "And if I want more? If I think we could be more?"

My lips parted. "What?"

"What would you say to that?"

I'd come to Raleigh to start over. Being close to Beaux had been my only option after leaving Melissa and Des Moines behind. The last thing I'd expected, two weeks after arriving, was this.

To meet Oliver Powell. To end up in his bed. Or to have him kiss me the way he did this morning, angry and adamant that I'd never say goodbye to him again. When he'd gone silent in my workroom, I was certain that was what he was doing when he walked away from me. When he'd come back and kissed me hard and long, he'd thrown me for my first roller-coaster loop of the day.

"I...I don't know."

I wanted to be honest. I also wanted to think of what I needed. I didn't want to get lost in his shadow, forgetting my passion and my desire.

"What if we drop the timeline we set forth and see what happens?"

I was still stuck on my last thought. "I won't stop Stamped for you."

He frowned. "I would never ask you to."

"That means I can't come to away games, or be there every time you need me to come running."

His frown changed direction and his hands left my hips to press against my cheeks. "Fucking hell, Shannon. I wouldn't demand that shit of you. You have your own business. You don't think after seeing it today that I wouldn't respect that?"

I didn't know what to think. If I was honest, I wanted a redo on the entire day. I wanted to not freak out in the shower that morning. I wanted to do everything different once we got to Stamped. I wanted to be able to sit on his lap, at that very moment and not be afraid I would lose myself in him.

"You scare me," I admitted, my voice breathless.

"Then we're even." He leaned forward and brought his lips to mine, nipping at my bottom lip and then soothing it with his tongue. "Because you terrify the shit out of me."

I laughed. He pulled me forward until our foreheads touched. Through his thick, dirty blond lashes, he looked at me, his hazel eyes swirling with amusement. "I still want to try this. Something with you. Something without timelines and restrictions. You in?"

I threw caution to the wind. I considered Melissa's advice from earlier...if it makes you feel good, makes you laugh and makes you happy, jump in and enjoy the ride. I considered my own feelings, along with the fact that he was as scared, too.

I considered the fact that sitting in his lap, I was already beginning to grow heated and wet in my center, longing for him. This morning, I'd gotten him off. I was still sore from last night, but disappointed I'd freaked out before he could return the favor.

I considered all of it, staring into his eyes, debating and making him nervous by the wait, based on the way his nostrils flared and his eyes darkened.

The doorbell rang, breaking the moment.

"Yes," I whispered and tilted my head to brush my lips against his. "Yes. Okay. No deadlines."

It was all I needed to hear. She swung a leg over mine and stood up.

I rolled to one hip and grabbed my wallet out of my back pocket, handing her cash. "Here."

"I already ordered it before you got here."

I gave her a look. "Take the money, Shannon. You knew I'd be here eating it and I'm guessing you bought twice as much knowing I was coming."

"Three times, actually." She grinned and swiped the money out of my fingers. "Thank you."

She wiggled her ass as she headed toward the front door for the pizza.

When the man was paid and tipped well, she disappeared into the kitchen.

She returned with three large pizzas, and stacked on top of the boxes were paper plates and bottles of water.

I moved to get up to help her when she stopped me. "Don't. I've got it and you need to rest your ankle."

It had been so long since someone had attempted to take

care of me, tried to help me, that I had to swallow the smart-ass comment.

"Thanks," I mumbled when she took her place next to me on the couch.

We ate. We talked about her jewelry business, about football and the season. Every time she offered up an opinion, I realized how much she truly knew the game. She'd studied it, loved it. It seemed almost as much a part of her as it was to me.

It only increased my attraction to her. Since Serena had walked out on me, angry I'd tossed her to the side for a dream I'd had since before I ever asked her out in high school, I hadn't met a woman like Shannon. Most of the conversations I'd had with women over the last several years revolved around my muscles and the way my ass looked in tight football pants.

I didn't know women like Shannon existed. Every layer I peeled back, every time I dug deeper, I continued to be pleasantly surprised.

She knocked me sideways and upside down as we watched ESPN highlights of the night's preseason games. She yelled and cursed when Beaux's old team won.

"What the hell?" I asked, surprised by her outburst.

My hand curled into her shoulder and I pulled her closer. I wanted her there. Loved her energy and her inability to hold back anything she was feeling.

"I can't help it," she said, bouncing on the edge of the couch. "I wanted them to lose."

"Typical girl," I said, pulling her so she fell against my chest. The ice on my ankle was long gone. I'd iced and rested it and I was tired of it. "Always holding a grudge."

She slapped my abs, and I grabbed her hand with my other one, holding her against me. "Shut up. I can't help it. They let him go and they could have used him and now their old quarterback doesn't have a decent backup."

I laughed and pressed my lips against the top of her head, inhaling the sweet scent of her shampoo. "Yeah, but then he wouldn't be here, in Raleigh and starting."

She relaxed in my arms—her fingers trailing circles on my abs. The light teasing touch, the scent of her, the feel and the weight of her all rolled through me, sparking and igniting interest and desire for her.

"Where's your room?" I asked when the attraction between us pulled tight and I didn't want to wait any longer. "Told Beaux I wouldn't fuck you on his couch."

"Oh my gosh." She groaned and buried her face into my chest. Her shoulders shook with muffled laughter. "You talked about me? In the locker room?"

I wasn't going to get into it. Not all of it.

"He simply said no fucking on his furniture."

"The bed I'm sleeping on is his." She grinned when she pulled back.

I was already pushing to my feet, bringing her with me until her legs were wrapped around my hips and my hands were holding her by her ass.

"Semantics. I also said we wouldn't wait up for him."

"Oh my God. I'm never going to be able to show my face around the team again."

"Hey." I walked her toward the room she gestured to and kicked the door open. "Does it bother you? You gotta know sometimes shit gets flung around, but between me and Beaux, no one's going to say shit to you. And if they do, we'll handle it."

She pressed her hand against my cheek and her fingertips played with the hair above and behind my ear. She always did that—found a way to touch me so gently that it drove me to distraction.

I wanted hard fucking, nails digging into skin, grips so tight they bruised, and yet she was the sweet to my spice, the light to my dark. Every time I wanted to dirty her up, she made me want to slow down and relish the moment at the same time.

So fucking different from the last six years.

I leaned into her touch while she pressed her lips to my jaw. "I don't care what they say."

Thank fuck. I didn't want to have to promise to kick my teammates' asses, but I would if it bothered her. Beaux would back me up, too, unless he was the one taking the first swing.

I bent forward and laid her down on the bed. She clung to me, not letting me go, and pulled me down on top of her.

"I love your weight on me," she said, her hands sliding down my shirt until she pushed her fingers beneath the waistband of my shorts. "And this butt."

I buried my face into her shoulder and pushed her further up the bed until I could kneel on it. "Get them off me. And my shirt."

I lifted my hips long enough for her to push my shorts down before I kicked them off, then I rolled us until she straddled me and helped her with my shirt.

Her fingers were cool on my skin as she dragged them up the planes of my stomach, the curves of my chest.

"You're so hard," she whispered, her eyes glazed over with admiration.

I worked on my body because it needed to be the best it could be at all possible moments, not for it to be admired. With Shannon's hands dragging through my chest hair, brushing across my nipples, light, teasing, and exploratory touches, I was fucking thankful I didn't have a desk job where I didn't have to work so hard.

"Stop teasing me." I groaned as her hand dipped across my lower abs, one fingernail trailing through the hair just above my waistband.

She scraped her nail across the edge of the waistband to my boxers and my hips jerked in response.

"Fucking touch me, Shannon. Wrap your hand around my dick."

She peered up at me through hooded eyes, her untamed hair draping a curtain around us. "In a hurry?"

"To feel your hot and wet pussy clenching and stretching around my dick? Yes." I rocked up again, pressing my dick against the center of her thighs.

She moaned in response.

"Take off your clothes."

She made a clicking sound with her tongue and her teeth. "Always so bossy."

"You like it."

I didn't wait for her to follow my command. I sat up, pressing her against my lap, and ripped off her shirt before pulling the cups of her bra beneath her breasts.

My mouth covered one of her nipples as my fingers teased the other. They were full in my mouth and my palms, spilling over from the pressure of her bra.

Her hands immediately went to her shorts and she wiggled out of them, shifting off me while I kept my mouth on her nipple, tugging and teasing and sucking on one before moving to the other.

"My God," she moaned, her fingers digging into my shoulders. I held her against me, pressed up against her before I pulled her down and I was on my back.

"Ride me. Show me how you like it."

I shoved my boxers down, pushing them off my hips, and held my dick. Shannon moved over me and I slid it through her wetness, both of us groaning.

"I want to play," she whimpered.

"Play later. Fuck me now before I take over and do it for you."

Her eyes narrowed on me, the haze of lust clouding the irritation she was trying to fake.

When she didn't move I grabbed her hips, and in one hard, forceful thrust I seated her all over my dick.

"No condom. Fuck!" I groaned and pushed my head back to the pillow. I couldn't move her off me. The slickened heat of her enveloped me—covering me and coating me with her wetness.

I rocked my hips up, pressing her further against me. God, she was incredible. When her hips rolled and her thighs began to shake, I had to fight the urge to come like a teenager losing his virginity. "I get tested before the season. I'm clean, I swear it."

Would you she trust me enough to have her bare? When I saw the quick flash of fear in her eyes, I bit down the disappointment.

She was already leaning over me, reaching for the nightstand drawer.

"I have a box."

"Shit," she muttered as I teased her clit with my thumb to keep her wet. Her fingers fumbled with the plastic wrapping before she bit it and tore it with her teeth. "Forgot how big of a pain in the ass these boxes are."

Any lingering disappointment at her not trusting me would have evaporated with that sentence, that it'd been a while for her. That she hadn't been with a man since her ex.

"You're going to hurt your teeth." I smiled, unable to stop it. When in the hell had sex been so fun? I imagined it wasn't that often, for that many people.

"Finally." She tore the box open and yanked out a strip, ripping one open. My thumb continued to press and roll around her clit and she fumbled again when I pulled her off me.

"Put it on." My voice had gone gravelly. Needy.

As her hand slid down my cock, she tugged and pulled before I pushed into her hand and growled again. "Fucking now, Shannon."

She looked up at me and grinned before sliding back down on my dick until I was seated balls deep inside her.

Thank fuck. "Good. Now fuck me like you mean it."

She took the challenge as intended and began sliding up and down on my dick, rolling her hips. I pulled her against me, her breasts brushing my chest, and dug one hand in her hair as I fucked her back, taking control. It wasn't my style to follow someone else's lead.

The sound of her flesh sliding against mine drove me wild and my hips bucked against her, faster and harder while one of my hands went to her ass, pressing her down against me when I pushed into her.

I fucked her hard, unable to slow down, unable to take my time. Every time she rocked against me, her pussy clenched around my dick.

Her whimpers increased, grew closer together as I took her to the edge and then backed off, not wanting it to end yet.

I wanted to drive her as crazy as she made me feel, both inside and outside the bedroom.

"Fucking hell," I groaned. "You're so fucking hot around my dick."

I'd been bare before, but not often. The heat I now missed around my dick made me curse the rubber fuckers I never wanted to use again.

"So close, Oliver." Her lips parted and she pressed them to mine. I sucked her tongue into my mouth as she slid toward the edge all over again, and this time I didn't slow down.

My thrusts increased. My fingertips on her ass slid to her crease and she bucked against me as my fingers pressed against her puckered hole.

"Holy shit." She gasped. "What the hell?"

"You'll like it," I assured her, watching her eyes roll back as I continued teasing her with gentle ministrations. "Someday I'll take your ass and you'll fucking love it. You'll come harder than you ever have before."

She shook her head. Not in argument, but because she was going wild with pleasure.

"Come, Shannon. I'll make it feel good."

"Oh shit...damn...yes...please, Oliver."

As her body began to clench around me, her pussy spasming with the beginning rolls of her orgasm, I bit back my own growl and pressed the tip of my finger inside her asshole.

Her body bucked wildly as she threw her head back. "Oliver! Holy shit, I'm coming!"

I fucked both her holes, gently pressing against her ass at the same time I pulled her pussy against me. I held on for the ride, taking her over the edge again and again, not relenting in my fucking until she'd screamed so loud her voice went hoarse and her body went limp.

I pulled her off me, grabbed her hand, and made her help me yank off the condom before I wrapped our hands around my dick. I shot my load all over my stomach, coating our hands and our fingers.

Coating *her*.

"Fuck," I groaned as her hand continued pumping every last drop of my cum out of my dick.

My chest was covered in sweat—it dripped along my hairline and I was breathless when she finally collapsed next to me. Our legs stayed tangled together and her hand rested on my stomach.

"I liked that," she whispered, her body boneless and liquid at my side. "When you pressed your finger into me."

I turned my head and brushed my lips against her cheek, tenderly, exactly the opposite of how I'd just fucked her and would again later. "You'll like it more when I have my dick in there."

Her eyes widened and she looked down at our hands still connected. Still covered in my cum. "It's really big."

"I'll make it good for you, stretch you, take my time. You'll come all over my mouth and my fingers before I ever put my dick in you."

"So sure of yourself."

Always. I was a cocky, arrogant asshole. Since I started high school, confidence had never been a problem for me. I knew what I was good at because I worked for it, so I didn't feel the need to defend myself to her.

I'd prove it soon enough.

"We'll get you a plug," I whispered.

Her body shook as a shiver rolled through her. Goose bumps burst onto her arm and I smiled.

"You love that idea, don't you? So fucking filthy for me."

She was silent for a moment before she began kissing my chest. "Yeah. I like the idea."

I slid my hand down her back and patted her backside. "We need to get cleaned up before this dries all over us."

She laughed and pushed off me. As she moved to slide off me, I tugged her back down so I could kiss her.

I kissed her slowly, tenderly. I kissed her with all the gentleness in the world, taking my time to explore her mouth.

She was sweet, pliable in my strong arms. When she pushed back, her cheeks were flushed and her eyes showed everything she was thinking. They showed desire mixed with apprehension.

I grinned. "Thank you for giving me this chance."

"Thanks for fucking me so well."

I laughed as she rolled off the bed, watching her when she went to the connected bathroom and turned on the sink.

She came back with a washcloth and placed it on my stomach.

I took over cleaning us. "Shower?"

"Your ankle okay enough?"

I rolled my eyes. "My ankle's fine, and I'm strong enough to fuck you in the shower, putting all my weight on it if you don't stop acting so worried."

"Such an asshole." She winked and grabbed the washcloth from me.

I jumped out of bed and grabbed her from behind, pulling her off her feet as she squealed in surprise.

Then I took her into the shower and did all the things to her I'd wanted to do that morning before she ran from me.

FIFTEEN

SHANNON

I pressed my hand to the headboard, the move keeping Oliver from pushing me toward the front of the bed. It had the added benefit of making me thrust back against him every time he pushed into me.

On his knees behind me, mine pressed together in between his thighs, the tightened space made his dick feel bigger. He'd woken me with his mouth all over my pussy, eating me like I was the breakfast he'd been starving for, before he flipped me over while I was still coming and pushed inside of me, already prepared with a condom like he'd taken his time getting ready before he ever began eating me.

When he was seated deep inside me, he pushed my legs closed, making me come again from the tight sensation.

"Come on, Shannon. Again." I'd already come twice. Once the night before. I wasn't sure I had another one in me.

I panted quietly, biting my tongue to keep from shouting out. "Oliver...please..."

His hand wrapped around my stomach and played with my clit, and his other hand curled around my shoulder. He had me completely restrained, completely held immobile for him except for the pressure I could put on his headboard.

I threw my head back as he thrust his hips against me fast, more powerfully. He didn't stop until I was screaming all over again, gasping for breath as my eyelids slammed shut. My orgasm took me over the edge with a deep, slow burn that wasn't any less powerful than it'd been earlier.

"Oliver."

"Fucking hell." He thrust into me, taking his hand off my clit and clamping it around my hip to hold me still while he chased his own orgasm, pumping into me with a precision and power I would think he'd reserve for the football field before he let loose his own groan. He pushed me forward so hard we both collapsed into the bed. His forehead rested against the back of my head and his groan made my scalp tingle. "Shannon, holy shit, honey."

I trembled at the endearment that fell from his lips.

When he'd caught his breath he slowly pulled out, rolled me over, and pressed his lips to mine, ignoring the fact that I had always hated morning breath and sweat. "Good morning."

"Mornin'," I muttered against his lips.

He gave me a squeeze before he rolled off me and headed toward the bathroom. "When do you need to leave? Do you have to set up your booth this morning?"

I brushed my hair off my face, reality setting in. Based on the light from behind the closed curtains, I had to get moving. It was the second day of the street fair and yesterday had been crazy busy, bigger and better than anything I could have imagined.

Last night when I'd finished closing everything up, I'd met him at the hotel for dinner and ended up staying.

"Yeah." I sighed and stretched my well-abused limbs. I had my hands above my head, pressing against the headboard and my body in a long, lean line when he walked out of the bathroom.

"Someday, I'm going to tie you to the bed, just like that and fuck you till you can't take any more."

My hips rolled, jumping at the thought. Oliver caught it and then swore before turning back to the bathroom, groaning and pressing his fingers to his eyes.

"What are you doing?" I asked, pushing myself to sitting and swallowing a groan. My muscles were uncomfortable and tight, a combination of sitting in the heat all day yesterday and the athletic sex sessions.

"Taking out my contacts. I keep fucking falling asleep in them and my eyes are killing me."

He wore...glasses?

I jumped from the bed, grabbing a shirt I'd tossed to the floor before, and met him in the bathroom. He splashed more water on his face before he patted it dry with a towel and removed a pair of glasses from the drawer next to him.

And holy shit. It changed the look of him. Took him from monstrous, sexy football player to sexy, forgetful professor in a heartbeat.

My lips parted. "You're going to have to fuck me with those on."

His eyes crinkled and he met my gaze in the mirror. He ran a hand through his hair, messing up the shaggy top and making it wilder. "What?"

A gazillion fantasies flashed in my mind and I nodded, breathless as I answered. "Oh. Yeah."

"You'll get your wish. Tonight." He turned then and pressed his lips to my cheek. "But I can't have you late for the festival today, and I have practice. I'll meet you in the kitchen once you're dressed, so get moving."

I hurried. The promise of tonight sparked all sorts of wicked thoughts in my head.

~

THE SUN BEAT down on my shoulders despite the tent covering overhead. It was going to take me months, if not years, to get used to the constant heat that made the pavement so hot that it steamed all day long.

The crowd was packed along the street, vendors set along the curbs of the arts district Festival like we were sardines.

I was hot and sweaty. I was miserable from being in the sun for the last two days.

I was also having the time of my life.

My jewelry was selling faster than I had thought possible. I'd made enough money in the last two days alone to begin to set aside a decent amount to continue not only making more jewelry, but to begin paying Beaux back for the paid lease on my building.

A week from Wednesday, my furniture would arrive from Iowa and I could finally move into my own place.

The past week had been insanely busy while the Rough Riders had been preparing for another preseason game coming up the next day. They were preparing to play last year's Super Bowl champions, and Oliver and Beaux had both spent the week acting like this preseason game was the AFC Championship game.

Not that I could blame them. The Seahawks had beaten the Rough Riders in the final playoff game last year, pushing them toward their Super Bowl win. The men—the entire team, it sounded like—were out for blood, and Beaux's natural competitive instincts wanted to be the one to take them there.

I had barely seen Oliver all week long, but the night before he'd stopped by Stamped, insisting I stop working after I'd been at the street fair all day and was still burning the midnight oil, making more jewelry to have a bigger selection to sell on the two following days.

My fingers were blistered and sore, my hands cramped from the work.

I was still smiling, handing out business cards, letting everyone who stopped by know of my new business that would have its grand opening in two weeks, just before the first home game of the real season.

Melissa was flying out for it, and I couldn't wait to see her, but I also couldn't wait to show off my new home, my new life... my new man.

I grinned at the thought as a small cluster of women slowed down and approached my table.

They whispered their appreciation of the jewelry as one of the women picked up one of the leather braided cuff bracelets. Those had yet to sell. A part of me still didn't like the way Oliver had mentioned that a friend of his would love them, and then dropped it without explaining who it was.

Not that it should have mattered—in the past week he'd shown me that when he decided to go all in for a relationship, to see what happened without a timeline ending things, he was really good at it.

It wasn't just in bed, either. On the nights we didn't see each other, he called and checked in. We didn't talk long, but he still made the effort—something that surprised me. But he was showing me, slowly, that he was the guy I'd seen beneath the hard layer of arrogance he easily wore like a well-tailored coat.

He was the guy I'd seen whispering to his horses, taking care of them, and being at ease on the farm.

Not that I'd been back there. The week before we'd spent

most of the time at his crash pad and not his home, needing to be out of the apartment when Beaux was around.

Beaux might have been okay with me dating Oliver, but I certainly wasn't going to force him to hear about it at all hours.

"These are beautiful," one of the women said, lifting a set of copper-colored bangles and inspecting the charms on each: *love, faith, hope, peace, kindness...* They sparkled from the sun hitting them before she placed them back down. "You make all of these?"

"I do." I slid a business card toward her. "Stamped is the name of my business. It opens officially in two weeks, just a few doors down on this side of the street."

I pointed toward the red brick building.

She took the card and smiled at me. She wouldn't buy today, but I knew, based on the smile on her face, that she'd remember me. The way she gently seemed to brush her finger along the copper told me she was being genuine.

"These are impressive, truly. I love every single one of them."

"Serena," another woman's voice called to her. "You have to come here."

The woman jerked her head, and I frowned at the mention of her name. I'd heard it before, but couldn't remember.

"What is it?" she asked, turning her head. Her face paled as the crowd seemed to part behind her.

My lips spread into a wide grin as Beaux and Oliver and three other men towered over most of the other patrons. Their bulk and their height made their presence noticeable to everyone around them.

Beaux was grinning, laughing at something someone behind him had said, when Oliver's eyes met mine before narrowing on the woman in front of me.

"What in the fuck are you doing here?" He practically

snarled, propping his hands on his hips as he walked straight up to her. "What shit are you pulling now, Serena?"

She smiled sweetly, a different smile from the one she'd given me earlier. If I wasn't mistaken, she also pushed her ample breasts forward and cocked her hip. "Oliver. So good to see you again. How are you?"

"Cut the shit, Serena. What are you doing talking to Shannon?"

Her head whipped back before she turned to me, that catty smile still in place. "How do you two know each other? You know Oliver? My husband?"

My mouth opened and closed with no words escaping. I flashed wide eyes to Oliver.

"Ex," he growled and didn't look at me. "And our meeting with the lawyers isn't until Monday, so what are you doing here?"

"Can't a girl come to town to visit friends? I do have them, you know."

A muscle jumped in his cheek, making his lips twist. "Leave. Now."

She walked up to him, and I curled my hands into fists. I wanted to reach out and tell her to stop, but I was frozen solid.

He jerked away, pushing Rudolph back a step. He had the same scowl on his face Oliver and Beaux had.

"Don't touch me. You lost that right and you know it."

"I'm sorry," she whispered, but not so quiet I couldn't still hear her. "I'm sorry for everything. For hurting you and leaving you. I'm sorry I was too young to be able to handle everything we went through. But if I'm honest, I'm glad I ran into you. Was going to call you before Monday. I'd like to get together and talk. See if we can maybe set some of this anger between us aside? I've missed you, Oliver."

Her voice softened further, almost pleading. It was gentle

and sweet and sounded like a beautiful song—one that made me want to vomit.

Oliver swallowed. The world seemed to shake beneath my feet when he looked at her, something in his eyes shining that I hadn't seen before—not directed at me, anyway.

This was his ex-wife. Essentially throwing herself at him. And he was standing there considering it.

He stepped back then, looked over her shoulder, and avoided my gaze. "I'll see you Monday."

She licked her lips and stepped back, turning to me as she did. The wounded expression in her light brown eyes evened out as she caught my gaze.

"It was lovely to meet you, Shannon. How do you know Oliver?"

"The new quarterback for the Rough Riders, Beaux, is my brother," I explained, my mouth feeling parched and thick.

Behind her, Oliver didn't argue. He didn't say a thing. He didn't tell her that I was with him now, or that he'd moved on from her.

It hurt more than it should have. More than it had the right to. When Serena's gaze traveled over my face and then lower before she looked me back in the eyes, something like relief shined in them. "Oh. That makes sense then. Hopefully we'll be seeing more of each other soon."

Still, Oliver said nothing. Did nothing. Didn't tell her she was wrong, or that she was outside her ever-loving mind if he thought for one second I'd have anything to do with her and why.

I couldn't respond to her, and she didn't wait for me to, anyway. Instead, she waved my card in the air before sliding it into her purse and telling me she'd see me soon.

Oliver turned and watched her walk away.

Conflict darkened his hazel eyes when he scrubbed a hand down his face. "We need to talk, Shannon."

An ice cold shiver rolled through me, making the hair on the back of my neck stand up. "I'm busy."

"Later then." He dragged his eyes to mine then, as if he was forcing himself to look at me instead of watching his ex-wife walk away.

Ex. The word seemed to grow louder inside my mind with every passing moment.

My lips were too dry to speak, too cracked and chapped. I could only stare at him while I Beaux pushed himself through the tent until he was next to me.

I jumped when he put his hand on my shoulder, squeezing it.

"I don't know when I'll be done, Oliver."

I didn't want to talk to him. I didn't want to hear any of it. Beaux stood next to me, radiating the need to protect me, but I didn't want that either.

I wanted to go back to this morning—or two weeks ago when Oliver and I had met, and I wanted to do everything different. The look he'd just given Serena wasn't the look of a man who was over his wife, but a look that screamed he still loved her, still wanted her, and would take her if given the chance. The fact that Beaux seemed to pick up on it as quick as I had made it more obvious. Not to mention humiliating.

"Call me when you're done here?"

It wasn't so much a question, but a demand.

When I nodded, he lifted his gaze to Beaux's and then looked at Rudolph. "I need to go," he muttered, pushing past Rudolph.

"Powell," he called out, but Oliver didn't turn around. He didn't look back.

He just followed the same path Serena had taken moments

before, like a man trailing after the woman he'd lost once and refused to lose again.

"Shit." Rudolph groaned and ran a hand through his hair. "I gotta go get him. See you later?"

He looked at Beaux, and I assumed he nodded, but I didn't hear if he said anything. Blood rushed through my veins as I sat there, frozen, wondering what in the hell had just happened.

SIXTEEN

SHANNON

I turned off the electric handsaw and rubbed my eyes, squeezing them closed. It was late and I knew I'd been in my workroom for hours, but I couldn't stop working.

I had to stay busy. After the festival had ended, I'd packed everything up and closed down. I should have been grateful for the amount of sales and new contacts I'd made, and I was, but I was also still thinking of the moment Oliver had turned to me, a distance in eyes like he didn't really see me, and then walked away. He'd hurried after his ex-wife, followed her like he still wanted her.

It stung more than it should have. I was trying to trust a man who not only had a reputation of being a huge player, a man who tossed aside women after only one night, but after I'd been cheated on.

My trust in men was shaky at best.

I had turned off my phone hours earlier, choosing to avoid the possibility of a reality that I didn't want to face.

Immature? Yes.

Necessary to my mental health? Most definitely.

I had a pair of pliers in my hand, twisting a braided copper design around another wide, dark-chocolate-colored leather band, when a loud bang sounded from the front of my building.

I jumped and turned toward my closed office door, dropping the pliers, before I moved to the counter and grabbed my phone.

As I turned it on, another thump hit the door, quickly followed by another.

I cursed and stared at my phone, willing it to restart faster in case I needed it, only to have it begin blowing up with texts and missed calls.

Almost all of them from Oliver. Three voicemails. Four missed calls. Seven text messages, each one becoming increasingly irritated.

Want to talk. Call me when you can.

Where are you? Tried calling. Call me back.

Damn it, Shan. Call me.

Then there was one from Beaux.

Hey, fucking call Oliver. He's trying to reach you and now I'm worried. Where are you?

Dread sank into my gut as the pounding increased. I opened the door to my office only to hear my name being bellowed.

The sight of Oliver forced my breath to stall in my chest like it always did. His one hand fisted and pounded on my front door while he shouted my name, looking into my building.

It wasn't his rage that I caught in his eyes first. That came after I couldn't help but notice the way he was dressed so casually. Khaki gray shorts hung fitted on trim hips and curved around his muscled thighs. Leather flip-flop sandals showed off perfect calves and feet, and a red-and-blue Captain America T-shirt, faded with that vintage look, stretched across rolling pecs and abs. A frayed black hat pulled down low over his eyes so I could just barely see the whips of his dirty blond hair peeking out from beneath it as he pounded on my building window beneath the street light.

"Where the hell have you been?" he shouted as he saw me frozen in my spot in the hallway.

Two perfectly arched brows disappeared beneath the bill of his hat.

Adrenaline buzzed in my ears as I became unstuck and hurried to the front door, unlocking it.

"What do you want?" It was snippier than intended, less rude than it could have been. Irritation couldn't be hidden at the way he'd lit up my phone, angry that I would have the nerve to avoid him after the crap he'd pulled earlier.

"You didn't answer your phone."

"I didn't want to talk to you."

"Why?" A small head tilt, a very brief look of confusion flashed through his eyes. "I said we'd talk later. That I wanted to see you."

My eyes went wide. The urge to slam the door in his face was strong. I withheld it, barely. "How was Serena?"

"Shit." His face scrunched up, and with one hand he removed his hat, smoothed back his hair unnecessarily, and flopped the cap back on his head. "I'd like to talk to you. But don't avoid me like that. It made me worried."

His eyes narrowed, as if the admission came before he meant it to, as if he wasn't used to giving a crap about people.

Perhaps he wasn't. He was great in bed. Fun to talk to. He was also strung tight and intense and not what anyone would ever call laid back, despite his current appearance.

"I would think by the way I didn't answer calls or texts earlier, you'd get the hint I didn't want that to happen. That doesn't give you the right to come down here and bang on my door."

His jaw tightened. "I was worried. When Beaux didn't know where you were..." Another hat-removal-hand-swipe.

A sense of disgust rolled through me. Immaturity wasn't the way I wanted to deal with obstacles. Neither was running. But staying had never worked out so great for me in the past, either. In all honesty, I didn't think I'd hear from him at all.

"Come on in." I relented and moved back, allowing him access to Stamped. Like the first time, he wandered to the display cases, most of them empty since I'd sold so much. The more expensive pieces were on display because I didn't think they would do well at a street fair. People tended to like less expensive things they could pick up while they wandered, so I'd left the larger, more elegant and intricate designs in their cases, showing them in photographs in a display book.

I was taking them the next day—the last day of the show. I'd had too much interest.

"Have you been working all night?" he asked, dragging his eyes to mine. They lacked the anger he had carried in them earlier, and now he looked tired.

Dark circles under his eyes, a slight slump to his shoulders. The man looked like he needed to go to sleep at least four hours ago.

Remorse for my behavior flickered down my spine.

"I can't get over how talented you are."

His praise washed over me like a gentle caress. "I'm sorry about my phone. I turned it off, but I shouldn't have done that." I waved it in the air. "At the very least, it's not safe."

"And you were pissed because I took off after Serena."

He laid it out there straight, no hesitancy, like he had nothing to hide.

"We'd been talking before you came up. You hadn't ever

mentioned her, although Beaux told me some. I was waiting for you to bring her up, though. It seemed like something you'd share with someone..."

My voice trailed. I had no idea how to finish that thought. Three weeks before, we were strangers; a week before, we'd ended a ridiculous timeline. Now...I had no idea what we were except great fuck-buddies and maybe friends.

"Someone I'm in a relationship with?"

He took a step toward me, but my eyes stayed fixed on where he'd just been. If he was expecting me to put that out there, I was too vulnerable. Too afraid.

"Shannon."

It was just a word, rolling off luscious lips that could be firm and sweet, soft and gentle, and hard and demanding. It sounded like a song.

"What?"

"I was going to tell you about her. I didn't know how. She's not someone I talk about—like to think about, for that matter."

He tugged off his hat again, another swipe of his hair. Unable to help myself, I hid a smile. Apparently, he wasn't the only one who played with their hair when they were nervous.

I made it easier for him, stepping aside like I always did. "You don't owe me anything, or any explanations. It's not your fault it hurt me when you walked away like that."

Looking so lost, like he just had to be with her.

"That's not it. It's not at all, but the story is long and twisted. Are you done here?"

"Yeah." I wanted to know. I had to know before anything could move forward, if that was the direction we were heading.

Plus, I'd been killing time in my determination to avoid him.

My phone buzzed in my hand and I glanced down. It was Beaux.

You don't fucking tell me you're not battered and beaten behind the alley in two minutes and I'm calling the cops or kicking your ass.

I'm alive. I quickly texted back. **Oliver is here. Stand down, cowboy.**

Don't do that to me again. Was worried sick about you, Sis.

I glanced up at Oliver. His eyes still on mine. "Sorry. That was Beaux. You made him worried."

"Glad someone else was."

It was sick and twisted. I liked knowing he cared enough to worry. When I went out with girlfriends, I would always text Patrick to let him know when I was coming home. He'd go out with friends and I'd never hear from him.

Some nights he wouldn't come home at all. But had he been alone those nights?

I shook the errant thought away and sighed.

"Sorry. Again. It was immature and not me—I was just angry. And confused that I didn't have the right to be."

"Of course you do." His voice tightened and his words clipped staccato sounds. "Fucking hell, Shannon. I've been fucking you for weeks. Don't you think that entitles you to at least some honesty?"

I would figure. I was also new to the fuck-buddy, dating-rebound stage.

"Fine. Serena then."

He glanced around the building and cringed. "You might need to sit for this."

"Fine. We can go upstairs."

"To your place? I haven't seen it yet."

"Don't be impressed. I've got a bed and a couch."

"Two of my favorite things." He walked straight to me and

pressed his hand to my check. "I'm sorry I pissed you off and hurt you."

Only honesty shone in his eyes.

I nodded. "Let me lock up and we'll talk."

"DON'T SAY a thing about the place," I warned him as I unlocked the upstairs door. It was beautiful—had the potential to be beautiful, anyway. But at that time, I hadn't bought anything new for it and I was waiting to get everything from the movers the following week. The only thing I'd stocked was the fridge with snacks while I was working, paper plates, and bottles of water. "I haven't done a thing with it yet."

I was planning on painting walls the next week, before the furniture showed up, so there were paint samples taped all over the walls.

Oliver's eyes went to those first, and he pressed his lips together at the empty space.

"You weren't kidding," he said, walking into the open area, shock in his features. "You didn't mention the kitchen table, but there really is only a couch."

"Bed's in one of the rooms."

He shot me a look that curled my toes.

"Do you want some water? It's all I have. I've got snacks, too, if you're hungry, but not much."

"No." He walked toward me and reached for my hand. It was in his palm before I could pull it back. "Stop blabbering. This isn't bad."

He laughed softly and pulled me toward the couch. I'd draped a sheet over it—something I pilfered from Beaux's place because the couch was old and gross. Oliver gave me a look before sitting on it, and I laughed harder.

"I know. It's nasty. My things are coming next week, though. Then I'll be all moved in." I spread my arms out to the open living space. The exposed brick walls and ductwork made it seem more like a loft-style building, but I loved the character. The doorways were wide and curved, and all the baseboards and wood floors were original and after a polishing would be in excellent condition.

"I like it. It suits you."

I was too nervous to ask what he meant by that.

He took his hat off and tossed it to the floor, then leaned to the side so he could face me fully before he let my hand go.

"Serena," he said with a groan and wiped his hand over his mouth. "God, I don't know where to begin. I haven't talked about her in so long with anyone but my lawyers."

"Beaux told me you'd loved her. That you didn't start acting like a dick until she left you."

"Yeah, well," he huffed. "That's what happens when the woman you think you'll be with forever walks out on you."

I gave him time and excused myself to get some water. I came back carrying two bottles, and when he didn't seem to notice I was offering one to him, I set it on the floor.

"We were high school sweethearts. Started dating when we were fifteen. Seems like forever ago and yesterday at the same time, you know?" He didn't look at me, didn't seem like he really wanted a response, and he continued talking before I could, so it didn't matter. His eyes glazed over and he stared at his hands when he wasn't running them through his hair or down his face.

"We grew up in a small town outside Savannah. All we wanted was to go to college and get out of that town and make something of ourselves. She wanted to see the world and I wanted to play football. And I loved her. God, I loved her. She has this energy, this wild and frantic energy that pulls you to her immediately. I was wrapped up in her, wrapped up in football, and she swore she'd follow me anywhere. Worse, I believed her. I proposed to her the night I was drafted, after we got back to the hotel, and we were married in my parents' backyard before I had to start the season."

His voice had softened and his eyes become so glazed that I doubted he even knew I was in the room. The familiar burn of jealousy—that after so many years he still looked like that when he thought of her—began to flame, twisting my stomach.

"What happened?"

He made a choking sound and pulled his eyes straight to me. "Raleigh happened."

My brow furrowed. "What?"

"We'd been in New England before here. Having the time of our lives. Newlyweds, exploring the big cities, traveling, partying it up like we always wanted to, and then I was traded to Raleigh."

"I don't get it."

"That's because you don't give a shit about where you live, I suspect, but Serena...she wanted lights and activity and shopping and she never wanted to return to the South. She hated it. A year after being up North, she started trying to forget everything about where we came from. Bitched around the holidays when I wanted to go home and see our folks and friends. I didn't want that stuff to change us, but she was changed by the fantasy before I ever got a paycheck. She wanted the high life—the condos in the city and the vacation homes in Greece. Raleigh...that was too big of a step down for her."

"She left you over it?"

He pinned me with a look that went straight to my stomach, icy and splashing out the burn of jealousy from earlier. "Said I had to get a different contract somewhere else or she was leaving.

Said that it shouldn't matter to me anyway, since I was never home. She didn't give a shit about football, or my dreams, or the fact this had always been our plan. I could keep our place in the city and just travel back and forth. I told her we were a family and I wanted her with me. That she knew having to move when I was traded was part of the deal she'd agreed to when we were married. But I hadn't thought of it as a deal, just something we would always do together. She said I either stayed or kept the place, found a way to keep her where she was happy, or she was gone."

"And she left."

"Yeah." He laughed and shook his head. "With half my money for a grand total of six years."

My eyes jumped open. His salary was public knowledge. Even I knew how much he'd made. She took half? "You were married three years!"

"Together eight. We hadn't even been married for three years before she filed and I came to Raleigh. But I just wanted to make her happy, I guess. I don't even know. She asked for what she wanted, my lawyer told me not to, but I couldn't tell her no. I'd never been able to tell her no until I said I couldn't stay in the city with her. I didn't even like it there. She knew I'd missed home. She just didn't care. The worst was that the night she left, she told me she'd always hated football, just used me to get out of our small town and knew it would happen. She felt like she'd invested enough of her life and now she deserved everything she'd asked for. I should have realized all of that when she quit coming to my games after my first season in New England."

"That's..." I sputtered, unable to think. "That's absurd!"

"Yeah, well, her support is almost up and guess who's broke?"

My eyes widened. "She...what?" I shrieked.

Three and a half million dollars a year, minimum, and she'd blown it all?

"How is that humanly possible?"

He flashed me a dumbfounded grin and shook his head. "I have no earthly idea. She's currently fighting to extend the support."

"You're fighting her this time, though, right?"

"I'm cutting her off, and she knows it. She's pissed. Today's display was a way for her to get what she wanted a different way."

His lip curled and I sat back. Wow. I'd met women like this. I'd seen it happen at bars and after-game parties and in the box suites where most wives and girlfriends watched the games. Serena had seemed so genuinely sweet when I first met her, I never would have pegged her as one of the women like that.

"When you followed her, you looked like…"

I couldn't finish the thought. Just remembering the way he'd chased after her, looking so lost, made my stomach roll.

"Like I loved her?"

I nodded.

"She's a memory, Shannon. She was also a part of me for most of my life. High school, college, my draft…football. Everything. She's wrapped up in all of it. I can't take that back. I grew into a man with her. And I can't lie and say that when I found out what she'd been doing all along I wasn't wrecked. I was. For a long time. I'm not sure when I quit caring about her at all, but I know I did. I went after her today to give her the attention she wanted and to make it clear that she'd never see me or my money again."

I understood so much of what he was saying. Hearing him confirm it, at least tell me he knew he was over her, helped.

We all came with baggage. Mine—mostly from Patrick— was losing trust in what seemed so good.

"I might have been projecting some of my own insecurities onto you this afternoon after what happened," I admitted.

"I'm not a cheater." He leaned forward and pressed his palm to my cheek.

I leaned into his touch, his scent, and the strength in his hand.

"I never have been. I wouldn't do that, and I'm not going to lie, it's not like I didn't have opportunity. But I was always faithful to Serena, and if we had stayed together it would have been a lifetime. I'm not that guy."

"I believe you."

We stared at each other for several moments, that familiar heat beginning to swirl between us.

My heart began beating faster, my pulse a little bit louder in my ears when he leaned closer.

"I'm going to kiss you now," he whispered. "And you're going to kiss me back."

I smiled, a puff of breath escaping my lips. "I'm sorry I got upset and ignored you."

"I'm sorry I walked away from you for Serena. *That* will never happen again."

His lips met mine then, soft and sweet and slow and absolutely delicious. I melted into him, pressed myself to his chest when his other hand wrapped around my back and pulled me to his lap.

We kissed for hours. And when we fell asleep, curled and entwined together on a lumpy couch, only a sheet to cover us, I woke up the next morning knowing with certainty that that night had been our beginning.

SEVENTEEN
OLIVER

"Oliver." Accompanied with her breathy little gasp, I knew Shannon was waking up, enjoying the ministrations of my fingers against her already hot, slick flesh.

Always ready for me. *Me.* Not the football player, because she didn't give a shit about that. If anything, that was a point against me.

It'd been years since a woman had looked at me and seen me. Didn't see the dollar signs or the endorsements or the potential photos in magazines with her on my arm. I never knew how much I'd missed it until the previous night, when Shannon had listened to me, understood me, and believed me at my word.

"Good morning." I pressed my lips along the exposed column of her throat, pushing back her wild and sexy curls. Goose bumps flared on her skin, following the trail of my mouth. My fingers continued teasing her, running through her pussy before drifting away.

Her hips began rolling, her ass grinding against my erection.

She said my name again, a breath and a plea wrapped up in one.

"I like this," I whispered as she shivered. Her cheeks were already flushed with want, her lips parted as she panted for me. "Like waking up with you, ready and hot for me."

"Always."

Hell. She was so damn sexy.

"I want you," I said, my voice gruff with need. I woke up every morning, hard for her. The few nights we spent together weren't enough. My body wanted hers, all the time. To show her what I wanted, I began pushing down the yoga pants she still had on from the night before, no underwear beneath them as if she'd been waiting for me the entire time. The previous night, I hadn't taken her like I'd wanted to. I'd kissed her until our lips were raw and we fell asleep, and it was a night I'd remember forever. Because she came to me, angry and trusting and believing and gave herself so fully, so completely without reservation.

This morning, she'd take everything I gave her.

"Please."

Her gasps became moans as I pushed her pants to her knees and removed her top. I removed my own clothing until we were settled on the couch, Shannon's back pressed against my chest.

My hands roamed her skin, teased her nipples while I rubbed my thumbs over them, and she gasped and arched into my touch. My fingers pressed inside of her, opening and stretching her for me.

"That feels so good." Her head pushed back into my shoulder and I began sucking on the sensitive flesh of her throat, tasting and touching her everywhere I could find.

"You're so wet, so tight for me. Do you want my cock, Shannon?"

"Yes." She pleaded and twisted her neck until her lips were

against mine. I took what she offered, rolling us until I was above her. My tongue slid into her mouth, my hands moved everywhere I could reach—her cunt, her tits, her nipples as I plucked them. Every time I did, she whimpered into my mouth.

I pulled back, sliding onto the couch, and spread her legs, opening her to me. I pushed her wide open until one of her legs hit the floor and the other was draped over the back of the couch. God. So fucking beautiful. Her wet, pink cunt swollen and pulsing for me.

"You're so fucking delicious. I want to taste you everywhere, all of the time." My lips trailed down the length of her body until I reached her neatly shaven pussy—just a small patch of hair above it that drove me wild. I teased her there, just above her clit, and her fingers curled into the sheet beneath her. Her hips bucked up while I ran my tongue along the outer edges of her lips, around her clit, and then sank it firmly into the tight, hot hold of her.

"Oliver," she groaned. Her whimpers increased while I drove her wild. I wanted to take her to the brink, over and over again, drive her wild, drive her out of her fucking mind like she always seemed to do me whenever I touched her.

My spine went hot, need beginning to heat my balls. Pre-cum dripped from my tip and I wrapped one hand around my shaft, pumping it hard and fast while I sucked on her clit. My fingers drove inside of her, curling deep within her until I pressed against her ridged flesh.

"Fucking come, Shannon," I growled against her as she tightened around my fingers.

She spread her legs further and fell apart. Her clit was swollen, her taste like sweet heaven on my tongue. A taste I never wanted to forget.

I groaned against her as she began shaking and trembling beneath me, signaling the first wave of her climax as it rushed through. I knew her signs now, the way her thighs began to shake. The way she pushed against the armrest of the couch as if she didn't know whether to flee from the sensation or thrust herself toward it.

As her orgasm started, I pulled out, eliciting a cry of frustration from her. "What the hell?"

I smirked and stood up. "You'll get there."

I was being cocky, and she growled at me in frustration. "Hurry."

I'd hurry. And then I'd take my time once she got off once, but I needed in her. I reached down and yanked her hips toward the armrest, flipping her over with ease before I hauled her over the edge of the couch.

Her hands curled into the sheets and I pressed my hand against her shoulder blades. Her toes barely touched the floor and I lifted her, standing behind her as I ripped open a condom and rolled it on. "Stay still."

She wiggled her hips, and I couldn't help myself. My hand smacked the globes of her ass. A sick thrill shot through me as her ass jiggled and turned pink from the sting of my hand on her.

I'd marked her with my cum and my teeth.

I wanted to mark her with every part of me.

"Oliver." She gasped my name, moaning and breathless, and I couldn't stop.

I smacked her ass again, rubbing it to soothe the sting. Instead of arching away, she pushed up, seeking my hand.

"You like this?" I asked, my teeth gritted. I took my cock in one hand and ran it through her slick cunt, biting back my own groan. With my tip at her entrance, I spanked her again. "Tell me, Shan. You like this? When I spank you? Do you know how fucking hot it makes me to watch your skin turn pink?"

She moaned my name again, and I grinned when she glared

at me out of the corner of her eye, her face pressed into the couch beneath her.

"You do, don't you? You don't think you should, but you fucking love it when I get my hands on you, however it comes, isn't that right?"

"Yes," she breathed, as I spanked her again. Every time my hand connected with her, she pushed back, until the tip of my dick slid right inside her.

She hugged me like a vise grip, and I lost the desire to tease her. I wanted to fuck her. Slam inside of her balls deep until she shouted my name, until my name was the only thing she thought. *Oliver, Oliver, Oliver.* I wanted her chanting it all day long.

"Are you going to come?" I asked as my hands went to her hips. I pressed into her, fighting the need to turn into a wild animal and fuck her relentlessly.

This woman. She took everything I gave and fucking loved it.

"Please," she whimpered. "Oliver."

I grunted as I hit the end of her, tilted her hips and bent my knees so I could go deeper inside of her. She contracted around my dick, sucking me in and holding me tight while her walls began convulsing.

I moved faster and faster until my fingertips grew wet from sweat. She came almost immediately as soon as I wrapped my hand around to her front and rubbed her clit. Her whole body tightened, muscles flexing in her arms as she held herself tight. Her pussy clenched around me and I continued fucking her harder, my hips smacking against her, my balls hitting her clit with every thrust forward. They pulled tight, screaming for relief, but I held off until another orgasm rolled through her, making her shake and shiver while the only thing she chanted was *oh God, oh God, yes, coming, Oliver.*

I powered into her, pushing her forward while pulling her back and threw my head back, roaring her name while I shot myself inside of her.

"Fuck," I groaned, grinding my teeth together. My throat muscles popped and tightened and I knew I'd bruised her from my tight hold on her. "So fucking beautiful." *Beautiful.* I whispered it again, over and over until my heart began to calm and she went limp in my hold.

"God, you're good at that," she whispered, her voice raspy and dry when I let her go and climbed back to my spot on the couch behind her, wrapping my arms around her. "I could do that all day with you."

I envisioned that: a whole day of fucking her wherever and however I wanted, listening to her repeat my name with a breathy voice, her curls wild and her eyes all smoky.

I pulled her tighter. "We should do that."

I meant it. I'd fucking skip a day of practice to have her in my bed all day, pliable and wanting.

She laughed softly, adjusting on the couch until she was on her back, and looked up at me. Her eyes shone with sated lust. "Someday. I have the festival today."

I leaned down and brushed my lips against hers, soft and slow, savoring the moment I had with her before our days took us in different directions. "And I need to get to morning workouts. But the first weekend I'm home, you're at my place."

It didn't surprise me like it did the first time when I'd taken her to my house without thinking. I wanted her there. Wanted her to meet the horses and get to know them. Wanted her to be in my house so I had those memories of her.

I wanted to fuck her in every room of my house so every time I walked inside, all I saw was her.

Her smile went soft as I pulled back, and with a finger she traced my jawline, feeling my morning scruff. "Your house?"

I nodded as she hesitated.

"I'd like that."

"Me too."

~

"THIS IS RIDICULOUS." I groaned and ran my hand down my face.

For thirty minutes I'd been waiting for Serena to show her face for our mediation, and she was late.

What else was new? The woman wore a watch as an accessory, was most likely always glued to her cell phone, and still couldn't manage to get anywhere on time. It used to be endearing. I had teased her relentlessly when we were dating. The night before our wedding, I'd teased her about being late to walk down the aisle. What I'd realized later, much too late, was that if Serena was going to be the focus of everyone's attention, she was always on time. When it was something important to me, or anyone else, she took her sweet-ass time, expecting everyone to wait around for her, demanding attention upon her late arrival.

This wasn't the first time she'd pulled the stunt since our divorce, and I was fed up.

I'd spent Friday night getting pummeled by Baltimore—a team we should have easily beaten, but our second strings couldn't pull their heads out of their asses long enough to make a tackle—and then I'd spent the rest of the weekend wrapped up in Shannon. I'd helped her after the game, bone-tired and muscles aching all over my damn body, but still energetic enough to help her finish putting away all of her designs and getting Stamped back to how she'd had it before the street festival.

It wasn't the first night we fell asleep without me burying my dick into her delicious cunt, but it'd been one of the best.

We'd talked. She told me about Des Moines, growing up in a run-down house on the east side of the city where nothing good had come from in the last fifty years besides Beaux Hale. She told me about her mom, working job after job to support them and they still managed to go hungry occasionally. I told her about life on the farm outside Savannah—where our town had two stoplights and half as many stop signs. Where everyone in town flooded football fields on Friday nights to cheer for the only good thing that brought them excitement outside the few who could have cable television. We laughed about the way we grew up, both of us dirt poor and desperately wanting more. The difference was that where I always wanted more for myself, she was the selfless one, doing everything she could, sacrificing everything she wanted for her brother.

It was that selflessness, that motive—to see her brother succeed at his passion and care nothing of her own ambitions—that sealed the deal that she was unlike any woman I'd ever met before.

No woman gave up everything for someone without growing bitter. With the closeness Beaux and Shannon showed each other, it was clear that wasn't an issue for her.

I was quickly becoming enthralled with not only her body, but her sweetness and her wit and her intelligence. She was the kind of woman men fought over, claimed, wanted to keep chained to them like some primal beast because they knew the prize they'd been given simply by her attention.

It unsettled me, less than it should have, that I was already feeling these things for her, so fiercely and so quickly.

I pushed the chair back from the table where my lawyer and Serena's lawyer had been waiting. The harsh sound of wood screeching gained everyone's attention. I didn't pay her lawyer any attention, but focused on Paul Costell.

"I'm leaving. You can handle this without me, right?"

After her play to find me over the weekend, a fortuitous event on her part that I'd run into her at the art festival, I'd gone searching for her.

She'd cried her fake alligator tears and clung to me, whispered how much she missed me. Missed *us*.

I'd repeated it was over. Would always be over. I didn't have a shred of emotion left for Serena except for annoyance and disappointment at who she still continued to be. Within thirty days, her extravagant lifestyle, or lack thereof, would be none of my concern.

"I can, Mr. Powell."

I fought the urge to roll my eyes. I'd known Paul for over seven years and he still refused to call me by first name. It was Southern respect, but sounded strange on his lips considering I'd shown up at his kids' seventh and ninth birthday parties.

"Mediation cannot continue without all parties present," Serena's lawyer said.

I'd gotten to know him as well over the last seven years. Never would I attend one of his kids' parties—not that he'd asked. I didn't even know if he had kids; the thought of that man creating offspring made me want to shudder on a good day. He was an asshole, and had most likely gotten rich off of my money alone from the cut he took before Serena got her hands on it.

"We'll need to reschedule."

"It is not our fault your client is late, as usual," Costell clipped, and I didn't bother hiding my grin. "Perhaps if you had stressed how important this meeting was, she'd be here."

"She will be. I said she's stuck in traffic."

It was Raleigh at eleven o'clock in the morning. There was

no traffic. And no construction. I'd checked after Paul had relayed the text.

"I'm done."

I was. Completely. Done playing Serena's games. Done with her lies and her need to be the center of attention.

Turning back to Paul, I grinned. "Tell me how this goes."

"With pleasure." He grinned back.

I turned on my heel, not caring at all about Mr. Gaines's threats. Paul would take care of me; he always did. I clapped my hand on his shoulder as I walked by him, and just as I reached the conference room door, Mr. Gaines' assistant opened it and walked through, holding it open.

"Gentlemen, Serena Powell has arrived."

I scowled at the name. The one thing I gave her I could never take away from her. For years after our divorce that ate at me—that she still had my name and wanted nothing to do with me except a pocketbook from a distance.

Now I just hated her for it.

I rolled my eyes as Serena practically floated in behind the middle-aged and kind-eyed receptionist. It wasn't the first time I'd seen her, definitely wasn't the first time I'd wondered how she worked for Gaines.

"Oliver, how kind of you to greet me."

Serena walked right up to me, looking more like she was getting ready for tea than preparing to lose millions. I stepped back before she could do her typical cheek kisses. They weren't the sweet ones Southern women used to greet their friends. Serena's dripped with vile poison.

"I wasn't. I was leaving. You're late and I have plans."

Her faux smile barely faltered before she concealed her surprise. And for probably the first time in my life, I didn't explain further.

"Goodbye, Serena."

I tipped my chin toward her and the assistant still at the door and walked out, leaving Serena behind, happily, for the first time I could ever remember.

I had found the one flaw in my old building—and most especially, in my apartment. A lack of decent air-conditioning had sweat dripping down my back, making me feel nasty and stinky while I unpacked boxes almost as quickly as the movers brought them in.

A thrilling sense of excitement had buzzed in my veins all day long, making me excited and terrified in equal parts.

I was really doing this: owning my own business, moving on my own, and starting a whole new life.

One that was becoming infinitely more exciting and terrifying with the surprising addition of Oliver. I hadn't been looking for him.

Hadn't even wanted a man so quickly after I'd left Patrick. I didn't think I'd be able to trust so easily, so quickly, and yet every time I turned around in the last couple of weeks, Oliver was there. Showing me he wasn't the man he was portrayed to be in the gossip news. Showing me that the man who had graced more GQ covers than I could count wasn't the egotistical prick he proclaimed himself to be.

He was kind. He was warm. He was rough and dirty when he wanted to be, but underneath all of it, there was tenderness to him that he hadn't allowed anyone to see since Serena. When he called me Monday to meet him at the hotel, I'd expected to find him upset or stressed after his appointment with Serena.

Instead, he'd told me how it went, how he felt absolutely nothing when he saw her, watching her try all her stunts to keep receiving his money—which had been relayed via his attorney since he had walked out. We didn't have sex that night. We talked.

It was more intimate than any time he'd taken me rough and fast. Over the past week, when we weren't working, we had been together. I barely saw Beaux except for our paths crossing in his apartment. Now that I was finally getting everything from Iowa, I would see him less.

I was unpacking a box of dishes in the kitchen when two strong and familiar arms surrounded me.

Hot lips brushed my neck as one hand rose and brushed my sweaty hair off my neck.

"Hello," Oliver whispered, his voice in my ear sparking desire immediately.

I stopped what I was doing and covered his hand on my chest with mine. "Hey. What are you doing here?"

I spun around and his hands dropped to my lower back. He dipped his head and went in for a kiss, making me rise up to my toes to meet him halfway.

"Beaux and I wanted to stop by and see how the move was going. See if you need any more muscle."

"You didn't have to do that. I think they're almost done here."

"Good. Then when they're gone, we can break in your

bed." He brushed his lips against mine again. "I missed you today."

I rolled my eyes playfully and stepped back when I heard more footsteps coming down the hallway. "You saw me this morning."

"Oh, I remember this morning clearly."

He shot me a look went straight through my body, all the way to my fingertips and toes. This morning had involved being woken up with my wrists tied to the slats in his headboard by two of his neckties. My skin was still sore, along with other parts of me that had nothing to do with a busy day on my feet, unpacking.

"Oliver." I blushed when a loud, booming voice hit the doorway.

"No kissing my sister when I'm around! Tell me it's safe to come in." Beaux walked in, one large, meaty paw covering his eyes, and bumped into a stack of boxes. "Oh, shit."

I laughed and stepped away from Oliver. "You're such a moron. Uncover your eyes before you break something."

Beaux grinned when he dropped his hands to his sides. "There are things a brother never wants to see. That's definitely number two on the list."

"What's number one?" Oliver asked, settling his hand at the base of my back.

Beaux quickly backed up as the movers pushed in.

"Where do you want your couch?" they asked, one of them looking at me as he continued walking backward. He lifted my couch over the boxes Beaux had just tripped over, essentially pushing him back into the wall at the same time.

"Where the nasty one currently is," I replied. They were taking that and the old bed to the dumpster on the way out.

Seeming to ignore them as soon as they entered, and

dodging their way as they began carrying out the old couch, Beaux glared at me teasingly.

"You remember when you were thirteen?" He shuddered as he asked the question.

"What happened when you were thirteen?" Oliver asked.

I rolled my eyes. "You were ten, and at some point you really have to get over it."

Beaux shivered again. "Never." Turning to Oliver, he said, "I walked in on her after a shower. All naked girl. Scarred me for life, I swear."

"Funny. That's one of the best things about your sister."

If it was possible to truly turn green, Beaux did it. His hand flew to his mouth as he covered a vomiting sound and gagged. "Oh God. I'm going to throw up."

I pointed down the hallway. Through my laughter, I said, "Bathroom's that way."

He hurried off, making exaggerating choking sounds, and when my phone rang I barely slid the screen a glance before I hit the speakerphone button.

Assuming it was Melissa, knowing it was getting close to when she'd be getting off work and calling to see how the move went, I answered and started talking.

"Hey, Mel! Thank you so much for—"

"Shannon."

My eyes popped open at the sound of Patrick's voice and my head whipped to Oliver.

"Patrick?" I asked, my throat going dry. Next to me, irritation began to prickle off Oliver's skin, making my already tiny kitchen seem even smaller. "What do you want?"

He softened his voice—that tender one that used to make me melt into him, seeking his promises. "Babe, I came home from work and all the furniture's gone. What's going on?"

Oliver glared at the phone, and I saw his muscles begin to

bunch beneath his short-sleeved shirt. He had a Rough Riders cap on, the bill covering his eyes and making it hard to see them, but I knew that hazel color was blazing.

"This isn't a good time, Patrick. And I tried scheduling this with you, yet you refused. I told you Melissa would take care of it for me if you wouldn't cooperate."

"Honey, I thought we'd talk. I thought you agreed to see me."

At that, those blazing eyes I couldn't see burned into my flesh. I gritted my teeth and glared at Oliver and mouthed *Stop it.*

His lip curled in response and I focused on the phone call.

"I did no such thing, Patrick. I've made it clear that I've moved on. You just refuse to listen."

His voice tripped a bit when he asked, "Moved on? But, Shannon, you love me."

"Not anymore, asshole." Oliver's thick, gritted voice came as a surprise and I gasped.

"What? Who is this?"

"The man whose dick was inside of your ex this morning, you fucking moron."

"Oliver!" I shouted and then flashed wild eyes at Beaux, who was walking down the hallway. This was disintegrating quickly.

"Shannon, who is this jerk speaking to me like this?"

I reached for the phone, but Oliver beat me to it. He clicked it off speakerphone and had it at his ear.

"Her man, dickwad. And she doesn't want you. You tossed her aside, and I picked her up. I've spent so much time inside of her, tasting her sweet pussy, that you're a memory for her. Now go the fuck away and don't call back."

Beaux made another gagging sound at Oliver's words, but I

couldn't even look at him. Embarrassment and anger burned my cheeks. Along with lust.

Damn it, even his words tossed out for the sole purpose of pissing off my ex still made me want to climb him like a tree until he was doing all the things he'd just said.

"Don't call again." Oliver punched a button on the phone before tossing it roughly to the counter.

"What the hell was that?"

"Don't talk to him again." Oliver pointed at me. "That guy is fucked in the head and you need to stay away from him."

"He's clueless, not crazy." I recognized my error when I suddenly had two insanely large men glaring me down.

"You defend him?" Beaux asked, appearing at Oliver's side. They were so big they blocked the doorway. "He hasn't left you alone in months, he cheated on you, and you're going to stand here and defend him when he acted like he didn't even know you'd left him? And yes"—he gestured with a wave of his hand down the hall—"I heard all of that. And if Oliver hadn't taken care of it, I would have." He looked at Oliver then and cringed. "Although I could have done without hearing the fucking and dick and sweet pussy part."

He turned green again at the mention.

I no longer found this funny.

Fortunately, I was given a brief reprieve when the movers returned, carrying my bed.

"Excuse me." I glared at both of them until they moved so I could get out of the kitchen. "Give me a few minutes."

I followed the movers to my bedroom and gave them instructions on where I wanted the furniture set up. Before returning to my overbearing brother and—apparently—severely overprotective Oliver, I took a few minutes in the restroom to fix my hair and wipe the back of my neck with a cool rag.

What he'd said had been rude. Partly disgusting.

And yet even with that, the area between my legs began to pulse with desire. The man undid me. He kept me on my toes, never knowing when he'd switch from domineering to sweet.

As bothered as I was by the way he'd taken control of my conversation, I found that as I calmed down from the shock of all of it, I was thankful.

I was tired of talking to Patrick. Tired of listening to his lies and his pathetic voice. Today's had been no different, a bit whiny. And after spending so much time around Oliver, I knew it wasn't anywhere near masculine.

His words and his voice still hurt, though. Five years of being with him and I wanted to move on like Oliver suggested.

Yet Patrick's continued efforts at contacting me constantly pulled me backward. Not because I wanted him back, or wanted to go back to him—that ship had sailed the moment I saw him plowing another woman in the bathroom. But he was still my past, still a huge part of me and what I had once envisioned for my future. His constant phone calls and texts made it difficult to forget him.

Blowing out a breath, I smoothed back my curls that had come loose in my messy bun and then opened the door to the bathroom.

I got one step into the hallway before I almost ran into a mountainous wall of curved and sculpted muscle.

"You okay?" Oliver asked, his hands on his hips and his head tipped down toward me.

I memorized the way his shirt curved around his pecs, his abs, and then the way his shorts fit loose and low on his hips.

Lifting my head to meet his eyes was difficult, and when I finally found the strength, he was smirking.

"A body like yours should be illegal," I said, my lips fighting a grin.

He'd caught me looking, admiring...soaking every perfect

curve of his body into the deepest parts of my memory banks. There was no use in hiding that I liked the way he looked.

"Why? Does it make you want to do illegal things to it?"

"I'm still here!" Beaux shouted from what sounded like the living room.

"Get over it, turd!" I shouted back before nodding at Oliver. "I'm okay. But you didn't have to go caveman on him."

He showed no sign of remorse. "I might have been more forceful than necessary, but you wanted him to leave you alone." His brow furrowed. "Didn't you?"

"I did. I just wasn't expecting you to talk about your dick on the phone to my ex, I guess."

I laughed then, softly, shaking off what had happened. Melissa would think it was hilarious. Maybe Oliver had a point: Patrick hadn't been listening to me, and the very fact that he seemed confused I'd actually moved my stuff out showed how delusional he was—that maybe he thought I was considering crawling back to him and taking his scraps.

"I have to finish unpacking."

Oliver checked his watch at his wrist. "How about we all go out for dinner first and take a break. You've been working all day, right?"

I had. I had been up at six in the morning when he left for early practice. I'd spent hours down at Stamped, making jewelry before the movers had arrived.

Putting my hands to his shoulders, I leaned up as far as I could and kissed his muscled throat. "Dinner would be good."

MY ORGASM WAS QUICKLY BARRELING down on me. I was on my hands and knees. My arms shook and my thighs trembled as fire and impending release spread throughout my body.

"Oliver." I panted his name through parched lips. He drove into me hard, hitting that perfect spot deep inside of me that made me quake for him. "Please."

"Get there," he growled. He was on his knees behind me, one hand on my shoulder, pulling me back to him as he continued powering into me, his other hand down by mine.

I dropped my head, unable to hold myself up, and reached my hand to cover his. My fingers dug into the back of his hand as my body lit with fire.

Needless to say, we were breaking in my bed, and it wasn't just great sex. It was fantastic.

"Come," he commanded. He lost his quick rhythm and just before everything inside me began to tighten in culmination, he pulled out, flipped me onto my back, and slid right back inside. "Fuck it. I want to see you."

My limbs wrapped around his body. My knees lifted high next to him, my heels digging into his lower back.

My hands dug into his shoulders.

"Coming," I panted, feeling it overtake me. It was powerful and long as the shocks rolled through my body and I clung to him, tightening every limb until I pulled him down, chest to chest, his lips inches above mine.

"Beautiful." He leaned down, claiming my mouth with his own. As I rode wave after wave of my orgasm, his movement jilted.

I heard something in the distance—like lightning hitting the Earth—right as he bellowed out my name, seating himself deep inside me, so deep it almost hurt, but damn it was good.

That crack I heard shook the floor beneath us and we fell to the floor.

"Ah!" I squealed and held on to him tighter.

"Holy fuck," he panted as his weight collapsed on top of me, jarring me and stealing my breath.

"What the hell?"

He lifted his head, his lips pulled back in amusement. "I think we broke your bed."

"Or we had an earthquake," I said, barely able to contain my giggle.

His eyes lit with fake fury. "Trust me. As hard as I just fucked you, we broke the bed."

"So sure of yourself."

"The bed is crooked." Oliver smiled, a beautiful mouth with shiny white teeth surrounded by full lips that had tasted every inch of my body.

I looked to my left, still clinging to him, and saw that he was right. One side of the bed was much higher than the other, and we were still lying at an angle.

Closing my eyes, I pushed my head into my pillow and groaned. "Damn it. The movers must not have set the frame right."

"Or your bed just can't handle my superhuman strength."

"Or the weight of your ego."

I smacked his butt, unwrapping my legs from around him as he slid out of me. I thought we'd fix the mess we'd made and get cleaned up, but instead he curled into the bed next to me, draped one hand over his face, and pulled me to him.

"Let me relax before we fix this."

I settled in, loving that he liked to cuddle. He didn't seem the sort—but like so many things about Oliver, he continued to surprise me.

At dinner that night, for example, I'd listened intently through most of it while Beaux and Oliver discussed the practice and some of the plays they'd struggled with. The coming weekend would be their first out-of-state game, when they traveled down to Miami.

The defense was clicking, but with so many new members on the offensive line, both Beaux and Oliver had said it was taking longer than it should for everyone to find their groove. I'd sat silent through most of the conversations, but still grinned as I realized that after Oliver had said he'd give Beaux a chance, all his animosity toward him seemed to evaporate. He could have been doing it for the good of the team, or to keep the peace between the woman he was fucking and her brother, but I suspected it was more than that.

Beaux was earning his respect, and Oliver was giving it freely.

After dinner, Beaux had taken off when I insisted I didn't need any more help unpacking. I had barely stepped inside my apartment before I was staring at the floor, flung over Oliver's shoulder, and then dumped onto my bed.

"You ready for the game this weekend then?" I asked as my mind replayed dinner and everything after that.

"It'll be hard. Miami's a good team and they have a great defense. If we can make our long-pass plays, though, and if Kolby can continue doing what he's best at, it should be a good game."

"That's good." My eyes drifted closed as I responded.

"You going to come?"

I heard a hint of hopefulness in his voice and turned to look at him, forcing one eye open. "I could," I admitted, "but I really need to keep working on getting Stamped up and running."

Oliver's mouth tightened for a moment before he smoothed it out by licking his lips. "Okay. Although I have to admit I don't know if it should scare the fuck out of me that I'm not going to like sleeping without you while we're gone or if I should just be happy about it."

It pleased me to no end—his open honesty and how much he seemed to show me that he really did like me. How much he wanted me around.

"I think you should just be happy about it."

"I'll think of a way to be with you anyway."

His eyebrows wiggled. I was sated, sore, and exhausted. It took that silly brow wiggle and a slow, teasing brush of his lips against my cheek to reenergize me.

"Do you know what I like?"

"What?" he asked, his eyes filled with wicked, scrumptious delight.

"Sleeping on a bed that isn't crooked."

I pushed at him when he chuckled. His arm loosened and I took the opportunity to roll away from him and toward the floor, landing on my knees facing him.

"Fine," he groaned playfully. "Go get cleaned up. I'll fix the bed so I can fuck you until it breaks again."

He flashed me a look full of promise before I reached for a shirt on the floor and scurried to the bathroom.

I took my time, hearing him bang around with tools he'd probably grabbed from the dining room table, and when I came back to my room he was standing up, dropping the mattress back onto a now straightened bed frame.

"Fixed?" I asked as I flung my hand towel onto a pile of dirty laundry on the floor.

Oliver's eyes followed the dirty towel as it landed on the heap, and he smiled.

Then he reached for me, tossed me back into the bed, and pushed my legs wide with his knees between mine.

"Yes. Let's see how many times in one night we can break the damn thing."

I laughed. "Another round with your stamina might break *me*."

His eyes darkened and went intense in a way I hadn't yet seen. Dark lashes framed shaded eyes, but it was impossible to miss the seriousness in his gaze.

"Never," he whispered, cupping my cheek with his palm. "I don't ever want to do that."

"Well, this is a nice surprise," Oliver drawled as he made his way to where I was standing, backside propped against the hood of my silver Honda. "What are you doing here?"

I slid my sunglasses to the top of my head and smiled. "I thought since you had the evening off and I needed a break from Stamped, we could go do something."

After the drama he'd had with Serena earlier that week, it had occurred to me that while we'd gone out for dinner a couple of times, we spent a lot of time between the sheets and not a lot of time talking. So that day I'd decided to surprise him when he got done with an early practice.

The next morning, the team flew down to Miami to get ready for their first game of the season.

Oliver glanced around the parking lot at the practice field and a line dipped between his brows. For a moment I wondered if I'd made a mistake. Perhaps he wanted to stay home and be alone, concentrate on the game ahead.

"We don't have to—"

He interrupted me and wrapped his hand around my waist,

pulling me to him while he held a duffel bag in his other hand. "No, I do. I'm just surprised to see you and I feel like an ass for not realizing we haven't been out much."

"Well"—I grinned and rolled to my toes, tilting my head back to kiss his chin—"we have been pretty busy doing other things."

He kissed my cheek and squeezed me tight before letting go. "All right, then. Let's do this, but I'm driving."

I laughed at the way he glanced at my car, like there was no way he was letting a woman drive him around.

"I wanted to go somewhere near my place, though."

A luscious look flickered in his eyes. "Then I'll bring you back here in the morning."

Considering that implied we were spending the night together, how could I argue with him?

"So where do you want to go?" he asked once we were settled in his car and pulling out of the lot.

"I was thinking Mexican. There's this great little restaurant down by the university I've been wanting to try."

"Mama Casita's?" he asked, barely giving me a glance. "I love that place. They have live Mariachi bands that play there on Thursdays."

"Which was why I wanted to go," I replied, grinning that he knew that information. When I'd walked by Mama Casita's while exploring the arts district, it seemed like any other restaurant from the outside, small, one-story brown brick building with the lettering of the name written in typical bright colors. Yet last week when I'd been walking down the sidewalk, the music had caught my attention and I'd wanted to go inside to check it out.

Oliver kept his eyes on the road in front of us and placed one hand on my thigh, squeezing firmly. "Trying to get me to dance with you again?"

I rolled my eyes. "Sure, if you think you can keep up with me."

He shot me a brief look and licked his lips. "I'm pretty sure we both know I can keep it up."

"Good." I smirked. "Because I have plans for you tonight."

The attraction between us, that electricity that was always there, simmering below the surface, sparked to life.

"How was practice?" I asked, my voice huskier than usual. Darn the man and his sexiness. I had to change the subject before we ended up in bed before our night began.

He flashed me a knowing look at the question and began running his thumb along the inside of my thigh. I had thrown on a simple dress earlier. The summer heat was killing me, so I'd grabbed a lightweight, baby pink dress with a pleated skirt, fitted bodice, and spaghetti straps. As Oliver began touching me, it felt like I was already naked.

"Tough. Feels like Pomville is treating every one of our games this season as if it's his last. He's not cutting us any slack."

"That's a good thing, right?"

"Yeah, but sometimes it makes me feel like I'm getting too old for this."

A frown pressed his lips down. I knew just as well as Oliver did that at over thirty years old, he couldn't have many years left.

"Given any thought to what you want to do after?"

"Not a clue. Tell me about your day."

His Adam's apple dipped down his throat as he swallowed harshly. I took the hint: no more talking football—at least not involving the end of his career.

I did as he wished and filled the rest of the car ride with talk of Stamped and moved on to telling him how Melissa and I met and how she started her own graphic design business. She was working on revamping my website again, so I'd spent most of the day emailing her back and forth while she sent me proof designs.

When Oliver pulled into a parking space in front of Mama Casita's, I smiled at the sound of music already filtering out of the restaurant and onto the sidewalk.

Oliver reached into the backseat and came back with a frayed Georgia Tech baseball hat. He slid it on his head, pushing it down low over his eyes. "There, now I'm ready."

I grinned and gestured to his hat. "I'm not sure wearing a hat with your Alma Mater on it will hide your identity very well." Another thought flickered in my mind and my smile vanished. "If you don't like going out in public, we don't have to. I just thought we could have some fun."

His lips pressed together before he answered. "I don't mind ending up in photographs and I actually do love the fans. I just don't always like having meals interrupted. Most of the time it's fine, though."

I'd been by Beaux's side enough to know that when one fan spotted you, the phones came out, the napkins were slid onto tables, and soon the quiet meal you'd wanted ended up with cold food, ice melted in drinks, and a constant stream of autographs being signed.

"How about a compromise?"

His eyes widened in surprised, like he couldn't believe I'd get it. "What?"

"We go in, get an order to go, and I get one dance while we wait for our food. Then we can go eat it somewhere more private."

I had the perfect place in mind. Mama Casita's was near the NCSU campus and I'd heard it had beautiful parks.

"How is it that you always seem to know exactly what I need?"

His hand was at the back of my neck and his lips were on mine, his tongue seeking entrance into my mouth, before I could respond.

"YOU HAVE A GREAT ARM," Oliver said, his hands extended to catch the pass I'd thrown.

"I learned from the best."

"I don't know if I'd call Beaux the *best*."

I clapped my hands and opened them, signaling for him to throw the ball. "Fine, I learned from one of the best. Happy?"

He threw the ball into my outstretched hands perfectly. When I did a hip-shake for a celebration dance, Oliver's gaze turned serious.

"Yes, I'm happy. Very."

We'd danced our Mariachi dance and laughed ourselves silly. I learned that while Oliver could move like a God in the bedroom, a master on the football field, and could roll his hips seductively to hip-hop music, he absolutely sucked at other forms of dancing.

We'd gotten our food after one song, like I promised him, and then we'd left Mama Casita's, Oliver holding on to my hand with one of his and our order of food in another, and gone straight to the perfect area of the university.

Fall term would start in a couple of weeks, so for the time being the campus was rather empty and Oliver had guided us to a small park that overlooked a nearby lake. When I'd started cleaning up our mess, he'd run to his car really quick and come back tossing a football in his hands.

I blinked away the emotion that his simple statement caused and threw him the ball.

"Your dad do this with you?"

He'd mentioned his parents a few times, but most of it was in passing.

"Of course," he replied. "Every day when we were done working on the farm, he'd have me out in the backyard throwing passes."

"Are you close?"

"Close as we can get, I suppose. He never really understood my passion for football, and I think a part of him still wishes I had stayed close and taken over their farm. But he's also always been supportive of me, behind me a hundred percent. Both of my parents were."

"It's good you had that." A small wave of sadness rolled over me.

"Your mom wasn't like that?"

Unlike Oliver, Beaux and I had pretty much done everything on our own, always. "Mom tried to support us, and she did with her words, but she was always so busy working that she didn't have the time to do much else."

He caught my next pass and tucked it under his arm before he started walking toward me. "What about your dad? Where was he?"

I snorted. "Drowning himself in a bottle of whiskey at the local bar."

"You know who he is?" His eyebrows arched in surprise.

Shrugging, I started walking toward the picnic table where we'd left bottles of water he had picked up. "Yeah, I mean, I know his name and he lived in town. But he and my mom weren't really together when she got pregnant, so he didn't feel any obligation to stick around when she got knocked up. It's not like he would have been any help. I only knew he was a worthless drunk."

He scratched the scruff on his cheek and frowned. "I'm

sorry. I don't know what that was like, but I bet it sucked. What about Beaux's dad?"

I scrunched my face. "My mom's not a slut, you know."

"I never said she was, Shannon. I'm just asking."

I squeezed my eyes closed and exhaled a breath. "I'm sorry, I'm defensive, but neither of our stories are pretty, I guess, and you come from such a normal family."

"All families have their problems."

"I know." I took another sip of water before explaining. "Beaux's dad was a one-night stand from a time when my mom worked the front desk at a hotel. All I know is that the hotel was fancy and the patrons had money. Lots of it. She didn't talk about it much, and I think she was ashamed, but she told me when she was sick that she was just lonely during that time. One small child, all on her own. She had a high school degree but nothing that could earn her enough money to give her kid what she wanted."

"That sucks," Oliver replied and set the football down on the picnic table. "I can't imagine what that was like for any of you, really. The fact that both of you have done so well for yourselves is a testament to her and your characters."

Tears burned the backs of my eyes and I forced myself to look away. "I miss her. All the time. I missed her when she was alive because Beaux and I were always alone, and then I missed her when she was gone."

His hand reached out and cupped the side of my neck, and his thumb began making small movements just beneath my chin. "How'd she die?"

"Exhaustion, I think. She was never officially diagnosed with a cause of death other than heart failure." Tears began blurring my vision as the memories slammed into my mind. "She got pneumonia one winter and didn't have paid time off. So she kept working, and it took forever for her to get better.

But she never really did, either. She kept getting sick, kept refusing to go to the hospital because she didn't have the insurance to pay for it. Once she lost her jobs and kept getting sicker, I think she just gave up."

His hand at my neck tightened and he tugged me forward until my forehead hit his chest. His other arm wrapped around my lower back and he held me against him while I began to cry. Swaying back and forth, he held me close, letting me expel all the emotions I worked so hard to keep bottled up.

And it was in that moment, with the sun beating down on us, the rustling of a breeze through the trees and the waves lapping against the shore the only sounds around us, I knew I was falling in deep.

So deep I was drowning, but didn't want anyone to rescue me.

I pulled back and wiped my tears away, my smile shaky when I looked up at Oliver. The understanding in his eyes made all his hardened features seem softer and made my breath catch in my throat.

"Sorry," I whispered, cleaning up my cheeks.

"Don't be." He leaned down and kissed my cheek, my jaw, my lips, back by my ear. "You have nothing to be sorry for. You ready to go?"

"Yeah." I sniffed one more time. I erased the sadness in my eyes and grinned, biting my tongue between my teeth. "I still have more things planned for tonight anyway."

His soft grin turned wicked. "Then by all means, let's go home."

"WHAT A FUCKTWIT," Melissa exclaimed after I filled her in on Patrick's phone call from earlier in the week.

I swallowed my sip of wine before I choked on it. It was Saturday, and for the first night since I'd been in Raleigh, I was alone. No Beaux, no Oliver, just my newly bought and set up television—complete with satellite so I never had to worry about missing a single football game all season—and Melissa's made-up curse words.

"But Oliver, man, he sounds like a man I wouldn't mind being claimed by. Not in that way, at least."

"Yeah, he's something else."

It was safe to say I was falling fast.

It seemed surreal at the same time that it was natural.

What didn't feel natural was the little white box I'd found sitting on the nightstand next to my bed this morning when I went back to grab my purse after Oliver had left.

It was too big to be jewelry. It was also way too soon for him to be giving me jewelry, despite the amount of money he made.

Maybe he left it by accident. Maybe it wasn't for me, but something he'd forgotten.

Maybe he wanted me to wait until he called me after the game like he'd promised he would.

I'd spent hours downstairs thinking of the rectangular box. It seemed to shout through the floor, down to my workroom in Stamped, "*open me, open me, open me, come on, you know you want to.*"

I'd caved two hours earlier, curiosity almost killing me.

Now, I was going to kill him.

The box hadn't contained jewelry. It hadn't even contained a memento, something cheesy to remember him when he played in his away games.

Nope.

A butt plug.

Butt. Plug. It wasn't a small one, either. He'd mentioned it once and, interested in what he'd done to me, I'd hoped we'd go there. We hadn't. For the past week he had backed off the backdoor entrance. After the first time he'd pressed a finger inside of me, though, I had looked butt plugs up online.

The plug he'd left surreptitiously next to my nightstand, giving me a clear indication he wanted this, was much smaller than him. It was also *not* a beginner, small-sized plug.

Hence the sudden need I had for wine.

"I tell you what, Shanna Banana," Melissa said.

It occurred to me that she'd been speaking, but I'd drifted off. I dragged off my eyes off the box I could spy down the hallway and focused on her.

"Patrick was never good enough for you. I know Beaux told you that, and now I'm telling you that. I stayed silent even though I never liked the guy, but you did and you deserved your happy, but Patrick was never going to be it for you. And frankly, I'm glad you've now got a large dick sticking it to you so you can realize that there are men out there who are real men and not the pussy guy Patrick is."

She was right, in a sense. I was tired of defending the guy, talking about him, and even thinking about him.

"Well, it's done now," I murmured and took another drink of wine. "Let's put it behind us."

"Yes, let's. Now, let's talk more about this hunk of a man you have. He is *fine...*"

She continued speaking and rambling, like she usually did, and I quit listening. The truth was, there was no comparison between Oliver's six foot four, two-fifty, muscled frame that held a bit of thickness around his sides and Patrick at five-ten and one-eighty. Both were built and in shape for their build, but Oliver was on another level.

A man who had spent years honing his body into a machine was no match, physically, for a man who occasionally ran on the weekends and lifted weights only when the spirit moved him.

While Melissa rattled on, I continued thinking about all the years I'd spent with Patrick, finally letting the truth everyone spoke to me sink into me like it should have long ago.

They were right about Patrick. Patrick had always expected me to bow to him, to go along with what he wanted because he was a McDonnelly.

I had fallen for it. I had craved the security his financial situation could provide someday, not to live a life of luxury, but to know with certainty that I'd never eat a week of bologna and cheese sandwiches again, and even then only eat twice a day.

But had I ever craved his touch the way I already craved Oliver's? Had I ever responded to him physically so quickly? So deeply? Did I miss him when we were apart, waiting for the minute I could see him again?

If they ever existed, they'd evaporated a long time ago.

Regardless of the passion we could have had in the beginning, it had long since burned out by the time he proposed. I had chalked it up to that's what happened when you moved in with someone. When you knew them so well after so many years that it was easy to settle into roommates with lackluster sex lives where you knew every move that would come before it happened.

We'd been stale. I hadn't even been bothered by it.

Already I knew that if that passion with Oliver waned, I'd fight tooth and nail to get it back, hanging onto it with everything I had to keep from losing it again.

"I didn't love him," I whispered.

The babbling voice on the other end of the phone went silent. "Jensen Ackles?" Melissa finally asked, confusion thick in her voice. "Because I was talking about—"

"Sorry, I wasn't listening, and I'll let you rant about *Supernatural* later, but I think I just had an epiphany."

"About Patrick?" Any other friend might have been offended by admitting they'd been talking and you'd totally drifted off. Not Melissa. Of course, her obsession with *Supernatural* rivaled mine with *Sons of Anarchy*—something she never understood.

"Yes. I didn't love him. Or if I did, I stopped a long time ago."

I didn't have to see her to know she was rolling her eyes. "Well, duh. I could have told you that."

I finished my glass of wine in one large swallow. "I love you. You know that, right, Pissy Missy?"

She snorted. "Sure, hooker. I know that."

MY PALMS WENT clammy as soon as I saw Oliver's name flash on my phone.

I was tipsy, having drunk more wine after Melissa and I hung up. Then more wine while I watched Raleigh cream Miami. For two guys who had seemed to think the game was going to be close, they had played a game that the sports announcers were declaring "prophetic of the rest of their Super Bowl-bound season."

I'd been so excited that I'd finished the bottle of wine while I cheered for every completed pass, every touchdown, every dodged sack and tackle.

Now, I was about to have a heart attack. If it was possible, the butt plug on my nightstand had grown throughout the day.

It wasn't even just a phone call that made me nervous. It was the small white video camera inside a green circle.

FaceTime? *Oh God.*

My stomach sank to my gut as I hit the Answer button. When we connected and I saw his eyes crinkle behind those sexy as hell eyeglass frames when he smiled, I swallowed past the lump in my throat.

"Hey, you. Good game tonight." I cringed as my voice cracked.

Oliver's smile disappeared as he noticed. "You okay?"

"I'm good. I promise. Maybe had a bit too much to drink tonight, excited to see you. You played great."

His eyes softened. His smile was a bit tremulous, as if he wasn't used to the praise. It was that vulnerability that made my heart skip a beat. "Thank you. Everything about the game was good, like we're figuring out our shit on the field."

"It looked like it." There was an awkward pause and heat crept up my neck to my cheeks.

"You're nervous," he said, adjusting in his seat. He leaned back, and that was when I noticed he wasn't wearing a shirt. All I saw on the small screen in my hand was tanned and firm muscles, slight bruises blooming on his ribcage, but I knew enough not to ask. Bruises and injuries were part of the game. "Would you care to tell me why?"

I blinked harshly and forced myself to look him in the eye. He smirked and ran his tongue along his teeth. Slowly.

Teasingly.

God. He knew why I was nervous and he was loving it.

"I found your present," I admitted, my voice thick.

His lips twitched. "And you're not going to say thank you?"

My voice went soft. "I'm a bit too afraid for that quite yet."

"You will." He nodded confidently. "When I'm inside you, with your ass full of the plug, you'll be thankful for it."

"You sound so sure." My body was already responding to the idea, to his words and his confidence. Warmth hit my inner thighs, making everything tingle.

He crossed his arms over his chest, excitement flashing in his eyes all while seeming so unconcerned at my nerves. "Tell me what you first thought when you saw it. And while you're doing that, take off your shirt. I woke up hard this morning, wishing I could put my mouth on your tits."

"God, Oliver." I was already practically panting. My breath quickened from nerves mixed with desire. I still listened. I took off my shirt and my bra, sitting in my bed in only a simple white cotton thong. Without being told, I adjusted my position on the bed and propped up my phone so I could talk to him without holding it.

Something told me I would need my hands soon anyway.

"When you saw the plug?" he asked, his hands disappearing below my line of sight. I knew what he was doing as he shifted his hips, pushed down, and then the muscles in one of his arms began to bunch and flex while he began working himself.

God, I wanted to see it. See him stroke himself.

"I liked it," I admitted, breathless now. "We talked about it but then you didn't mention it again. I've been curious."

"Scared?"

I nodded, then blinked as he continued working himself. "I want to see you," I blurted.

He barked out a quick laugh but pushed back from the desk. Shit. He was naked. Completely, except for those glasses I wanted him wearing sometime when he was on top of me. They made him seem less like a god and more like a man. A completely edible man. His hard dick stood straight up while he wrapped his hand around it. His thighs were spread wide, unashamedly.

Always so confident.

I dragged my gaze off him masturbating and blinked quickly. "I've never done this. Or that," I admitted, thinking of the plug and him taking that part of me. "It makes me nervous. Scares me. But I want it, too."

"You'll fucking love it. God, do you see how hard I am for you? So damn hard for you all the time. And all you have to do is listen to what I say. Can you do that, Shan?"

I nodded, dropped my gaze back to his dick. Wetness dampened my thong.

"Take off your underwear, then. As sexy as you are covered, I want to see you."

I shifted again, listening to his rich voice, the way his hazel eyes had gone as dark as the forest. Every muscle in his face was tight and his abs bunched and rolled while he worked himself. He was just as turned on as me.

When I was naked, I fought for my confidence and planted my feet on the bed, knees up and legs spread wide so he could see all of me. I was completely exposed to him.

The look in his eyes told me he liked it. "Good. Now run a thumb over your nipple, tease yourself while I watch you."

I listened without hesitation. My nipples were already hard as diamonds anyway. Each brush of my thumb sent sparks of pleasure straight to my sex. Without being told, my other hand drifted down my stomach until I was rubbing two of my fingers over my clit.

"Oh, God," I gasped, arching into my hand. My eyes grew heavy, but I forced myself to keep them on Oliver.

"Dirty fucking girl," he groaned, watching me. His half-lidded eyes were focused on my fingers at my pussy. Seeing how much he liked it, watching his own cheeks flush while I got myself off spurred me on. I slid my fingers through my folds, gathering the moisture there, and dragged them back to my clit. "You fucking love this. And you'll love it when I'm inside your ass."

"Yes," I breathed out, unable to hide it anymore. His hand worked his dick faster and his commands returned.

He told me how to pleasure myself. To twist my nipples, tug on them. He told me when to push my fingers inside of me and fuck myself. I listened to every word he said, needy and panting and wanting and driving myself so absolutely crazy my skin glistened with sweat.

"Oliver," I panted rapidly, chanting his name while my orgasm danced around the edges.

"That's it, honey," he grunted, softening his voice while he ferociously worked his own cock. "Let me see you fall apart. I'm so damn close. So hard. So fucking jealous it's your fingers inside you and not my tongue."

It was all I needed to hear, the last thing I heard before I squeezed my eyes closed and fireworks exploded behind my closed lids as my climax rolled through.

I threw my head back into my pillow as my body tightened and quivered, and drained every ounce of my orgasm from me as I heard him growling in that gravelly voice of his.

"Give me your eyes, Shannon. Watch what just the sight of you does to me."

I barely peeled my tired eyes open in time to watch him. His heavy balls were drawn tight, his hand moving hard and fast around the tip of his cock.

He didn't take his eyes off me when his own orgasm hit him. His jaw clenched. His abs tightened until I saw every single indentation on his chest and sides and hips and thighs. When he came, he was staring directly into my eyes, my name rolling off his thick and swollen lips, his eyes lit with fierce desire. "Fucking shit," he growled as he slowed down the ministrations of his dick, his climax rolling through him.

A tremble rolled through him as it left him, shaking off the final twinges of a climax that I knew had hit him as powerfully as my own did, and then a blush hit his cheekbones and he winked. "So. That was fun."

I laughed, my eyes crinkling, and my lips stretched into a full smile. "Yeah," I exhaled. "That was fun."

"Go get cleaned up. When you come back, I want to hear all about your day."

"Are you ready to open Stamped in a couple of weeks?"

We were winding through the back roads on the way to my house, and next to me, Shannon was strung tight.

I knew why. Earlier, after I'd told her I wanted her at my house for the weekend and I'd pick her up after practice, I had hung up and sent her one text.

Don't forget to bring the present.

I had smiled when I hit Send, knowing she'd get it and her already large brown eyes would flash in surprise and they'd widen even further. I fucking loved that look on her. I loved knowing I could make her nervous, yet some part of her trusted me enough to do whatever I wanted.

A simple text saying *okay* had been replied, and then I hadn't responded until I pulled up to Stamped just as she was locking up, an overnight bag slung over her shoulder.

She'd barely spoken during the forty-minute drive out of the city to my place, asking me questions about Sunday's game, the last preseason game which should be an easy win.

I'd ignored the elephant in the car. I wanted her ready to

explode. I wanted to reach out and touch her and feel the heat of her flushed skin. I wanted her on edge, so that when I did finally take her this weekend, she'd go off like a firecracker, without any warning.

Next to me, sitting in a simple tank top, frayed jean shorts that barely covered her ass, and her hair piled high and wild on top of her head, she jumped as I asked the question. She was beautiful. Not classy beautiful. Not elegant. In fact, there were probably thousands of women in the world you could line up next to Shannon and the other women could be classified as "more beautiful."

But I thought she was perfect. She was the complete, perfect package, and every time I talked to her, every time I was around her, I began to realize more and more that I didn't just love fucking her, I was starting to fall for her.

Her voodoo pussy and handful-sized tits sucked me in, but it was her intelligence and her smile and her sass that pulled me toward her in a way I hadn't experienced in so long, I'd forgotten what falling in love felt like.

And this was it. It took weeks.

It didn't matter. Shannon Hale was a woman you didn't just want on your arm or in your bed, you wanted her pulled tight next to you, walking through life with you. She had the potential to be my biggest supporter, my greatest cheerleader, and my largest pain in the ass.

I wanted all of it.

"What?" she asked and brushed a tendril of hair behind her ear. "I'm sorry, what'd you ask?"

One side of my lips lifted into a grin. "I asked if you're excited about Stamped. Are you ready for the opening?"

"Yeah, I think." She paused and brushed her hands down her thighs. They were tanned now, and I knew when she wasn't working or at my place, she'd found access to the rooftop of her building that had a small deck. She had told me one night on the phone that she went up there on her lunch breaks to see the city and get some fresh air.

I had thought of all the things I'd do to her up there once the sun set.

She continued after pulling in a long, trembling breath. "I mean, I still need to do some marketing, and that's been hard even though Beaux put me in touch with someone before he ever closed on the place. I've got ads going out and my website is up and running now with the information for the first physical location. That's been getting a lot of excitement. I didn't realize I had so many customers online that live nearby, which is good."

"It sounds like it's all falling together." She'd been working her ass off ever since I'd met her. I'd met few women in my career who wanted their own. It was the price of having so much damn money that you attracted women who didn't care about having their own, just spending someone else's. In my gut, I knew that if I blew out my knee tomorrow, heaven forbid, or if I lost all the money in the stock market, Shannon wouldn't give a shit.

"Yeah. Or it's all going to fail and I'm going to fall flat on my face."

She'd mentioned her concerns. One night in her bed, she'd trailed a finger down the center of my chest, through my chest hair down to the waistband of my shorts. I'd gone hard at her languid touch while she'd told me all about how, for so much of her life, she'd been so focused on helping Beaux succeed that she'd never had time to achieve anything of her own. She'd bounced from office job to office job after college, spending most of her free time at night selling her jewelry and working to increase that dream she'd started in college.

"I think it's brave," I said and slid a hand to her thighs.

She jumped from the contact, and I wrapped my hand around her. She was so small compared to me. My hand easily covered her leg and slid to the sides where I tightened my grip.

"I think you have more drive and more ambition than most people I've met in my life, Shannon. You won't fail. You don't have it in you."

She laughed softly. Nervously. "It's just jewelry. Silly little bracelets and baubles and charms and earrings."

"You make women feel beautiful and happy and excited. You're selling yourself short."

"Yeah," she huffed and looked out the window. "I've learned recently that I have a habit of doing that. I'm working on it."

"You'll succeed at that too. I have faith in you." I did. The statement rolled off my tongue so easily it didn't even surprise me. Based on the way she gaped at me, it surprised the hell out of her, though.

It just reminded me I had one more thing to do this weekend—show her exactly how much she was beginning to mean to me.

I pulled off the road and into my driveway, noticing how her breath hitched when we were finally at my house. We hadn't been back since the first night, when we'd had to leave earlier than I wanted. Now, we had an entire thirty-six hours to spend together before I had to get to the game on Sunday.

She was nervous as hell.

I was excited as fuck.

I pulled up to the garage and pulled in, leaving the door open behind us.

I knew that Shannon was expecting me to take her some-where and fuck her right away. I wanted it. But more than feeling her cunt spasm around me as she came and feeling like she was sucking the life out of me through my dick, I wanted to show her something else.

Me. Who I really was. No hiding, no walls…I wanted to be completely transparent with her, and I'd planned an entire weekend of how to do it.

I met her at the back of my car, popping the trunk and reaching in to grab a shopping bag for her. I'd bought the boots earlier in the week, before she'd agreed to spend the weekend with me, I wanted her to have her own, something she could wear here.

"Here," I said and handed the bag to her.

Her eyes jumped wide as she gingerly reached out and took the handles from me.

I slammed the trunk closed and her brows furrowed.

"Don't we need to take those inside?"

"No. We'll get them later. I have something else planned first. Now open your present."

I flashed her a wicked grin as I said the word, knowing exactly what she'd be thinking of.

"I'm not sure I'm ready for another one of your presents." She gave me a timid grin before she peered into the bag like I'd loaded it with rattlesnakes. Then those brown eyes popped open and her grin widened.

"Boots?"

"Yup." I nodded and took the box out of the bag for her. I'd also made sure to include thick socks so she didn't get blisters on her soft feet. "These are yours, for when you're here with me. I need to run inside and grab mine while you put them on, and then we're going for a ride."

"On the horses?" she gasped, clearly surprised.

I smirked. "I could ride you another way, but I thought you'd like the horses first."

She bobbed her head energetically. "I do. I want that. The

horses." Her cheeks burned hot pink and she winked. "Then later, it's going to be me riding you."

We'd see about that. The thought made my dick come to life in my pants, though, so it wasn't an altogether bad idea. I bent down and wrapped an arm around her back, pulling her to me. Her fingers instantly entwined behind my neck when I tilted my head. My lips brushed against hers and I slid my tongue inside her parted lips, tasting her slowly. She responded immediately, letting me take control the way I enjoyed it. She tasted like heaven and mint, soft and sweet in my arms. God. I was falling fast for this woman. "Get your boots on," I said when I pulled away. I smacked her ass before I stepped back and grinned. "I'll be right back."

LEE HAD ALREADY PULLED out Ralph and Winne by the time I'd changed my clothes and grabbed the lunch I'd had him ask his wife, Sue, to make for us. The small cooler was slung over my shoulder and I hurried to the fence where Lee and Shannon were talking.

"A picnic, too?" she asked, brown eyes sparking in the sun when she saw the cooler.

"My wife made it for you," Lee chimed in, grinning like the cat that ate the canary. "Thrilled when Oliver asked her to. Can't remember a time when he'd asked for a picnic lunch. To Sue, it was like Christmas, so excited she danced and sang in the kitchen all morning, preparing a feast for you two."

I glared at him, but it lacked heat. "Tell Sue thanks."

"Will do." He tipped his hat to me and winked. "Now you two kids don't do anything I wouldn't do today."

Next to me, Shannon giggled, and I waved him away. "Scram, you old coot."

"I'm going, I'm going. Be back Monday."

I kept an eye on Lee as he climbed into the truck, and when he'd turned and driven down the driveway, both of us waving goodbye to him, I turned back to Shannon and arched a brow. "You ready to ride?"

Her eyes lit with unabashed excitement. "I can't wait."

"Let's go then." I took her hand and pulled her through the gated fence. Winne and Ralph danced a bit before settling down when we walked up to them. "You'll sit on Ralph because he's calmer and won't throw you."

"Wow, you know how to calm a girl's nerves."

"Just preparing you," I said, smacking her rear end. "I'll take Hulk out later and exercise him, but he's too ornery for a slow ride, and I didn't want him getting the other horses excited. Next time, when you're ready, I'll put you on Winne. She's a bit more feisty, but something tells me you'll be able to handle her in no time." I brushed my hand down Ralph's crest to his shoulder until I knew he was calm. "Ready, boy? Be good to her. She's new to this."

As if he understood, he neighed and dipped his head and met Shannon's gaze.

"Hey, Ralph," she whispered, reaching out to touch his neck. "You'll be nice, right?"

"He'll sense your nerves," I warned her. "So he might be jumpy at first, but hold on tight and sit with your back straight, centering your balance, and he'll calm once I'm on Winne. When I get on her, I'll take your reins and guide him for a bit, okay? All you have to do is hold the pommel of the saddle."

I pointed to where I meant on the saddle and waited for the sign that she was ready.

It rolled through her like it did every time I suggested something outside her comfort zone. It was usually about sex, but her nerves brightened and then evaporated much the same way now as she blew out a breath.

"Okay. I'm ready."

I told her how to hold on to the saddle of the horse and helped her up, holding on to Ralph's reins around his throat to keep him steady. He wiggled a bit once she was on, and I saw her eyes flash wide when he sidestepped, pulling me toward him a bit, but he quickly settled back.

"You good?" I looked up at Shannon and the force of her smile hit me like a meteor straight to my chest. It made my lips part and my ribs burn as she grinned down at me, so fucking excited she could light up the sky.

"Ready, old man."

"I'll show you old man," I grumbled teasingly and hoisted myself onto Winne. Once I was saddled, I reached over and took Ralph's reins. Shannon's giggle echoed through the air every time Ralph moved in a way she wasn't suggesting.

We took two laps around the large ring while I helped her with her balance and gave her basic instructions for digging her heels in and how to pull on the reins to make him stop or slow down.

The entire time, her grin kept her lips spread wide and she continued that sweet giggling sound even though I knew she was focused on paying attention and learning too.

She was like Beaux in that moment, enjoying the hell out of life while at the same time focused on doing her best.

For the first time since I could remember, it made jealousy burn deep inside me. That both of them lived like that. Carefree and focused. Kicked back but paying attention. I'd been so focused on one thing for so long, I hadn't realized until that moment with Shannon how much I'd forgotten to have fun along the way.

"Thank you," I said, walking Winne next to Ralph until I

could reach over and place my hand on Shannon's thigh. "Thank you for doing this with me today."

I let my sincerity shine in my eyes, hoping like hell she could read everything I felt in that moment. It was perfection. Something I wanted to remember forever.

"I should be thanking you," she said, her voice awed and soft. "For teaching me this. I can't remember the last time I've had so much fun."

Neither did I. Something told me this wouldn't be the last time I had this much fun, though. Not with Shannon next to me.

"Ready to hit the trails?"

"Trails?"

"Yup. You didn't think we'd stay in the ring all day, did you?"

She frowned a bit and then shook her head. "Well, yeah. Sort of, but let's do it."

I was on a horse on my way through a wooded trail with Oliver on my left side, and we were going to have a picnic lunch.

It was not what I was expecting us to do the minute we arrived. I figured it'd involve seduction and fucking and lube and butt plugs.

I hadn't determined if I was disappointed by this or thankful. Apprehension had chilled my skin when he'd first sent the text telling me to remember the plug. I could practically see the glimmer in his eye as he'd sent it, knowing what that one sentence would do to me. Yet I hadn't hesitated in packing it either. What he wanted involved a certain amount of trust, and while we hadn't been together long, Oliver was showing me that he was the guy who could be trusted with everything I had to give him.

I was falling for him, against my original plans of moving to Raleigh to make something of myself and figure out who I was without a man. Oliver didn't detract from those plans, though. With his obvious interest in my day and in my business and in his appreciation for my work, plus his sexy, alpha side I saw all the time when we were together, he was proving to be a man who could stand at my side, supporting and encouraging me in equal measure to what I gave him.

Yeah. I was falling—falling fast and hard, and I didn't even care about having a safety net.

Next to me, Oliver led us to the left a bit farther and then pulled the horses to stop at the tree line.

I gasped as I saw where he'd brought us.

"Wow." I sighed. "This is beautiful."

In front of us was a small lake that jutted up against the tree line except for the small, beachy area where he had led us.

We were surrounded by trees, the sun high in the cloudless sky. Cerulean blue and emerald green filled my vision as my gaze wandered around the water until I was looking at Oliver. In the bright sun, the baseball cap he generally wore was turned backward. His eyes were as bright as the trees.

"This place is beautiful."

"I come here a lot," he said, dismounting from his horse. "Helps me think after a shitty game."

I licked my parched lips, taken aback at the admission.

He was always so strong and confident, arrogant and bossy. I imagined after a shitty game, he went and punched something or ran six miles or did something manly like wood chopping or hay baling to release the adrenaline.

Visions of Oliver in his glasses, hands pushing back his hair while he sat in the stillness of this location, never would have occurred to me.

"That surprises you," he stated as he walked around Winne and reached up to help me off Ralph.

I grinned, thinking of wood chopping and hay baling again. I must not have hidden my surprise very well.

"Yeah, a little." I threw a leg over the side of the horse and placed my hands on Oliver's shoulders. His hands went to my waist and he slowly helped me off the large and gentle beast. "Thank you for the ride," I whispered, running my hand down Ralph's's shoulder. "That was great."

"I take you on the ride and you thank my horse." Amusement lit Oliver's voice and I turned back to him, rolling to my toes so I could reach his lips with mine.

"It was beautiful," I whispered. "Thank you, again."

His gloved hand gently brushed along my cheek. "Anytime."

I wanted to be on that horse again. Lots.

He reached around Winne and unsecured the cooler he'd brought with him. He nodded toward a thick, low branch hanging from a tree a short distance away. "Can you hold this while I secure the horses?"

"Of course." While he led the horses away, I stepped through the knee-high grass and out onto the sandy beach area. Kicking off my boots, I bent down to pull off the thick socks he'd also given me and then slid my toes deep into the hot sand until I reached the cool, wet sand beneath the top layer.

"I should have brought a blanket," Oliver said, stepping up to my side and slipping the cooler out of my grip.

I was thinking of cool sand and clean water and sunshine when I replied, "I don't mind getting a little bit dirty."

The bright summer sun had nothing to do with the heat that suffused my cheeks.. I looked at Oliver through half-lidded eyes and his expression said he noticed.

"I know. It's one of the many things I like about you."

"That's not what I meant." I shoved him playfully, not moving the large man a single inch as I laughed.

"I know that, too." He slung his arm around my shoulder and pulled me closer to the water. "But I still mean it."

"You're incorrigible."

He tugged at the messy bun on top of my head and

grinned. "I know. It's one of the many things you like about me."

He was right. Besides being stubborn and arrogant, his playful side was often hidden behind his surly veneer, but I liked it when he shed that for me.

"Come sit with me." He kicked off his own boots and took a seat in the sand. Pulling his knees up, he set the cooler in between his spread feet while he opened it. I didn't waste time joining him as he dug through the cooler, emptying the contents before I saw the meal Sue had prepared for us.

"Wow. Lee wasn't kidding when he said Sue made us a feast."

There were containers of pasta salad, fruit salad, two sandwiches filled with thickly sliced prime rib on large hoagie buns, crackers, cheese, and several small bottles of water.

"It all looks delicious." I didn't know what to choose first when he handed me silverware.

I chose the pasta salad and closed my eyes when the cool flavor hit my tongue. "So good."

When I opened my eyes, I found Oliver's gaze fixed firmly on me. "How can you be so sexy even when you're eating?"

I blushed and looked away, pushing a small chunk of escaped hair behind my ear. Changing the subject away from me, and the way his words affected me, I looked out at the water and asked, "Do your parents come to your games often?"

"Yeah, they come whenever they can, although it's easier for them to get away after the harvest in August and September. But come fall, they travel wherever they can get." His voice trailed off a bit and he took a bite of his food. "Dad's getting older, moving slower than he used to. He wouldn't admit it, but I know keeping up the farm and all the traveling is getting hard on him."

I saw in my memory banks my own mom, too young to be

so frail and working herself to the bone. Stress and depression along with pneumonia and exhaustion stripped the life right out of her. "I'm sorry." I leaned over and rested my hand on his knee and squeezed. "It's hard to watch your parents decline and get old."

"Yeah." His voice softened along with his eyes. "But they'll be there at the first home game in a few weeks. You'll get to meet them then. I know you usually watch the game in the seats Beaux gets for you, but it'd mean a lot to me if you and Melissa would watch it with them from the box."

My body stiffened from the shock before I could hide it and his jaw hardened.

"You don't want that?"

I shook the surprise away and found my bottom lip sucked in between my teeth. "No, I do, I guess I was surprised you'd want me to. It's soon."

I realized my mistake as soon as I said it. His eyes flashed.

"Game's not for three weeks, Shannon. That's almost two months together. That is what we are, isn't it?" He leaned forward, setting his sandwich down before he moved to me, stealing the breath from my lungs with his intensity. "Tell me I'm not the only one thinking we were building something here."

"God, no. I'm sorry." Shit. Damn it. I didn't want to hurt him. I hadn't meant to hurt him. It was clear that I had, and I hated the pain mixed with anger I saw warring in his hazel eyes. I set down my pasta salad and scrambled into his lap, loving that not only did he let me, but he settled me right against him, holding me tight at my waist. "I'm sorry," I said again, dropping my hands over his shoulders. "I was just surprised, that's all. Of course I'll meet them. Melissa and I would love to."

His lips fell to mine, his tongue demanding entrance into

my mouth. I acquiesced quickly, loving the taste of him and the feel of his hot skin against my fingers, burning through his thin shirt.

"We're together," he commanded, pulling back and leaving me needing more of him. The kiss was over too soon, and too intense to end at all. His hands cupped my cheeks firmly, his gaze seeking mine, seeking the truth in my eyes before it spilled from my lips.

"Yes," I gasped. "Of course we are."

My body heated against his as he held me there, not doing anything except roaming my face and my body with his eyes before he pulled me back to him. Right before he closed them and pressed his lips to mine again, I swore I saw something different...something softer and filled with longing and relief, as he kissed me.

"Eat," he growled when he pulled back this time. His thick erection pressed against my sex.

Food had been forgotten and my lips parted at the one-word command.

When he saw my eyes flicker with confusion, he smirked.

"Eat and then we'll get back to the house. You'll need your energy later."

A full-body tremble rolled down my spine, making him laugh when he set me back to the ground and handed me my sandwich.

I smirked when I saw him adjust himself and let loose a low groan.

Biting into my sandwich, I grinned back at him. "Can't wait."

I couldn't. I couldn't wait for whatever it was he had planned, because I knew that like everything else that was Oliver Powell, I was going to love the hell out of it.

~

"RELAX," he murmured, sliding his hand down my back.

My body was slick with sweat. My hands were together in front of me with another tie of Oliver's. It was patterned with black and gray, tiny diamond shapes, and it was the only thing I could focus on while he tried to get me to further relax. I was fully restrained to his headboard once again, depleted from the orgasm he'd already given me with his mouth and his fingers before he'd flipped me over, pulled up my ass, and demanded I spread my knees.

"Please," I whispered, shifting. I knew what was coming. He'd already dug through my bag and taken out the present he'd given me, the present that had mocked me and scared me and filled me with trepidation, but was now the only thing I wanted inside of me besides his cock. "Hurry."

He leaned over me, his chest brushing against my back, his full lips and warm breath at my ear. "No. We go slow."

I'd burst into flames if he went slow. One orgasm was suddenly never enough with him. As soon as I'd climax, he'd bring me to the brink, setting me on fire with his touches and kisses.

He'd played with my puckered hole while he ate me out, licking me and teasing me, igniting my entire body. His fingers had pressed and opened me slightly, and when he'd done that, I'd exploded into a ball of heat so great that I thought I might set the house on fire.

Now he was doing more, preparing me for him but killing me in the process.

"Fuck." I gasped as his hand ran through my crease at my backside. He gathered my wetness from my slit and pushed it toward the back, making me tremble.

"You're on birth control, right?" he asked and my breath

stuttered. He'd been inside me once before, told me he was clean, and at the time I hadn't given him that trust.

"Yes." He slid two fingers inside of my pussy, and I groaned, closing my eyes. "Please, Oliver. I'm dying."

"You won't. I want to be bare inside of you tonight." He pushed and pulled, twisted his fingers and drove me to the edge so quickly I thought I might shatter before he did anything else.

"Yes," I breathed. "I want that."

I did. I trusted him with every part of me. He'd shown me who he was and who he wanted to be. There was nothing about Oliver Powell that wasn't making me fall in love with him.

His fingers paused and slowly slid out of me, making me groan with frustration.

"Thank you," he whispered, his voice thick with need and emotion. He pressed his hand to my cheek and turned my head so our eyes met. "Thank you for that."

I swallowed thickly, feeling a burn deep in my throat as I saw how overwhelmed he was with what I'd given him.

He'd wanted me to trust him. Needed to know I did.

"Please," I whispered, begging now and not caring in the least. I pushed against his fingers still inside me. "Fill me. I can't wait anymore."

His expression turned wicked with desire as he grinned and kissed me with a ferocity, stealing my breath, before he pulled back.

The click of the bottle of lube echoed in the air like a fog horn and his fingers slid out of my pussy.

"Relax," he murmured, coaching me again and soothing me with a hand on my back and my ass. "It won't sting if I go slow, but it'll feel better if you don't fight against it."

I pressed my forehead into his bed, gripping his tie with my fingertips. "Ready."

He coated me with lube, the cooling sensation sparking

goose bumps on my backside, before he slid a finger inside me *there*. It burned and stretched but was so deliciously wonderful at the same time.

I pushed back into him, groaning at the sensation I was already beginning to enjoy.

"Damn, this is so damn hot," he growled as he removed his finger.

The rounded tip of the plug that had once terrified me brushed against my opening. Now, curiosity and need toppled it. He pushed, twisted it while I forced my body to relax.

And then he pushed in. I braced myself with my elbows and knees, pushing into the bed at the same time his other hand snaked around to my front. He played with my nipples, ran his hand over my stomach, and whispered encouraging words to me as he slowly pushed it in farther.

"Fuck." I gasped as I let the plug begin to widen, stretch me open and further than he had before. The burn was minor compared to the sensations rioting inside me.

"You're doing so well," he crooned, sliding his tongue and his teeth against the column of my exposed my throat. "So fucking good. I can't wait to fuck you while you're full of this plug. You're going to lose your damn mind."

I already had. Everything he did made my thighs tremble, made me wetter. Made my core tighten and pulse.

"Ah." He pressed the plug inside of me and I groaned. His hand at my stomach drifted lower, his thumb running along my clit.

"Fucking hell, you're soaked."

"I know. Please." I wanted more. Needed more. I had never been so restrained, so full...so fucking needy I thought my heart would shoot out of my chest. "Oliver."

He kissed my cheek again and moved back until he was

behind me, his knees pushing me apart, and then he was pushing his thick cock inside of me.

My back arched at the sensation—the fullness in my backside along with him now. Bare. Hard.

So *damn good.*

"Hell, you're so tight now, I can hardly move."

"Do it."

My plea frayed the last thread of his control and Oliver moved. He pulled out and thrust in, slamming inside me until he pushed me forward. My arms slid out in front of me, his hands on my hips kept me open for him. I gripped his tie feverishly as he fucked me, slamming his dick inside of me before slowly dragging it out. Every sensation intensified tenfold as he slid along the ridged flesh inside of me

He fucked me frantically, burying himself inside of me. He was splitting me apart and at the same time putting me back together.

"Oliver!" I screamed his name as my orgasm hit me out of the blue. I squeezed my eyes closed against the onslaught of his hips pounding against mine and the wild sensations shaking my body.

"Fucking beautiful," he groaned, slowing down as the aftershocks left my body. He leaned forward, and with one hand quickly untied my wrists before he slid out of me and turned me to my back.

He slid back inside, pushing my legs wide and high. "Hold on to your legs. Keep them spread for me."

I gripped them despite my arms feeling languid and my body like jelly.

"Eyes on me," he growled as he dropped down closer to me. "Every fucking time I slide inside of you I feel every part of you."

Every time he slid inside of me, I gave him every part of me.

It was unavoidable and I'd long since quit trying to hold anything back.

I pressed my legs to his sides and rested a hand to his cheek. "You feel amazing inside of me."

Every shift of his body made the plug scrape against me, causing delicious friction inside me and sending myriad sensations throughout my body.

I kept my eyes on him, my hand pressed to his cheek as he continued fucking me, sliding in and out quickly and smoothly, until his jaw tightened and his teeth gritted together. "Fucking hell," he groaned and dropped his head and his eye contact from me. "I'm going to come."

"Please," I urged. "Inside of me."

I wanted him, all of him.

He thrust three more times, seating himself balls deep inside of me and at the same time filling me with him as he came, and as he did, he groaned, "Damn. I fucking love you."

Shit.

I'd said it.

It was too soon. Way too fast. I hadn't meant to say anything, but it had been pulled from my lips with the force of my orgasm, rendering me incapable of holding anything back from her.

She gasped from surprise and her fingers on my cheek flinched. Beneath me, her abs flexed.

I could mask it. I love fucking you. That was what I meant.

Except I didn't mean that and I'd told her I wasn't a liar.

"You're freaking out, aren't you?" I asked, unable to keep the humor out of my tone in an effort to cover my nerves.

I kept my dick inside of her warm, amazing-feeling cunt and forced myself to meet her in the eyes.

I had never been a sissy, never run from my fears, and I wasn't going to do it now. Not when I'd laid everything out on the table for her.

"You don't need to say it back," I said as I lifted my head and met her gaze, the way she nibbled on her bottom lip. "And I didn't mean to scare you. Didn't mean to say it either, but that doesn't mean I don't mean it."

"You..." She blinked rapidly. Her chest thundered against mine as fast as mine was beating against hers. "You love me? Like love me, love me? Or love fucking me love me?"

"I'm beginning to think..." I said, bracing myself on one elbow and pressing my fingertips to her hairline with my other hand. I trailed my fingers through her curls, untangling them from where they'd bunched around her shoulder. "...that there isn't a part of you that I don't love, Shannon."

"Wow." She swallowed and blinked harshly. "I just...it's so fast. I wasn't expecting this."

"You don't have to feel the same way." After her freak-out at meeting my parents earlier, I wouldn't be surprised. Didn't mean I didn't have the fucking urge to hear it, though—to know someone looked at me and felt the way about me as I did about them.

"No," she said. She relaxed beneath me. "I do. I do feel the same way."

A slow grin began stretching my lips. "You do?"

"Of course I do. You consume me. Everything about you is something I'm falling in love with. It's just...the speed of every-thing scares me."

"Fuck the speed," I said, sliding out of her despite wanting to be buried in her forever. "I live my life full throttle, no looking back. No regrets."

She paused before whispering, "No looking back. I like that. Full speed ahead."

I rolled to the side and pulled her with me. She wrapped her legs around mine, tangling us together as I brought her lips to mine.

"I love you, Shannon."

Her lips twitched before her shoulders relaxed and she

smiled up at me, thick black lashes rimming her beautiful chocolate-colored eyes. "I love you, too."

I hugged her to me tighter, kissed her softly so I could show her without words exactly what hearing that from her meant from me, and when she relaxed into my hold, softening toward me and giving me everything she had without words, I pulled away.

"Let me go get a cloth and get us cleaned up so we can sleep."

Her eyelids opened slowly, as if she was already halfway to dreamland.

I felt the same way.

I OPENED my eyes in the morning and grinned as soon as I saw Shannon sleeping next to me. She had small freckles dancing over the bridge of her nose, her pink lips slightly parted and long black eyelashes fanning from closed lids.

I wanted to kiss every inch of her but withheld myself. I'd worked her over hard last night, multiple times after we'd rested and eaten dinner, taking her again and again long into the night. I should have still been sleeping, but it was the curse of a man who grew up on a farm and lived a life that required earlier mornings that prevented sleeping in.

The sun wasn't up yet and I had work to do.

Adjusting my already hard dick, I groaned as I brushed against Shannon's cheek and slid out of bed, careful not to wake her.

She didn't move at all as I pulled away and threw on the shorts and shirt I'd worn the day before. I didn't need clean clothes to muck out some stalls and feed the horses.

When I came out of the bathroom after putting on my

glasses and brushing my teeth, she was still lying in the same position, both of her hands pressed together beneath her cheek, eyes still closed and lips still parted.

I started a pot of coffee and took bacon out of the freezer while I took a few minutes to wake up. While the coffee brewed, I stared out the window, thinking of the night before, the things we'd said to one another.

I meant every word.

I loved her. Loved her in a way that I knew if she walked away from me like Serena had, it would take infinitely longer to recover from. I hadn't planned on it—had never planned on being married again or loving a woman. For the past seven years, I'd taken what I wanted when I wanted it without remorse for the behavior. The women I took to bed wanted the same things as me or only wanted to use me for my money.

I had no qualms about using them for their pussy when they were using me for what was in my wallet.

I had no regrets about the previous night, or telling her I loved her. I only hoped that when she woke, she still felt the same way—that she hadn't said the words back to me out of a sense of obligation or because of the crazy, hot fucking sex we'd had.

"Nice, asshole," I muttered to myself, chuckling while I filled a mug of coffee for myself. "You think your dick is so perfect it can fuck with a woman's common sense."

"It can."

I flinched at the voice behind me and turned to see Shannon. Her shoulder rested against the doorframe to my kitchen, her eyes still sleepy and only half open.

"What are you doing up?" I asked, smiling at what she'd said.

She walked toward me, collapsing against my body when she reached me and lazily wrapped her hands around my waist.

"Smelled coffee. Woke up without you. What are you doing up?"

"Need to feed the horses."

She tilted her head back and grinned. "Can I help?"

"You want to?"

"Yeah, it'll be fun."

Goddamn. She blew me away at every corner.

"This is the second time, you know, that you've ruined my plans for wanting you to sleep in so I can fuck you awake when you've been here."

Those sleepy eyes went hazy with something entirely different from tiredness.

"Then you should do the fucking first and worry about the horses and coffee later," she suggested, wriggling her brows in response.

"You really want to help me?" I asked, still surprised she'd be willing. She didn't need to.

"Yeah...you can get me dirty and then clean me up." She yawned over her words and covered her mouth.

"Don't you know, Shannon," I whispered, unable to hide the gruffness in my tone, "that I like you filthy?"

She laughed softly and yawned again. "Of course you do. I need coffee before I go feed the horses."

I let her go after dipping down and brushing my lips against hers, giving her a sweet, closed-mouth kiss.

"By the way," she said, turning to me with a coffee mug pressed close to her lips, "you still haven't fucked me with those sexy glasses on."

I adjusted them on the bridge of my nose and winked. "We'll see to that later."

～

"YOU DOING OKAY?" I asked, my voice tight with the need to sink inside of her. Instead, I had three fingers in her ass as she writhed beneath me, her legs spread wide on my bed.

It was Sunday night, and I'd had the weekend of my fantasies. I now had a memory of fucking her everywhere in my house, every way I'd wanted to take her. She'd worked beside me with the horses, and when we weren't walking around my land where I showed her all my favorite parts on horse and on foot, we'd spent time in front of the television hanging out, cooking meals together.

This morning she went to the game with me, sat next to Rudolph's wife in the seats Beaux had bought for her, and cheered us on to a victory.

And the best part? It was only the beginning.

I'd wanted to fuck her one last time in my bed, slowly and passionately, taking all the time we had left. But then she'd looked at me and grinned, blush hitting her cheeks, and she'd timidly asked, "Can you fuck me...there...with your glasses on?" I'd changed course immediately.

I'd oblige her anything when she looked at me like that.

"I'm good." Her lips parted and her eyes widened, looking down to where I was taking my time preparing her.

"You're beautiful, you know that?"

She nodded, but doubt still warred in her cocoa-colored eyes. That was okay, too. I had all the time in the world to prove that to her.

"Please, Oliver."

I loved it when she begged. Loved it when she bucked her hips toward me, seeking more of what she wanted from me. But the begging hit me straight in my already hard dick every damn time.

"You need to be ready," I said, looking down at her glistening pussy. If I rolled my tongue around her clit, she'd come in a heartbeat. "Bare?" I asked again. I'd taken her that way every night, but this was different.

"Yes," she answered immediately, panting. "Now. I'm good. Ready."

I leaned down, laughing softly while I kissed her and used my fingers to continue stretching her. I swallowed her groans and my balls grew tight and heavy.

Fuck. I'd shoot as soon as I was inside her. She was so tight. So hot.

So fucking deliciously naughty.

There was no way I wouldn't have fallen in love with this woman.

Sliding my fingers out of her, I placed my tip at her entrance. "I'll go slow," I assured her, pressing against her. "Tell me if you need me to stop."

Her hands hit my hips and she stole my breath with the desperation in her voice. "Don't stop. Never."

Slowly, I began to slide into her, watching her expression as I stretched her wider than she'd been before.

Her eyes widened in surprise and then she flinched as I pressed the head of my cock inside of her.

"Just a minute, Shan. Let me get inside and I'll stop."

She nodded frantically, her fingers digging into my hips. "Hurry."

I pushed inside of her, sliding my fingers against her clit to give her another sensation to focus on.

"Just relax. There you go, good girl." Her hips arched up, seeking more, and that one quick move from her pushed me deep inside of her.

"Fuck," I groaned, closing my eyes. She was like a damn vise, squeezing my dick hard and tight while sucking me into her at the same time.

"Move," she moaned. "Move something, anything."

I bit back a laugh at her desperateness and slid my fingers against her clit. She was so fucking drenched. Hot and wet, her cream glistened all over the lips of her pussy.

I slid my dick in further, waiting for a sign that it hurt too much but every time I pushed in, she pulled me closer.

"So good," she whimpered when I'd finally sunk inside of her. "Please. I need more."

That *please*. It undid me every time.

"I can't go slower anymore," I warned her, resting one of my hands on her hips, holding her against me. The walls of her ass clenched tight, her pussy and clit were swollen and dripping, and all of it was about to send me over the edge.

She cried out my name as I pulled out and pushed back inside of her. Then I began moving, pressing my thumb against her clit before teasing her cunt with my fingers.

"Fucking hell," I groaned, watching her legs begin to shake as she quivered from head to toe.

I let loose, fucking her like an animal, like I needed her to breathe.

Some deep part of me whispered that I did.

I fucking needed this woman. I needed her cunt and her mouth, and I needed her damn heart and soul.

"Oliver!" she cried out as her orgasm took her over the ledge.

I was mesmerized by the way her body bucked wild beneath me. My thumb and finger pinched her clit as she began to slow, sending her straight into another orgasm.

My own climax started at my spine, that fucking buzz of heat that went straight to my balls and my dick.

I thrust myself inside of her deep, exploding all of me into her, hoping it was enough to keep her connected to me forever.

"Shannon," I groaned as my dick still twitched deep inside her ass. "You're so damn incredible."

Her hands slid from my hips to my back. Her fingertips lightly trailed down my spine and around to my sides. "You're pretty amazing yourself." She opened her eyes, blinked slowly, and smiled before she frowned. "I love you. Please don't hurt me."

Damn.

Her vulnerability, her fear, went straight to my chest and I pulled out of her slowly before I fell between her legs.

"Never," I promised. "I'll try my best, every single fucking day to never hurt you."

I was a man of my word. Always had been.

I hoped like hell I'd prove it true with her.

It was official. I was completely freaking out.

"This is amazing," Melissa said, bouncing up to me with two glasses of champagne in her hand.

We'd been busy since one o'clock with the official grand opening of Stamped. We had champagne and tiny cupcakes and bite-sized cookies brought in from a bakery just down the street, and we were almost out of the hundreds we'd ordered.

I'd made more money in one day than I had in almost six months.

My head hadn't stopped spinning.

The last two weeks had completely flown by. I'd spent most nights with Oliver at my place or one of his. Sometimes we met at his hotel crash pad, and on weekends we went to his house. Other nights he came directly to Stamped and had to almost physically haul me out of my workroom.

I was in way over my head. My online sales had started booming after the street fair, from mostly local customers who had stopped by my booth. I'd had dozens of previous customers contact me wanting more jewelry after seeing my website had been updated with the information of my first physical store location.

My fingers were cut and callused and bandaged and worn down from all the work I'd been doing.

The first day had completely blown my mind and I owed it all to Beaux, his faith in me, and the marketing company he'd hired for me to help with the opening.

"I don't know what to do with all this," I said as I took another glass of champagne from her hand. It was only my third of the day. I'd been sipping it slowly despite wanting to chug bottle after bottle to assuage my nerves. "This is more than I imagined. I'm going to need help, I think, to keep up with the production." I slid her a glance. "Know any jewelry designers who could help?"

She shot me a look that was clear. "Hell no. You're the only person I know who's this talented. I'm just glad you're finally seeing it for yourself."

I shook my head and looked around, awed at the amount of people in my store. It was packed full. Product was flying off the shelves faster than we could replace it.

I was going to have to do something if this wasn't some rare Thursday fluke.

At least hire someone to help me work in the store so I could spend my time creating.

Needless to say, my time with Oliver had been helpful in more ways than one. He listened to me bitch, he supported me, he gave me ideas on advertising when I was stressed out, and then when I was super-stressed, he found multiple ways, almost nightly, to help me relax. I did the same for him, I knew it. He never hesitated to bounce ideas off me. Some nights we talked plays. Some nights we just hung out in front of the tele-vision, barely watching whatever was on and talking about our lives.

I had fallen in love with him quickly, painlessly. So easily that some days I wondered if it was all a dream.

If it was, I never wanted to wake up from it.

Especially not on this day.

I'd made other decisions in the past few weeks, too. While I'd told Oliver that I didn't want to be in his shadow, with all the support I knew he was giving me, I wanted to do the same for him. Because of that, and partly still out of my fear of failing at this whole running-my-own-business thing, Stamped was only open four days a week. My marketing coordinator, Lacy, assured me we could use that to our advantage. I wanted it closed on Sundays so I could at least make sure I was able to attend home games. We were open from Wednesday through Saturday, when the arts district had its busiest foot traffic anyway.

Based on the day's opening, it seemed to be working.

I walked around for a few minutes, speaking with customers, unable to keep the thrilled grin off my face before I moved back behind the counter to help Melissa ring up several sales.

"Thanks for being here, by the way."

She rolled her eyes as she said goodbye to another customer, handing her the hot pink bag filled with purchases. "You're so stupid. You've thanked me a thousand times, and where else would I be? Plus"—she turned to me and wiggled her brows—"I can't wait for the game this weekend. All those hot, sexy men on the field. Me watching you be a nervous wreck around Oliver's parents."

"Don't remind me," I groaned and tossed back a large swallow of bubbly champagne.

"It'll be fine." She hip-checked me as she came close, wrapping one arm around my shoulder and waving the other out at the sea of people. "And so will this. You've done good, amazing things in a short amount of time, and I'm really proud of you."

Emotion burned the backs of my eyes and I blinked it away. "This feels like a dream."

"It is." She turned to me, both of her hands on my shoulders, and stared directly into my eyes. "And it's your dream, finally come true. Now you get to enjoy it."

She winked and turned away when her eyes popped open and her mouth dropped. With the sudden quiet in the space, you could have heard a pin drop—and then it changed to quiet, quick murmurs and people reaching for their cell phones.

Oliver and Beaux and Kolby paid none of the women any attention as they pushed themselves into the doorway.

They headed straight for me, all wearing ball caps but clearly unable to hide who they were.

"Hey," I said, breathless as Oliver sauntered directly to me on the other side of the counter. He didn't care about the space between us as he reached out, cupped my neck with his hand, and pulled me toward him.

He kissed me quick and hard, pulling back with a large smile. "This place is packed. We had to park blocks away. Good day?"

"Amazing," I said, breathless from the kiss and the surprise at seeing him. "What are you doing here?"

"You think we'd miss this?" He tilted his head, not giving me much space to back away.

In truth, I did. They had their first home game in a few days and their practices had been brutal. I figured they'd all be too tired to stop by, and I didn't blame them.

He must have noticed I thought that because his grin faded and he shook his head. "Someday you'll realize you're not the only person who will do everything they can for the person they love. Until then, I'll have to work harder to teach you."

He kissed me again and pulled back.

I was quickly turned and twisted and pulled into Beaux's arms. For a brief second, I saw and heard the clicks of flashes from phones.

"Hey, Sis!" Beaux boomed, I was guessing more for the crowd than me. "Congratulations on this! This place is the shit."

I slapped his shoulder when he put me down and quickly turned away. I couldn't let anyone see me cry now, not even happy tears.

"Thanks." I sniffed and reached for my champagne. "How are you guys doing?"

"Sore as hell, more ready than anything for Sunday," Beaux said, helping himself to a glass of champagne. Before giving me time to prepare, he raised his glass in the air and shouted for everyone to hear, "To my sister! And to the best damn jewelry shop in town!"

Dozens of women raised their glasses in their air, stars in their eyes as they looked at the men in front of me and next to me, as if they couldn't believe what they were seeing.

"To Stamped!" Beaux shouted again.

"To Stamped!" the customers shouted back.

I glared at Beaux as he tossed back his champagne in one quick chug. "I'm going to kill you."

He winked at me. "Think of this as more free publicity. Chicks think they can come here and see me and you'll have a line wrapped around this place for months."

"Your ego knows no bounds."

He rolled his hips, eliciting more cheers for an entirely different reason. "Hey. If you got it, flaunt it."

"You're a dork."

"And you're my sister, who's always supported me and cheered for me. Now it's my turn. Get fucking used to it."

With that parting shot, he grabbed another glass of champagne and walked out from behind the counter, pulling me with him.

Quickly, Beaux and Kolby were surrounded in a sea of women clamoring for their attention and autographs.

Oliver sidled up next to me, one arm wrapped around my back while other women asked him to sign anything they could find in their purses. Never once did he take his arm off me, indicating exactly who I was to him.

There was something about that—his desire to be honest and forthright, to not hide our relationship from anyone—that caused me to take another sip of champagne, lean into his side, and enjoy the hell out of the ride.

I looked up and caught Melissa's gaze. Her light blue, happily shining eyes flickered from Oliver back to me, and then she winked. *Dream*, she mouthed. *Love you.*

She turned away to ring up another sale before I could respond, but I took her point.

This was my dream. All of it. And I was going to live it.

"FASTER," I whimpered into his throat as Oliver moved inside of me.

"Slow," he responded, looking down at me. "I want to feel you."

It was morning, three days after Stamped's grand opening, and nothing had slowed down.

That day was the first home game of the season. The team was 2-0, hoping to make it three wins that afternoon. I hadn't expected Oliver to wake me up that morning, his tongue doing delicious things to my pussy before I'd fully awakened, but I'd quickly gone with the flow.

Now, he was driving me mad.

He slid out and in again, my knees pulled up high to the sides of him so he slid in deeper.

I was close, so close, but his frustrating pace was keeping my orgasm just out of reach.

"Oliver." I gasped, as he hit a new spot deep inside of me. My fingers pressed against his shoulders as I arched into him.

"Tell me you love me."

"I love you," I said without hesitancy.

His eyes seared into me as he gritted his teeth together.

"Please." I pressed one of my hands to his cheek. "I'm so close."

He grunted as he thrust into me hard. "Like this?" In. Out. Harder. Not faster.

God. He was killing me.

My hips arched up and into him, trying to get the friction I needed that he was keeping from me.

"I need you."

"You have me," he responded, so forcefully that I knew he was losing control.

He pulled back, and I took the small break in our skin pressing against skin to slide my hand between us.

"Fuck, yes. Do it. Get yourself off."

It didn't take long. His long, hard dick inside me, moving slow, grinding against me when he was fully inside, my fingers helped take me over the edge and I tightened around him, my heels digging into his lower back as I came.

"So damn beautiful when you come," he growled and dropped his forehead to mine. "Hold on to me tight."

I did what he asked, wrapping my limbs around him while he pounded into me, his speed finally increasing like I'd asked for, drawing out my orgasm.

"Oliver."

"Fuck, Shannon." He seated himself to the root and came on a growl, my name reverberating through the walls of the bedroom in his hotel room.

We'd stayed there the night before when he'd dragged me out of Stamped, my fingers cramping from working so hard.

Melissa had been with me even though she was staying at Beaux's since I had yet to buy any guest room furniture. When Oliver had shown up, his interest and desire clear in his eyes, she'd practically shoved me out the door, promising she'd find something to do to keep her busy for the night before I picked her up for the game. His parents were in town, staying at his house for the weekend, and he said he wanted the night alone with me. I'd meet them for breakfast before a driver took them to the game early, but I was still trying not to think about that part yet.

It had taken only a few hours before photos of us at Stamped on Thursday had surfaced on local gossip sites. Then they'd gone viral on social media platforms. My notifications had been dinging through the roof so much that I'd finally shut down my phone earlier in the day.

I was terrified as to what Oliver's parents would think about me. When I had met Patrick's parents, they'd made it clear they didn't think someone from a run-down home with a single mom was anyone close to being good enough for their son.

Based on the things the media had been saying about me when they saw Oliver's arms wrapped around me, or the kiss we'd shared when he'd first shown up, it was also clear that half of America thought the same thing about Oliver and me.

I'd tried not to let it bother me. I knew the truth. In some crazy way, Oliver and I fit.

But his parents might not think so, and I was terrified to

spend three hours that afternoon watching a game with people who might hate me.

I blew out a breath at the thought as Oliver slid off me, draping a sheet over my hips as he moved. "Stay here. I have something for you."

"Another present?" I asked, my face paling.

He laughed and sauntered to the bathroom to clean up. "You'll like this one, I promise."

I'd liked the last one, eventually. I'd liked it so much I'd wanted him to take my ass over and over again—and while there'd been play in the last couple of weeks, it hadn't happened.

I thought about asking him for it then, but remembered his game later.

When he came out of the bathroom, still naked and completely confident in his body he walked directly to the closet and came out holding a white box—the kind of box dress shirts came in.

"What's this?" I sat up and brought the sheet with me to cover my breasts.

Oliver sat down next to me, his hips to the side of mine on the bed. He reached out and tugged the sheet until it fell down. Before I could reach for it, he leaned closer and pressed his lips right between my breasts, softly and slowly, making my nipples harden at the sensation.

"Hey," I whispered, running my hands lightly through his shaggy blond hair. He dragged his eyes up to mine. "Careful or you'll start something you won't be able to finish."

"I'll finish," he promised. "Later. But I want you to have this."

He sat back up and held the box out to me. His bottom lip disappeared between his teeth.

He was nervous.

It wasn't a look I saw on him frequently, if ever, and my hands trembled slightly as I took the box from him.

"You always wear Beaux's jersey at the games," he said as I set the box in my lap.

I knew instantly what it was and my pulse kicked up a notch.

"The last few days have been crazy with media and everything, and I know it all took you by surprise, but I want you to wear this today." He cleared his throat and that vulnerable side of him peeked out before he vanquished it with a blink. "I want you to wear my jersey when you cheer for me."

"Oliver," I breathed out. I opened the box, and inside it was as he said: his jersey, the blue and teal colors of the Rough Riders, and the number eighty-seven stamped in bright blue right on the front. I held it up and smiled, looking at him. "I feel like you just asked me to go steady."

He laughed softly, his eyes narrowing with that look I knew so well. "Later, I want to fuck you in only this, my number and my body all over you."

"Well, that's something to think about when I'm with your folks today." I chuckled with him then and pressed the shirt to my chest. "Thank you," I said, trying to erase the nerves that assaulted me at the mention of his parents. "Of course I'll wear it to the game."

"And later?" He leaned forward and pressed his lips to mine.

"You'll have to wait and find out."

Grace Powell pressed her soft, warm hand to my cheek and smiled. "Well, you're even prettier than the pictures we saw this week, aren't you?"

Next to me, Oliver groaned. "Ma."

"Well, she is." Her kind, hazel eyes, which were exactly like Oliver's, came to mine. "It's lovely to meet you, Shannon."

"You too." I grinned and held out my hand for Sean to shake. "You too, sir."

"None of that," he said and pulled me in for a hug that was tighter but faster than Grace's when she'd hugged me. "We're huggers in this family."

Oliver snorted. "Or you're just pretty and he likes the ladies."

Sean pulled back and winked. "That might be it, too. But my son knows how to pick 'em, that's for certain."

I tried and failed to stifle my giggle as Oliver groaned again.

I was obviously meeting his parents. They'd driven from his place to The Maytower for an early breakfast before Oliver had to be at the stadium. He was dressed in a suit, and that black-

and-gray tie he'd tied to my wrists when he'd taken my ass. My eyes had gone hazy and half-lidded when he'd walked out of his closet earlier, him in that suit and tie, and he'd smirked.

"Guess that tells me what we're doing later," he murmured, pulling me in for a long and wet and *heated* kiss.

I had pushed him away, my cheeks burning with heat, and next to him I still felt ridiculous. I was dressed in frayed skinny jeans and sandals and his jersey like he'd asked. With him in his suit, we didn't look like we fit.

"Let's eat some breakfast," Sean said, patting his small, rounded stomach. "I'm starving after working the horses this morning."

"You didn't ride Hulk, did you?" Oliver's concern was obvious. In the past few weeks, I'd learned that nobody but Lee and him rode Hulk. He was too wild, still—too unpredictable.

Sean flicked a hand in the air, dismissing him. "It was fine. Quit worrying about me."

Oliver growled at his dad and looked at his mom. "You let him do that?"

She rested a soft hand on his forearm. "It's fine, dear. Honest, he was okay."

"He looks tired."

"You worry too much."

He rolled his eyes and looked at me. I was chewing my bottom lip. In truth, Sean looked exhausted and his skin was a bit pale. I had never met him, but he did seem like a man Oliver had the right to be concerned about. He'd told me frequently over the past few weeks that he thought his dad was constantly overdoing it, not taking into consideration that at nearing seventy, he wasn't as capable as he used to be.

"Somebody needs to worry," Oliver muttered, but followed his mom into the restaurant.

When we were seated, his frustration seemed to evaporate

while we sat around and ate. His parents were kind and quick to laugh. Sean was boisterous and had no problems criticizing Oliver's playing to which, shockingly, Oliver took with a quick nod and "yes, sir" even while I knew he was trying not to roll his eyes. In front of me, he seemed to change from superstar, cocky football player to respectful Southern son in the blink of an eye.

Both sides of him had me squirming in my seat. Was there anything he did that didn't make him sexier to me?

I doubted it.

Grace, on the other hand, was quiet with a serene presence. She added in her two cents in a way where you wanted to lean in and listen more closely. Soft-spoken and mild-mannered, she held a wisdom in her eyes that made you respect her instantly, and at the same time want to sit next to her with a cool glass of lemonade and just *be*.

I was in love with the entire family by the time breakfast was done.

"I need to get to the stadium," Oliver said, kissing me on the cheek after he'd had our bill charged to his room. His parents had excused themselves for the restroom and we were alone at our table. "You sure you and Melissa are okay getting there on your own? I can have a driver pick you up."

I shook my head. He'd already asked and offered, but Melissa and I wanted to enter the stadium like regular fans. There was always something about the excitement in the air, the hope of victory, and the spark of a new season that made the first home game different from any others.

It'd be a pain in the ass, but worth the experience.

The driver he'd ordered for his parents was going to be there any moment. They would go to the game and enter the stadium through the family and players' entrance so they didn't have to deal with the crowds.

"We'll be fine," I said, stressing each syllable. "Don't worry about us, I swear. We'll be in the box before kickoff and I'll cheer for you and Beaux every play."

His lips pulled tight and he frowned. His gaze flickered to his dad's empty chair before returning to mine and he dropped his voice. "Do me a favor? Make sure Dad doesn't get too excited. He looks worse today than he did last time I saw him."

"Okay."

"I'm probably being stupid," he said, still whispering. "I just don't have a good feeling about today. Or the game. Or something."

I pressed my hands to his cheeks. "It'll be fine. He'll be fine. You'll win, and it's probably just nerves."

A line deepened between his brows before he nodded. "You're probably right."

"I love you," I whispered, leaning in and brushing his lips against mine. "Go kick some ass. Score some touchdowns. All that good stuff."

He laughed softly before he deepened the closed-mouth kiss. "Be good."

"I will," I promised and pulled back. "I love you. And tell Beaux I said good luck, too."

I'd already texted my brother, and he'd responded, but it wasn't often I didn't see him before a game I attended. Usually, he was the one driving me.

"Will do. Love you, too." He pushed back from his chair before leaning over me, kissing me again like he couldn't leave without the taste of me on his lips.

"Go Rough Riders!" I cheered, pumping my fist in the air.

A few people turned and looked our way but most didn't hear me. So when Oliver leaned back down and playfully growled, "I'll show you a rough ride later," I was thankful no one saw the blush that stained my cheeks when he tugged a lock of my hair before he walked away from me.

"I CAN'T BELIEVE this game is so close," Melissa said, sitting next to me on the chairs just outside the box. Sean and Grace were inside getting more food, because I'd learned that while Grace was soft-spoken and kind earlier, she also really liked to take care of her husband. Making sure he kept his plate and drink filled during the game seemed like her duty.

"I know." My fingernails had been in between my teeth all game. Two of them were completely gone already. The crowd was insanely loud, and more than once I'd wished we were down at the fifty-yard line, cheering from my usual seats. There was something different about being up so high, in your own little box. It made me feel removed from the excitement and wonder of the game and the anticipation in the crowd.

I'd seen my face on the Jumbotron while sitting next to Sean and Grace after Oliver had made a great play, and twice when he'd dropped a pass.

It was halftime and we were only up by one field goal against the Denver Cavalry, a team we'd been projected to beat by double digits.

The Cavalry was doing an excellent job at shutting down the passing game, effectively leaving Kolby scoreless for the entire first half, which was keeping our scoring down.

"They'll come back in the second half," I said and stood up. I wanted another drink and some snacks. I needed something to help settle my stomach. I gestured toward Melissa. "Want another glass of wine?"

"You betcha," she replied and raised her glass without taking her eyes off the field.

One of the things I loved most about Melissa was her love of sports like mine. I didn't know if she'd learned it from me or had always been a football fan, but when we'd met in college, she started watching every game with me, often coming back to my high school to watch Beaux play. She'd been just as much of a big sister to him as I had since we'd met ten years before.

I walked into the box suite and headed straight for the bottles of wine that had been staffed for us. Oliver had gone all out for our spread for the day. There were selections of all types of alcohol and a buffet that could feed thirty. There'd be way too many leftovers thrown away, but I appreciated he thought of everything we could possibly desire.

"You guys doing okay?" I asked Sean and Grace as I refilled our glasses.

"Fine, darlin'," Sean said, scooping a corn chip filled with chili dip into his mouth.

We'd spent most of the first half of the game talking and cheering. I could tell he appreciated my knowledge of the game, and they'd both made it easy to talk to them. They were just as sweet and simple as Oliver had promised they'd be, and just like over breakfast, our conversations were easy.

I took a sip of wine.

Sean pressed his hand to his chest, grimacing. "You okay, Sean?"

"Fine, fine." He cringed again but waved me off. "Chili's spicy a bit, that's all."

Grace dug into her purse and muttered, "How many times do I need to remind you to take your medicine, Sean?" She looked at me and grinned before pulling heartburn medication out of her purse. "I tell ya, this man is as stubborn as his son. Every day he gets the burn, and every day he refuses to take the pill until he's unbearable. Train my boy better than I trained my man to follow common sense, would you?"

I grinned into my glass of wine. "I'll do my best."

A cheer erupted on the field and I looked out to see the teams running back onto the field.

"I should get these drinks to Melissa. You two coming out?"

"Soon, darlin'." Sean coughed into his hand and flinched. "We'll be there soon. As soon as this pill kicks in you won't be able to stop me."

"All right." I patted him on the shoulder and went back to the game.

Soon, Sean and Grace joined us and the four of us nearly lost our voices while the game continued to be close.

It was the third quarter, five minutes to go, and we were finally up by ten points, having scored another touchdown. Cavalry could pull off a win—or at least a tie—and they had the ball, moving it slowly but steadily down the field.

It was the third down, eight yards to go for them, and they were nearing field goal range when they threw the long pass they had to get.

The play unfolded perfectly. Cavalry's quarterback dropped back to pass the ball, and as it flung into the air I was on my feet, holding my breath while it sailed through the air, thirty yards down the field.

Right as their wide receiver jumped to catch the ball, too far behind him even though he tried to double back, our safety appeared out of nowhere and snagged the ball into his hands.

"Hell yes!" Melissa shouted next to me.

Smith, the safety, bobbled the ball once then twice before he got a firm grip on it and started running down the field.

We all jumped to our feet and shouted, cheering as Smith ran for fifteen yards, almost ending up at half field before he was tackled by Cavalry's offense.

"Yes! We did it!" I shouted, turning to give Sean a high-five as I did. But he wasn't there.

He was in his chair, his hand fisting his shirt, his lips twisted in pain.

"Sean?" I asked, dropping to my knees in the small space.

Grace must have heard me because she turned, looking down at us.

"Sean!" she shouted, and he dragged listless eyes to hers.

"My chest," he rasped, barely able to breathe, "hurts."

His body began shaking and I stood paralyzed before I realized what was happening.

"Call nine-one-one!" I began screaming. "Call nine-one-one!" I flashed terrified, panicked eyes to Grace and realized hers matched mine. "I think he's having a heart attack."

"Fine," he gasped again.

Melissa's hand wrapped around my shoulder. "I'll do it," she said. "Get him inside and lying down on his left side."

She took off then, running toward a phone at the wall of the box suite for emergency uses.

"Come on," I said to Grace. "Let's get him inside."

"He has to be okay," she chanted repeatedly. "My Sean."

His hand reached up and held hers, but I could tell it was taking everything in him. "Love you, honey. All the love in the world."

"Stop it," she hissed, and tears began falling down my cheeks. "You'll be fine."

We moved him inside, his weight difficult for us. When we had him on the floor, resting on his side, Grace dug into her purse again and popped out an aspirin. "Swallow this, Sean. Now."

He did, working his throat like he was swallowing shards of glass, and I stepped back while they whispered to each other, things I couldn't hear.

It was minutes that felt like hours before the stadium's

paramedics rushed through the door. We could do nothing except stand there and watch. Waiting.

Hoping.

A loud cheer in the distance and the vibration of the stadium shaking with applause pulled my eyes to the field. "Oliver." I snapped my head to Grace. "We have to tell Oliver."

She shook her head. "After the game. We'll get word to him."

"Should I wait for him?"

"No. Come with us. He'll meet us there. The driver will be quicker anyway."

WE WERE at the hospital sitting in waiting room seats much too uncomfortable for anyone scared out of their mind.

I'd spent much of the time pacing, unable to sit still while we waited for word from the doctor.

Grace and Melissa had sat down, Grace the epitome of calmness with hope in her eyes while she sat there, hands clasped together and stared out the windows. Melissa looked as scared as I was, and I didn't know if it was because of what we had seen, or what we were afraid the result would be.

Damn it. Oliver had been right—Sean had looked too tired this morning. Too worn down. And the way Oliver had looked at me, so concerned about his dad and asking me to keep an eye on him, promising him I wouldn't let his dad get too excited.

I'd failed him. I hadn't listened. I'd trusted Sean and Grace when he'd waved off the earlier pains in his chest.

I couldn't close my eyes, I couldn't blink. Every time I did I saw Sean's large frame, almost as tall as Oliver's, lying there on the floor, motionless and pale as the paramedics worked him over before rushing him out to an ambulance.

It was a memory forever ingrained in my brain.

Movement coming from the double doors caught my attention and I whispered Grace's name.

Two doctors hustled through the doors, stopping only at the nurses' station before looking at us when she gestured in our direction.

"Sean Powell's family?" one of the doctors asked.

"I'm his wife, Grace." She stood and held out her hand, smiling as if she wasn't terrified out of her mind. There was something in her eyes, something that hit me after I'd watched all of this play out. She had been calm. Too calm and it didn't feel right. She was either a chunk of granite in the face of horror, or she knew something she hadn't shared. "How is he?"

The doctor smiled, tugging down his mask so it bent beneath his chin. "Sean's going to be fine, Mrs. Powell. But he shouldn't have been traveling—not so soon after his last heart attack."

I gasped. Heart attack? Oliver had never said anything.

He shot her a look full of recrimination, and she rolled back her shoulders. "You try telling that man not to be there for his son's games."

I choked on a laugh, equal parts shocked and amused at the tone she'd just taken with the doctor when he sighed. "He's still sleeping, but we can show you back. You know what this means, though, right? Did your doctors in Savannah explain it?"

"Surgery...stints..." Her voice trailed off as she flicked out her hand. "I'll make sure he listens this time."

"See that you do." His voice went soft and kind and he reached out, squeezing Grace's hand. "The next time he won't be lucky. He won't get a third chance, Mrs. Powell. There's too much damage to his arteries."

She turned to us then and fear flickered in her eyes as well as her remorse. "We didn't want Oliver to know," she said as she met my eyes. "He would have told us not to come, and Sean —well, Sean said if he didn't have much time, he needed to see one last game."

"I understand." I didn't. Oliver was going to be furious and it was warranted. I nodded toward the doctor. "You should go see him. I'll send Oliver back when he gets here."

"Thank you," she whispered, reaching out and squeezing my hand. "Thank you for being so kind and loving my boy."

I smiled with tears in my eyes. "It's my pleasure."

As soon as she'd disappeared behind the double doors and Melissa had her arms around me, I was quickly pulled away and my shoulders gripped by strong, firm hands. "What in the hell happened, Shannon?"

Oliver's grip was so strong, so fierce, my head snapped back and my eyes flared.

"Oliver..." Melissa started as I winced from another hard shake. "Calm down."

"Stay out of this," he clipped, his hazel eyes flaring with fury. "What the hell happened? And why didn't you call me? They could have gotten me during the game. I should have known what was going on. How could you let me go out on the field, knowing what happened and you knew how worried I was about him?" He scrubbed his hand through his hair and shouted at me. "I told you to watch him!"

I stumbled backward, rubbing my arms where he'd gripped them so hard they might bruise. Tears dripped down my cheeks and I swiped them away. "I did watch him, and your mom told me not to call you. He said it was heartburn." I inhaled a long breath before exhaling. "He's fine, though, Oliver. The doctors just came out and talked to us. He had a heart attack, but he's fine. Sleeping. Your mom just went back there."

"Damn it." He swiped a hand through his still-wet hair and

cursed again. "I knew it. I knew something wasn't right. How in the fuck could this have happened?"

I shook my head, unable to comprehend the vitriol he was shouting at me. He was scared and hurt. Probably terrified. I'd take his anger for him if it helped him.

"I tried, honey," I whispered, reaching out for him.

He jerked away from my touch and scrubbed his face with his hands again and then tugged on his hair. "Not well enough," he barked. "I'm going to go see him."

"Do you want us to wait?"

"No," he said. Any emotion he had for me this morning was now gone in his cold, angry eyes. "I think you've done enough. Just go."

I gasped, my fingers flying to my mouth when he turned and hurried away. He talked to a nurse before she opened the double doors for him, smiling at him with stars in her eyes while he rushed down the hall and disappeared.

"He didn't mean it," Melissa said, pulling me into her arms and squeezing tight. "He didn't mean it. He's just angry and scared. You'll see."

I'd seen Oliver lose his temper and say shit he didn't mean often. He was usually quick to apologize.

I reminded myself of that, focused on the truth Melissa spoke, and hoped like hell I was right.

He'd realize that in his anger he'd just been an asshole to the woman he loved, and he'd make it right.

Melissa looked down at me, her pretty little nose all crinkled. "You smell."

"I'll shower later." I rolled my eyes at her before staring back at the television set.

ESPN was now the only way I was getting any updates on Oliver or Sean other than the texts Beaux got from the team manager's updating the team on Sean's condition. He was getting released from the hospital that night.

It had been two days and I hadn't heard anything from Oliver. I hadn't received a single text message, not a phone call. And after I sent one message the day before, asking him how his dad was doing when I'd heard he made it out of surgery via Beaux, I hadn't gotten a response.

Was it possible for a heart to actually break? I understood he was busy. I understood he needed to be with his dad, and I had originally believed Melissa: he'd freaked out on me because he was scared and angry that he hadn't known about it as soon as it happened.

Two days later, and radio silence from him, and I no longer believed her.

My chest hurt. After we'd left the hospital, Melissa and I had gone to Beaux's house. I didn't want to be alone in my apartment.

He freaked out and shouted when Melissa had relayed what happened and then he'd stalked off to be with the team at the hospital. Visions of him giving Oliver a black eye for being a dick to me popped into my mind, but I pushed them away. Beaux wouldn't do that to him...not yet, anyway. But if I knew my brother and his protective instinct, it'd come at some point.

Melissa bent down and picked up the remote. She clicked the button and the television screen faded to black immediately. "We have to go out. And you have to get back to work tomorrow."

I should have been working for the past two days. There was too much to do and not enough time for any of it.

"I will. Tomorrow."

"Fine. Then tonight we go out. Beaux said the team's finally celebrating their win and he wants us there."

I pushed off the couch and fixed my messy bun. I cringed at the feel of it. I really did need to get cleaned up.

"I'm not going out with them. Not now." Before she could protest, I smiled at her. "But I will go shower, we'll go to Stamped so I can check the mail, and then we'll get drunk here."

She pouted for a moment before her blue eyes shone when she smiled. "Deal. Now go, before I hose you down."

"I'm not that bad," I shouted as I walked away.

Melissa's fake gagging sound was the only response I got.

I showered quickly, throwing on minimal makeup and comfortable lounge clothes while I got ready. And while I did, I hatched my own plan. I had stayed in a crappy relationship once, knowing it was going downhill but too afraid to stand up and ask for answers then. I wouldn't be that woman again, and I wouldn't wait around, eating my weight in food and drowning my sorrows, waiting for him to come to me.

I refused to believe that only shortly after telling me he was falling in love with me, Oliver truly meant the things he'd said.

"Let's go," I said to Melissa when I returned to the living room.

She was dressed just as casually as I was, both of us in tanks and short yoga shorts, our hair pulled up and off our necks.

She turned to me and must have seen the determination that had set in my eyes because her glossy lips spread wide. "Well, that shower seemed to have worked."

I laughed and walked toward the door, digging my keys out of my purse. "Yup. And tomorrow, I get the rest of my shit together."

I'd give Oliver the day, one more day to help his dad and be there for his parents, but I knew from Beaux that he was staying at the hotel in Raleigh while his dad was in the hospital.

THE ELEVATOR BELL DINGED, jarring me. Wiping my palms down the sides of my skirt, I inhaled a breath as I stepped out of the elevator car and onto Oliver's floor. I was surprised when the doorman at the hotel had given me permission to go straight up, but took it as a good sign. I hadn't yet been removed from visitors allowed to head to Oliver's place without a phone call first.

It was mid-morning. The night before, after getting done at Stamped, Melissa and I had sat around Beaux's condo drinking and talking about everything and anything that didn't involve Oliver Powell. Instead, we'd talked about her job as a freelance graphic designer while she continued to tell me how she loved the Raleigh area. Despite the heat that was going to take me years to get used to—but much less time to get used to in the winter, since I'd get to avoid Iowa's bone-chilling windchill temperatures—I agreed with her.

Raleigh was beautiful. Not too large of a city that it was intimidating, and it had everything I could possibly want.

The bonus was definitely that my online sales of Stamped were still going strong. Soon, I'd be able to start paying Beaux back for everything he'd done for me.

Hopefully sooner than that, Oliver would apologize for being a complete prick and we could move past this small hitch in the road. All couples had problems. All couples fought. All couples said things out of anger, and he had to have been beside himself with worry.

I was counting on all of those things when I found my nerve to exit the elevator and turned toward his door.

I was three steps away when his door flung open and a woman—a beautiful woman—flew out, laughing as she did, her waist-length blond hair flying out behind her. "I'll see you later, then!"

She turned around and froze, just as I did.

"Oh! Hello!" The beautiful woman—shiny pink lips, glassy-eyed—was looking directly at me, and she instantly looked familiar, although I couldn't place her. *Gorgeous.*

She had to be one of the most beautiful women I'd ever seen. Curvy, blond, so beautiful and sweet-looking my teeth almost ached. Or they would have...if I could have felt anything.

Everything went numb as I gasped.

What she must have caught on my face wiped the smile right off hers.

My heart froze inside my chest.

No. He wouldn't...

Then her eyes went wide and she looked down following my gaze. She was wearing nothing. Not *nothing* nothing, but all I could see of her was a pale pink, silky robe, wrapped and tied tight at her waist.

I took a step back.

I couldn't breathe.

She looked back at me and followed my movement, coming closer while I backed away.

"You must be Shannon," she said, walking toward me.

Without looking, I pounded on the elevator button with the palm of my hand. It had to open. It couldn't have left yet.

He did. He wouldn't, though...would he? Oliver had always promised he wasn't a cheater.

And how did she know my name? I opened my mouth and closed it like a fish, unable to speak to her. I couldn't draw air into my lungs to breathe.

Behind me, the elevator door opened.

Her hands went up. "This isn't what it looks like, I swear to you."

I said nothing. What could I say?

As I stepped back into the elevator, I heard Oliver's voice.

I hit the button to close the door. "Bethany...you forgot..." He stopped as he saw me.

He had on pajama pants. Nothing else. Dark blond hair a shaggy mess that told me he'd just woken up. A woman's purse in his hand at his side.

I made a choking sound and began slamming the button to close the elevator door.

I was standing there dressed in a super-cute tank and skirt and sky-high heels, looking my absolute best, and this woman—who looked so vaguely familiar, but I couldn't place her—was dressed in just a robe and *ohmygod* so much more beautiful than me without any makeup on at all.

"Shannon..." His voice trailed off as he looked at me and then at Bethany.

His eyes went hard.

My heart dropped to the floor beneath my feet.

The doors shut right as he dragged his hands through his hair.

It was the last thing I saw and tears flew down my cheeks, unbidden, before I could stop them. Before I realized I was crying, my vision blurred and sobs wracked my shoulders.

I flew out of the hotel, only thankful I'd managed to park on the street and not valet.

That look in his eyes when he'd seen me.

I cried when I got to my car, my hands shaking so badly that I couldn't control myself, couldn't get my key in the ignition.

Everything about that moment.

It hurt more than when I'd seen Patrick. Then, I'd been angry.

This wasn't anger rolling through me so hard it seemed to take forever for me to stop crying enough that I could drive away.

Never, in all of that, did he come to look for me. He didn't call. He didn't text or explain.

He had just stood there, looking at me like I was nothing to him.

TWENTY-SIX

OLIVER

Fuck. Fuck fuck *fuck.*

"Well, you totally screwed that up."

I dropped my hands to my sides and glared at Bethany. Bethany who was in only a damn robe and had just come over to drag my ass out of bed because the night before I'd gotten so fucking drunk in the hotel bar that she'd had to practically carry me to my room.

She'd only come over that morning to make sure I was still alive and bring me coffee.

"What the fuck?" I asked. My mind was moving too slow—the result of too much tequila. It barely registered that Shannon was inside that elevator before it closed.

"If it helps, I told her it wasn't what it looked like." Her nose scrunched and she looked at the elevator doors. "I don't think she believed me."

A harsh laugh escaped me. "You think? Damn it." My hands went to my face again and I tried to scrub away the remainder of the hangover pounding at my temples.

I'd been a dick to her.

A complete, fucking dick. I had no excuse and I had to make it right.

"Bethany," I said, turning toward my friend. "She'll never forgive me for this. Never, not after her ex—"

She rolled her eyes and let her Southern drawl flow free. "Not if you stand here talking to me. Go *after* her. You spent hours last night droning on and on about how much you loved this woman, and she was here even after you said those things to her. Go explain it. All of it."

I couldn't. Not now. Not when my head hurt too much to think straight. Not when she'd just seen what she thought she saw.

Fuck. We were both half-naked.

There was absolutely no way she was going to believe me.

"Damn it!" I balled my hands into fists and forced myself not to punch the wall.

For two days, I'd sat with my father, fucking pissed at myself for the awful things I'd said to her, the way I'd handled her. Beaux had said nothing when he'd shown up at the hospital with most of the team to support me and my dad. He'd wanted to hit me.

I could see it in the glare in his eyes and the tenseness in his body.

"Oliver, go to her. Go talk to her. Make her understand."

Bethany was sweet. Too innocent for her own damn good. The very fact that she thought that would work—after Shannon's past and her lack of ability to trust again—told me she didn't fucking get it.

"I can't. I've got to shower and get my parents home. Damn it."

"Oliver—"

She called to me again and I turned. "What?"

"My purse?"

I tossed it to her and shook my head. "I'll handle it. I just don't have the time. Not right now."

"You let it go too long and you're screwed, you know."

I rolled my eyes to the ceiling and sighed. "I already am."

It'd been a full twenty-four hours since I'd been to Oliver's hotel room.

The pain wasn't any better. I'd slept like shit, but had orders to fill and work to get done, so I'd dragged myself out of bed early in the morning to get to Stamped and start working.

I'd already changed my entire life after one horrific breakup. I couldn't let this dream of mine fail, despite wanting to lament my inability to find a decent man.

"You know," Melissa said, getting my attention from where she'd been perched on my worktable for the past few hours trying to keep me company. She'd brought her laptop with her and was working on some website designs for a few clients, but mostly she was talking, trying to keep me from not thinking about Oliver and the blonde.

I turned to her. She was holding a pair of pliers, opening and closing them repeatedly. A scary, maniacal grin on her face. "I really liked Oliver. Liked how he was with you. But this little tool is giving me some great ideas." She winked at me.

I looked away and back to the metal bands laid out in front

of me. I had to string them with charms before I finished embellishing them. "I don't want to talk about him."

"I don't want to talk about him, either. Or talk to him." I heard the squeak of metal as she squeezed and played with the pliers. "But hearing him scream while I wrap these around his balls—"

"God," I said, unable to stop the laugh at her description. "Stop, Melissa. Please."

She dropped the pliers and picked up her laptop. "I just wanted to see you smile."

Rolling my eyes, I turned back to my work. "You're a nutjob."

"That's what I was talking about. A smash-and-crush nutjob."

I glared at her out of the corner of my eye at the same time a bell at the front door rang. We weren't opened for business, wouldn't be until Thursday, but I had deliveries scheduled.

"Can you go take care of that, please?" I asked as I began twisting a fine piece of sterling silver.

"Sure thing, hooker."

I snorted as she walked out of my office, listening to her quick feet take her down the hallway.

She was back within seconds, and when she spoke, her voice had lost its playfulness.

"Holy shit, Shannon." She grabbed my shoulders and spun me around, her eyes wide and her hands trembling. "Bethany Carlson is in your store...looking for you."

Who?

"Who? What?"

"Bethany Carlson. Famous country singer?"

My eyes bugged out and I dropped my tools, my bracelet forgotten. "What the hell? Me? Why?"

"I don't know," Melissa breathed, the awe clear in her voice.

My hands began trembling at the same time she pulled me to standing.

"Go see her!"

My hands went to my wild hair. I'd forced myself to take the time to get ready that day because I was going to be at the store, but Bethany Carlson? She was famous. I freaking *loved* her music. I had tried to talk Patrick into taking me to her last concert that went through Des Moines two years before and then acted not that disappointed when he'd twisted his lips and went, "Eh. Really? Not really my thing."

Dick. I knew how to pick 'em.

I brushed the errant thought out of my mind and blew out a breath. "Okay. Okay, I'm going."

We rushed out of the office, Melissa close on my heels, and then I froze when I reached the end of the hallway.

In front of me was a woman with her back turned to me.

Blond hair flowing to her waist. A tight, short skirt that barely covered her ass. Tanned and toned legs that went to gold strappy sandals I would *die* to own.

And all of it—from the hair to the waist to the legs—had all been parts of the woman that had been burned into my brain since the morning before.

"Holy shit," I breathed, slamming to a halt in my tracks at the same time I reached out to squeeze onto Melissa's hand.

"I know," she hissed quietly, totally awed.

I shook my head and whispered back, "No. That's her. That's the woman who came out of Oliver's yesterday. I knew she looked familiar then, but I couldn't place her."

Her eyes jumped open and her lips pulled back to a sneer. "That whore. Oh my God, what is she doing here?"

I wanted to hug my friend and her loyalty. To go from being in awe to getting her claws ready to attack, Melissa was the shit.

"Fuck," I whisper-hissed. I forced my feet to move forward. As I walked toward her, Bethany turned to me and exhaled slowly.

"Hello, Shannon. I'm Bethany. We didn't really get the chance to meet yesterday."

She was famous. A country rock star who toured with the best of the best and had won handfuls of CMA awards.

She'd also walked out of my boyfriend's home—or ex-boyfriend's—dressed in barely anything and giggling about seeing him later.

I *hated* her.

I forced myself not to be enamored with the first part, to focus on the second, and didn't take the hand she offered to me.

"Can I help you?" I asked, my voice dry and hoarse and blood rushing through my veins.

Her hand fell to her side and she sucked her lip between her teeth. "I, well, I'm not sure what I'm doing here, but I thought maybe it'd be best for me to come talk to you myself."

To mark her new territory? She already had it. Oliver lost claim to me when he slipped his "I've never cheated and would never cheat" dick into her.

I crossed my shaking arms over my chest and said nothing.

"I'm really sorry," she said, the words rushing out of her. She waved her hands in the air while she spoke, making her seem even sweeter. "Oliver and I, nothing happened, I swear. We're friends. I stay in the room next door to his and I'm only in town a few days. I saw him at the bar the other night and he was so drunk, I helped him to his room. That's it, I swear. I went there yesterday to make him coffee and make sure he was okay."

She seemed honest, almost pleading with me to believe her and God, I wanted to.

It didn't change anything, but I still really wanted to believe that Oliver hadn't cheated on me. Or fucked another woman so quickly after kicking me to the curb.

"Thank you for letting me know," I said. "Is there anything else I can help you with?"

"You don't believe me."

Her pretty blue eyes turned sad and she sucked a lip between her teeth again. "I can understand why, I really do. But well, I haven't always had the best luck with guys, and sooner or later they all turn out to be assholes. But Oliver's not like that, and he wouldn't have...we've never, I swear, Shannon, nothing happened with us. Nothing ever has. We're just friends and we get together occasionally when we're both in town, but it's never been anything more than drinks and laughter."

I believed her. Her sincerity was too genuine, the pain in her voice was too obvious. "I believe you," I finally said. "If that's all..."

"So you'll forgive him?" The pain switched to hopefulness so quickly I almost got whiplash.

Bethany was younger—around Beaux's age, I figured, but she'd hit the music scene even before she was twenty-one and flown to the top of the charts where she'd been for *years*. I knew all this because I'd been a fan of her music and seen her perform on television during the music award shows. My hands still shook from overwhelmed excitement.

Sighing, I forced down my sudden, overwhelming need to fangirl. "The thing is, is that you're here explaining it to me and he's not. And he hasn't." Tears burned the backs of my eyes. The way he'd stared at me. "Thank you, I suppose, for explaining it to me. It helps, honest. But Oliver and I—"

"He loves you," she cut in, stepping forward.

I held my ground even though I wanted to run from her.

"He told me. He talked about you for hours, felt so shitty

about everything he said to you. I swear to you, if you give him a chance, he'll explain it."

"I'd have to see him for that to happen." And it hadn't.

"I know. He's being an asswipe, but if you want to know the truth, all he talked about the other night was you."

Tears filled my eyes, making her go blurry as I blinked them back. "I don't know what to do with that."

She looked lost for a bit, her gaze roaming my store as if she'd run out of her own things to say before she looked back at me and shrugged. "I don't know either. Boys suck."

I laughed then, unable to help myself.

Before I could respond in the affirmative, she clapped her hands together. "Now, this is totally off topic, but he also told me about these fabulous bracelet cuffs you made that he saw one day and had wanted to buy. Do you still have them?"

"Um." What? "Yes," I said, once again getting whiplash by this girl. She was too sweet to resist, and suddenly Melissa was at my side.

"Hi, I'm Melissa. How about I help you out with those?"

Bethany grinned. "I'd like that. And it was really great meeting you, Shannon. I hope I see you again."

I doubted it. "Thank you," I said, for lack of anything better.

"Go to the back and fix your mascara," Melissa whispered before she guided Bethany over to the displays of cuff bracelets. "Take a few minutes. I'll help her out, but you're shaking so hard you might fall over."

I hadn't realized it until she said something, but my entire body shivered.

I nodded and went to the back. Then I dropped my ass to my chair in the office, put my head in the palms of my hands, and cried out all the residual pain I'd been feeling.

This changed nothing. So Oliver didn't cheat. He still

didn't love me. There was no way he could, not after hurting me so deeply twice and ignoring me.

Another slice of pain hit my chest and more tears fell. He would tell another woman what he thought of me, how bad he felt for hurting me, but he didn't have the time to make it right.

What good was it knowing any of it?

LATER, after Melissa had helped Bethany and then brought me a bottle of iced tea and a salad from down the street, and after I'd finished up two more bracelets, I was finally able to try to focus on my work again.

I had just sat down to work after taking a small break upstairs in the apartment, and Melissa was out front, dealing with the deliveries that had just arrived.

Another bell chimed, and I assumed it was the UPS man leaving, when Melissa's voice went shrill and she snapped, "What in the hell are you doing here?"

I jumped in my seat as a male voice murmured in response, and was on my feet and moving toward the front of the building when I heard Melissa's angry demand.

"I don't care. Get out."

"What is going on?" I asked, turning the corner only to once again stumble on my feet.

"Hey, sweetheart," Patrick said, turning toward me and smiling.

I blinked rapidly, unable to move.

"She's not your sweetheart," Melissa clipped harshly, baring her teeth like she wanted to rip him to shreds. "Go away."

Patrick glanced at Melissa, a quick sneer twisting his lips

before he ignored her and turned back to me. "I was hoping we could talk."

That one look in his eyes he gave Melissa before quickly being able to erase it told me everything I needed to know.

"No, Patrick. I don't know why you're here, but I don't want to talk to you. We broke up. Hell, I moved almost twenty hours away to get away from you. I don't know what you're doing here, but I think I made it clear I want nothing to do with you."

"Yes," he said, his voice dropping in a way I used to think was sexy, but now I realized was arrogance. "I remember the last time we spoke."

"Then you know she doesn't want you," Melissa said, still glaring at him.

Man, I loved my bestie. Now wasn't the time for her to defend me. She and Patrick had always hated each other. "Melissa, please...give us a moment."

"But—"

"No buts," I said. "Please. This will take two minutes."

She huffed, and I waited until she'd gone to the back before I turned and faced Patrick. He spoke before I could.

"I miss you, sweetheart. I know, I know I messed up, and I'm so sorry. But I love you. I still love you. Please, let's go somewhere, let's just go somewhere and talk."

I shook my head, crossing my arms around my waist.

They were the right words, coming from the wrong damn man and for the wrong damn reasons.

I knew it.

Patrick was handsome. He was attractive in the pretty-boy way, and he took care of himself. Dressed in a long-sleeved plaid shirt, sleeves rolled up to his elbows and wearing gray linen shorts, he looked everything like the perfect, kind gentleman he'd always portrayed himself to be. I had been drawn in by his looks and his body and the security he'd offered me. His well-groomed ginger hair and light green eyes helped. He was just *pretty*.

I couldn't summon up a single emotion for him. His eyes were hard as steel, his voice lacked sincerity.

"You're here because you found out another man has me and you're pissed I don't want you. That's all this is, Patrick."

"Powell?" he asked, almost choking on the word. "He's no good for you. Come on, he's a rebound for you. Someone who wants to fuck you until he's tired of you. You know football players, you've always said the same thing about them, and don't think for a second I haven't looked into his reputation. He's a player. He fucks women, doesn't go back for more, and leaves a trail of pussy who have spread their legs for him in every city he travels. You're nothing but a meaningless fuck to him. But to me, you're everything."

My heart pounded in my ribs. My cheeks heated. There was no way for Patrick to know the full extent of the pain he'd just lanced straight through my already broken heart.

I shook my head back and forth rapidly, trying to shake away the pain he was dishing out. "Patrick," I said and took a step back. My chin wobbled. Fuck. I couldn't cry in front of him. I wouldn't.

"Shannon," he said and closed the space between us in three quick strides. His hand reached for my forearm and I gasped from the surprise. His other hand pressed to my cheek. "Let me show you how sorry I am. It's killing me. I hurt you, and I'm sorry. But it won't happen again."

"You don't want me," I said as I flinched again at his sudden hold on me. "You're mad you can't have me. We both know it, Patrick. I'm never coming back to Des Moines. I'm staying here."

"With Powell?" he asked, his green eyes beginning to glint with jealousy. Damn it. I knew it. "He's no good for you."

"That may be," a masculine, *very* familiar voice said.

I gasped and pulled back only to see him...Oliver...standing in my doorway. I'd been so focused on Patrick I hadn't heard the bell chime at the door.

"But if you don't want my fist in your face, you're going to get your hands off my girlfriend."

The asshole's eyes narrowed on me.

Shannon's widened in surprise.

"You're still touching her," I said, stepping closer.

Red blurred the edges of my vision. Ever since the day before, I'd been trying to figure out what to say to Shannon to get her to believe nothing had happened with Bethany, to apologize for being such a fucking dick at the hospital. All of it sounded like bullshit. There was no way I could go to her without being able to explain everything in a way that made sense—that would make her forgive me, like I needed her to...desperately.

On top of all of it, I'd driven my parents back to Georgia the day before, turned around, and driven home. I hadn't slept in almost forty-eight hours, but when I got a text from Bethany telling me she'd gone to explain to Shannon, I had come as soon as I could.

I'd almost wanted to strangle the little shit for not minding her own business.

"What are you doing here?" Shannon asked, wide-eyed as

Patrick finally let her go when I got close enough to punch him. Screw my catching hand. I'd love to jam my fist into his face. That she thought I wasn't any better than him, thinking that I could have cheated on her—*her*, of all people—made me want to punch my own face, too.

I glared at Patrick and reached out, wrapping my arm around her waist and pulling her to my side. She stiffened immediately, but fuck him. He wasn't touching her again. If she didn't forgive me, that was her choice and my fault, but there was no way he was leaving there thinking he had a chance of putting his hands on her again.

"I thought we had dinner plans," I whispered, brushing my lips against her temple.

Patrick's face flushed as I kept my eyes glued to him while I kissed her.

Shannon flinched again, but I held her tighter. Fuck, there was nowhere else I wanted her to be. Ever.

"You should go," I said, glaring at Patrick. "You've lost her, and you won't have her again. Leave before you make an ass of yourself."

"He already did," Shannon said. Her gaze had stayed fixed on him while I held her. "Go, Patrick."

"He'll throw you away," Patrick said, his hands in fists like he wanted to rip her away from me.

Like fuck that would happen. Now that I had her in my arms, I wasn't letting her go. I'd stay glued to her side until she forgave me.

"Never. You had something good and treated her like shit the entire time because you thought she had to work to be as good as you. I'll never fucking throw her away like you did."

It was a vow. I meant every word. As soon as I spoke them, Shannon stiffened before relaxing next to me.

God, I hoped she believed me.

"We'll talk later," Patrick said, deepening his voice and looking at her.

I pushed her behind me until I was in front of her. Fuck that.

"You don't get it," I said, unable to stop myself from practically growling at the obnoxious dickhead. "She's mine, and she's not going back to you."

"I can handle this, Oliver."

"You can," I said and turned to look at her, "but you won't. You've dealt with enough shit lately and you're not taking this on."

A flutter of something softened her eyes, but I turned back to Patrick before I could read it.

"Go. And honest to God, I hear you've contacted her again and you'll regret it."

"You're threatening me?" he said, pulling back. "Wonder what the media will say about that."

"If you knew anything about me, you'd know I don't give a shit what anyone says about me. Are you going to go, or do I need to help you out the door?"

"God, Patrick. Go." Shannon's annoyance rang thick and clear. "I mean, my God. You had me and treated me like shit. You took advantage of me, you killed any love I had for you long before you screwed Priscilla. Can't you just do one decent freaking thing in your life and leave me alone?"

"I love you."

She glared at him and then walked next to me. She was stiff and angry, and I saw it in her eyes, but I still fucking grinned when she slid her arms around my waist. "You don't know what love is. If you did, you would have cherished me when you had me, not hung me out to dry and expected me to stay with you. You're selfish and egotistical and you're pissed you lost a toy. Now go, or Oliver will help you."

He ground his teeth together before snarling at me. When he looked back at Shannon, his green eyes turned to ice. "You aren't worth it anyway."

A frustrated sound left her lips and her fingers dug into my waist. He left, the door slamming shut behind him, and as soon as he'd disappeared past the windows, she let me go and stepped away.

I reached for her, but she held up her hands, looking up at me with tears in her eyes.

Damn it. I'd done that. Patrick played a part, I was sure of it, but most of those tears were for me.

"Don't," she said, shaking her head. "I want you to go, too."

I scowled at her. "No."

"God, Oliver." She paused and pressed her hands to her cheeks. "This is too much today. Too much this week. Please, I don't know why you're here or why you did all that, but you have to leave. I can't do this right now."

Tears dripped down her cheeks. I was frozen helpless—unable to reach for her, unable to soothe her.

"Everything I just said to him is true."

"And yet you treated me the same."

Fuck. It was true. Mostly. "I know, and I'm here to apologize. To beg your forgiveness."

She took another step back. I was losing her in front of my eyes. Pain sliced my chest as more tears fell.

"Please, Shannon. Let me hold you. I'm so sorry for the hospital, for yesterday, for not chasing after you. I was a dick, and I know it. I didn't mean it. I was angry and terrified. It was my *dad,* Shannon—the guy who taught me everything, and I was thinking the worst." Emotion clogged my throat and I pulled in a breath. "I was fucking terrified and angry I wasn't there for him. Was pissed he hadn't listened to me and stayed home. So fucking pissed that they went to that game when he wasn't feeling well. It wasn't you—honest to God, it wasn't you."

"This was a mistake," she said, her chin wobbling. God, I hated that I'd done this to her. "We…it was sex…and then, we just got swept away in all of it. But we don't work…"

"We do." Damn it like hell we didn't. We worked better than anyone I knew. "Give me this chance. I didn't fuck Bethany. I didn't touch her, except when she helped me to my room. But I swear to God. I knew I had hurt you. I had so much in my head, I just…didn't handle it right. I know that."

"I know you didn't do anything with her. I believed her."

Not me. Her words made her point, punching me in the chest. "But not me. You wouldn't have believed me."

Shit.

Fuck.

"Listen to me," I said, reaching for her again as she stepped back. I took her hands in mine and held them, despite the urge to pull her to my chest, to wrap my arms around her so she couldn't get away. "Fuck, I'm so sorry for hurting you. I shouldn't have. I shouldn't have said anything at the hospital. I should have hugged you and let you help me. I should have let you be there for me, but besides my parents I'm just so fucking used to not having someone in my corner—not really, not genuinely. I didn't think, and I hate that I hurt you. Yesterday I had to get them home, and I was hungover and I wasn't thinking clearly. I should have come after you. I should have dropped to my knees and begged your forgiveness. I'll do it now, if you want." I stopped and tried for a grin that failed.

"You hurt me," she whispered. "Patrick always did and I always gave in."

"I'm not him." She had to know that, at least. "I'm not him. You know that. I've shown you I'm not that guy, but it doesn't mean I'm perfect, either. We'll hurt each other. Frequently.

That's the ugly truth of life, but it doesn't mean we stop trying. It doesn't mean we can't use it to make us stronger instead of ripping us apart. Please. Give me a chance to make this better."

She choked on a cry, and I stopped resisting. I pulled her to me until her head hit my chest and my hands wrapped around her lower back.

"God, I'm so sorry. I love you, Shannon, and I hate that I hurt you. It fucking kills me. Forgive me. At least give me the chance to earn it."

I held her while she cried and sniffed.

I held her until she collapsed her weight into me.

I held her until a shiver rolled through her and she finally... fucking *finally*...wrapped her arms around me and held me back.

"Okay," she whispered. She looked up at me, pressed her chin to my chest, and all the pain I was feeling evaporated when her eyes met mine. "Okay. I forgive you."

"Don't." I pressed my hand to her cheek. Satisfaction and victory rolled through me when she melted into my touch. "Let me prove to you that I've earned it."

"You have," she said, her lips twitching. "You're here."

Fucking Christ. She slayed me.

A low groan bubbled from me and I pushed her back just enough so I could reach her lips with mine.

"I'm going to kiss you now," I whispered, my nose brushing against hers. "And you're going to fucking love it."

She laughed softly and nodded. "Please."

I took her mouth harshly. My need was too great, my desire to show her how much her trust and forgiveness and love meant to me. I slid my tongue into her mouth and devoured her, unable to stop my hands from roaming her sides, pulling her to me. The kiss was frantic and wild, like so much of what we were.

I lost myself in it, lost myself in the feel of her and her scent and her taste, and before I knew it I had her in my arms, my cock against the center of her, and I placed her on the top of a counter.

Her fingers dug into my shoulders, through my shirt. I relished the pain. I wanted her to hurt me, give me the pain I'd caused in her.

She whimpered as I held her against my hard dick, rocking against me.

I swallowed her cries as we lost ourselves in the moment, lost ourselves in each other, and it was only a humored throat clearing that pulled my attention away from her.

We were both panting when we turned our heads toward the sound.

"Fuck," I whispered when I saw Melissa leaning against a wall, arms crossed over her chest, a very amused smile on her face.

"I forgot she was here," Shannon whispered and then giggled.

Fucking giggled.

"Now that's what I like to see," Melissa said. "I very much like you making her laugh rather than making her cry."

Melissa's smile disappeared and I sobered.

"Me too."

"See that you do it more often then."

With fucking pleasure. "I will," I promised Melissa. "Now can we get back to it?"

"Oliver!" Shannon smacked me against my chest, but it lacked any heat.

"Oh no," Melissa said, lifting her hand in a wave. "I'll let myself out. You two..." She paused and winked. "Well, you two just get back to whatever it was you were doing before."

"I love you, Missy Pissy," Shannon said.

I could have let her go to hug her friend, but I didn't. She was in my arms, and I was going to keep her there until I was done with her. And I'd had days to plan out our make-up sex. I was stocked full of fantasies.

"I love you too, Shanna Banana."

I laughed at their crazy nicknames and said goodbye to Melissa before she walked down the hallway.

"We should finish this somewhere else," I said, turning back to Shannon.

"I have work to do," Shannon said, and my gut tightened. My dick was still hard against her. I needed inside of her.

Now.

Then she grinned and ran a finger down my jaw. "But it can wait."

ONE OF MY hands slid around to her front and pressed against her clit.

My other hand went to her ass and I pressed my thumb against her puckered hole.

I wasn't fucking her this time. She was on her hands and knees, fucking me, rocking her hips back as she slid along the length of my shaft—and damn, she was so fucking gorgeous taking everything she wanted from me without shame that I had to fight to not explode before she did.

"Yes," she whimpered. She faltered in her hurried movements when I pressed my thumb against her, not entering, just teasing. "Oliver, please."

"Your ass?" I grunted. "You want me filling your ass? You like it, don't you? So fucking naughty for me."

"Please."

"No." I pulled my hand back and smacked her ass, loving

the way she jumped at the sting of the pain and reared back into me at the same time. "Fuck me, Shannon."

I held her against her hips as my orgasm began to coil tight in my balls. Bending over her, I hit her deeper. I wanted her to be consumed by me.

We'd made love earlier and we'd eaten. Then we'd taken a nap, naked and tangled in her bed, before I'd woken up with her mouth wrapped around my dick.

She sucked me until I was hard and ready and then rolled to her knees, a soft, pleading tone in her voice when she whispered, "Fuck me, please. I've missed you."

And hell if it hadn't undone me. I'd missed her too.

I always would when she wasn't around me.

"Shannon, honey." I grunted and pulled her against me.

Her hands slid out from beneath her until she fell to her elbows, and I knew she was close. But fuck, she felt so good.

"You're so fucking hot and tight wrapped around me, honey. Take me. All of it. Show me what you like."

"You," she whimpered, her cunt beginning to get tight around me. "I like you."

I reached down and wrapped a hand around her throat, pulling her up to me until her back was to my chest. I didn't put pressure there, but held her firmly. "You love me."

She cried out from the change in position and her hands flew to my wrist in front of her. The fingers of my other hand pressed and rolled against her clit.

"Say it," I growled in her ear, fucking her harder. Her eyes closed and her head fell back against my shoulder. Damn it, she was so tiny and malleable in my arms. So fucking turned on by everything I did to her. I would never get sick of her.

Never stop desiring her body or her laughter or her smiles or her cunt.

I'd never stop loving her.

"Say you love me," I said. "I need to hear it."

She must have heard the depth of my voice, the honesty buried inside that she'd always seem to rip from me whether I wanted it or not.

"I love you," she panted. "I love you, Oliver."

She came then, my thumb on her clit, my hand at her throat, and my dick buried deep.

It still wasn't enough, and as she came in my arms and around my dick, I followed quickly, grunting that I loved her too while I shot my load deep inside of her.

I pushed her forward, cushioning her fall, and settled my weight over hers, bracing up on an elbow to avoid crushing her. We rode out our orgasms connected, slowly, and when she'd drained every drop from me and she'd stopped tightening around my dick, I stayed inside of her, pulling out and pushing in at a languid pace.

She trembled beneath me, and I saw her lips tilt to a smile. "I like it when you do that," she whispered. "Just like this."

"I like it when you're beneath me," I replied and brushed hair off her cheeks until I could see her eyes. "I'm still really sorry, Shannon. I'm so sorry I hurt you so bad. I'll do my best to not let it happen in the future."

"I know," she said softly. "But I forgive you, and I love you."

I brushed my lips against her cheek. "I love you too."

I did. I'd take this chance she gave me and prove to her exactly the kind of man I wanted to be. I wanted to take her to my house, burn it down and build another one in its place that was everything she had ever dreamed of. I wanted to plant my babies inside of her and watch them grow up, flourishing under her kind and crazy love.

I wanted to have her by my side after every game, celebrating every win and commiserating after every loss.

I would spend the rest of my days proving to her exactly

how much I loved her, how much I cherished her, how much I never wanted to hurt her again, and if I did, I wanted to prove to her that I wouldn't be a fucking dumbass and I'd make amends immediately, not letting it fester until it became buried deep inside her.

Shannon Hale swooped into my life at a time when love and laughter and forever were the last damn things on my mind, but she changed my mind about all of it almost as soon as I'd touched her, before I could admit it to myself.

Now, I just had to spend the rest of my life showing her how much it meant to me.

It'd be the dirtiest game of my life.

EPILOGUE

SHANNON

Confetti rained down on me and the massive crowd allowed on the field after the final field goal had determined our victory.

The Raleigh Rough Riders were Super Bowl Champions.

My cheeks ached from grinning so wide as I searched through the horde of people, trying to find Beaux or Oliver.

Next to me, Jillian Rudolph squeezed my hand and pulled me closer to the stage they'd set up immediately following the game.

"Come on!" she shouted, turning back to look at me. Mascara stained her cheeks from happy tears and I knew mine looked similar. "They're this way!"

As soon as we got close, elbowing our way through the reporters and ducking beneath their oversized cameras, I came face to face with one of the men I'd been searching for.

"We fucking did it!" Oliver pulled me into his arms and lifted me high into the air, squeezing me so hard I was breathless. "I can't believe we pulled it off."

I wrapped my arms around his shoulders and hugged him

tight. "You were amazing. That last catch right on the two-yard line you had will go down in history as one of the best ever."

He swung me in a circle before setting me on my feet. "It was a hard-fought game, by both teams."

I rolled my eyes before I planted my lips on his. Oliver wasn't known for his humility. I blamed his statement on shock. He was right, though: Raleigh and Seattle had battled back and forth all game, making it a nail-biter of epic proportions. An interception with less than a minute left had ended in our game-winning field goal and a final score of 27-25.

"I'm so proud of you," I whispered into his ear.

"Hey. What am I, chopped liver?"

I turned to Beaux, and Oliver let me go so I could immediately be swept up in my brother's arms. He squeezed me almost as tightly as Oliver just had, but I clung to him more tightly. "I'm so damn proud of you," I whispered, holding him so tight around his neck that I thought I might choke him. "Can you believe you've done it?"

"Feels fucking awesome."

He let me go, and Oliver's hand went to my lower back. A look I didn't understand passed between the two of them before we heard another roar rumble through the crowd.

"That's Coach," Beaux said, nodding at Oliver. "Need to get to the podium."

"Come on." Oliver pressed me forward, stopping briefly to accept congratulations and pats on the back from media and fans and family members of teammates while he pushed me toward the podium with him.

My feet halted as he reached the bottom of the stairs.

"Come with me."

I glanced between Beaux and Oliver. "I should stay here."

"Fuck if you are," Beaux said, a teasing glimmer in his eye.

"Family's allowed up here when the MVP trophy is presented."

My eyes widened. "MVP? You?"

"What am I, chopped liver?" I laughed as I turned to Oliver, who repeated Beaux's exact question from earlier.

"You?"

He nodded, lips twisting into a smirk. "Of course. You said yourself that catch would go down in history as the best ever."

"You're an asshole," Beaux said, slapping him on the shoulder. "Of course it's me. Wouldn't have gotten the win without my arm of steel."

My gaze jumped between both of them and their banter. I had no idea who was being serious and who had won, but it didn't matter. They were both incredible and had played an amazing game.

Reluctantly, I let Oliver guide me onto the podium. There, I was met by Jillian, who had found Danny, Kolby with his daughter, Mya, on his hip, and the coaches with their families.

As soon as we made it up there, Oliver pulled me to his side as Coach Pomville gave a speech that sent the throng of people in front of us into another hysteric cheer.

When he was done, he turned to Oliver and winked. "And now, for our MVP! A man who has been with this team for the last five years, who has fought the hard battles, celebrated the victories, and helped lead this team into what it became today. Our Team Captain...and our MVP, Oliver Powell!"

The sound from beneath the podium became so loud that I fought the urge to cover my ears, but my grin spread so wide I thought my cheeks would burst.

Oliver tugged me forward with him to accept the trophy, not dropping his hand from mine until he had the MVP trophy in his hands and raised it above his head.

"Thank you," he said into the microphone, smiling down at

his parents, who had made it into the front row. After his dad's heart attack at the first game of the season, they'd gone home and he'd had surgery. Then he'd sold his farm, but it took him so long to recover from surgery and then finish the sale that they hadn't been able to make it to many games during the year. Tears dripped down both his parents' cheeks when Oliver smiled at them and began thanking the crowd for the honor, thanking his coach and his team. I barely heard it over the noise, despite him being next to me.

"Now, I'd like to thank the most important woman in my life." He turned to me then and my jaw dropped. Next to him, I saw Beaux pull something out of his pocket and slide it into Oliver's outstretched and waiting hand.

My brow furrowed when Oliver set the trophy he'd been holding on the podium and grinned out at the crowd.

"Earlier this year, I had one thing on my mind: this game. I wanted to win and wanted to make it to the Super Bowl more than anything else. But then, this beautiful woman standing next to me walked into my life and my entire game plan changed."

My hands went to my mouth when I saw what Beaux had placed in his hand. A box. A black box. A small, tiny, black velvet ring box.

I shook my head frantically and tears began falling down my cheeks.

"You're not doing this," I said, glancing at the crowd behind us and in front of us. He couldn't be doing this. Not in front of television cameras and millions of viewers.

"Oh, I'm doing this," he said, pulling back from the microphone so only I could hear him. He turned back toward the cameras, and I was almost blinded by the constant flashing. "Shannon Hale, I love you and I want everyone in America to know it. Make me the happiest man in the world, knowing that on the day I finally won the ring I've been wanting my entire life, that you also agree to this ring for the rest of yours. Say yes, and have this day go down in history as being absolutely, one hundred percent, the best day I could ever have in my entire life."

"You're insane," I whispered, not realizing my voice carried to the microphone.

"Say yes!" someone cried out from beneath the podium. The entire New Orleans stadium began shaking while I swore, and every person in attendance chanted, "Yes! Yes! Yes!"

Oliver leaned toward the microphone and smirked. "They're waiting for your answer, honey." He opened the box, and I saw the ring that sat inside. It was gorgeous, a huge emerald-cut diamond that had to have cost more than his Audi sports car.

My entire body trembled from the shock, the rush of the day, and the way the podium seemed to shake.

"Yes," I finally managed to choke out. I nodded repeatedly and stepped toward him until he draped an arm at my lower back, pulling me flush against him. "Yes, of course I'll marry you."

"You hear that?" he called into the microphone. "*Now* it's the best day of my life."

He slid the ring onto my ring finger and bent down, enveloping me in his arms, and kissed me while the thousands of people in attendance roared their approval.

THANK **you for reading Dirty Player! Need more Rough Riders in your life? The Rough Riders**

Series continues with Beaux Hale's story, Filthy Player. Check it out today by clicking on the title.

CLICK HERE to sign up for my newsletter and receive information about all upcoming releases, sales, and other exclusive content. Plus, as a thank you, you'll receive a FREE E-Book.

THANK YOU

Eeeek! Dirty Player was so much fun to write. I hope you've enjoyed delving into the dirty mind of Oliver Powell just as much as I did.

Thank you first, to all of my early readers of this book. Kathryn, Lisa, Laura, Kelly, Brittainy, and Tonya...I absolutely love all of you and your input. Thanks for helping me tighten this up and make it even better than the original version I sent you.

Special thanks to my "team" that takes my manuscript and makes it into an actual book...Amy, Emily, Summer, Shannon... from cover design and editing to proofreading and formatting, any success I have with a book is largely due to all of your hard work, too, so thank you all so much for working with me, for putting up with my craziness, and my last minute ideas or schedule changes.

To all my author buddies and FTN...F*ck It. You all rock. Here's me flashing you the middle finger.

To all the readers and bloggers who read my stories and leave reviews or send me emails and private messages, thank you for not only taking the time to read my books, but to go the extra step and contact me directly or leave a review. They all mean everything to me.

To Christy and Kelly, just because I love you. I am so thrilled to have met both of you this year and forming friendships I know will last forever.

And finally to my family...you may not always understand my special brand of crazy, but you manage to put up with it. You're the best and I love you all to pieces.

ABOUT THE AUTHOR

When Stacey Lynn isn't conquering mountains of laundry and fighting a war against dust bunnies and cracker crumbs, you can find her playing with her children, curled up on the couch with a good book, or behind closed doors, imagining the next adventures she'll soon write.

She lives off her daily pot of coffee, can only write with a bowlful of Skittles nearby, and has been in love with romance novels since before she could drive herself to the library.

Stacey Lynn lives with her husband and children in North Carolina.

If you would like to know more about Stacey Lynn, follow her here:

Website: www.staceylynnbooks.com
Facebook: www.facebook.com/staceylynnbooks
Twitter: www.twitter.com/staceylynnbooks
Instagram: www.instagram.com/staceylynn.author

If you enjoyed this book, please leave a review on the site where it was purchased.

OTHER BOOKS BY STACEY LYNN

Love In The Heartland

Captivated By You

This Time Around

Long Road Home

Before We Fell – April 2019

Crazy Love Series

Fake Wife

Knocked Up

28 Dates

Weekend Fling – coming soon!

The Rough Riders Series

Dirty Player

Filthy Player

Wicked Player

The Luminous Series

Dominate Me

Crave Me

Long For Me

The Fireside Series

His to Love

His to Protect

His to Cherish

His to Seduce

Tangled Love Series

Entice

Embrace

Enflame

Just One Series

Just One Song

Just One Week

Just One Regret

Just One Moment

The Nordic Lords MC Series

Point of Return

Point of Redemption

Point of Freedom

Point of Surrender

Standalones

Remembering Us

Don't Lie To Me

Try Me – A Don't Lie To Me Novella